How Do You Spell Beautiful?

How Do You Spell Beautiful?

AND OTHER STORIES

Patrick Lane

Fifth House Publishers
Saskatoon, Saskatchewan

Copyright © 1992 by Patrick Lane

All rights reserved. No part of this publication may be reproduced in any form or by any means, electronic, mechanical, recording, or otherwise, without prior written permission of the publisher, except by a reviewer, who may quote brief passages in a review to print in a magazine or newspaper or broadcast on radio or television. In the case of photocopying, users must obtain permission from the Canadian Reprography Collective.

Edited by Seán Virgo
Cover art, entitled *Andromache*, by Cheryl McFie
Cover design by Robert Grey

Printed and bound in Canada
93 92 2 1

Canadian Cataloguing in Publication Data

Lane, Patrick, 1939–

How do you spell beautiful?

ISBN 0–920079–98–9

I. Title.

PS8523.A53H68 1992   C813'.54   C92–098021–X
PR9199.3.L35H68 1992

The publisher gratefully acknowledges the assistance of the Saskatchewan Arts Board and The Canada Council. The author wishes to thank both The Canada Council and The Ontario Arts Council.

Fifth House Publishers
620 Duchess Street
Saskatoon, Saskatchewan
S7K 0R1

Contents

Mill–Cry	*1*
Survival Kit	*10*
Rabbits	*21*
Honey	*29*
Irene Good Night	*37*
Sleeping Annie	*43*
All of Their Hearts	*51*
Apple Peels and Knives	*58*
Jack on the Queen	*62*
Blue	*70*
What Is It You Want, Exactly?	*79*
How Do You Spell Beautiful?	*87*
The Babysitter	*92*
Whatever Was Going to Happen	*102*
The Bear	*108*
The Judge Sisters	*127*
Marylou Had Her Teeth Out	*139*
Burning Wings	*148*
Sing Low	*166*
Ned Coker's Dream	*181*

This book is for Lorna

Acknowledgements

These stories have appeared in the following places:

"Apple Peels and Knives": *Grain*; *The Old Dance*, Coteau Books

"Honey": *NeWest Review*

"How Do You Spell Beautiful?": *West* magazine

"Marylou Had Her Teeth Out": *Journal of Canadian Fiction*; *Best American Short Stories 1991*, Houghton Mifflin

"Rabbits": *Canadian Forum*; *Best Canadian Stories 1985*, Oberon

"Survival Kit": *Event*

Blue Monday,
Bitter Tuesday,
Long Wednesday,
Everlasting Thursday,
Friday, will you never go?
Sweet silver Saturday in the afternoon,
Sunday, may you last forever.
Amen.
Two nights in the straw and three meals ahead.

Anonymous
(found written on a wall in an
abandoned sawmill, circa 1958)

Mill–Cry

THE YOUNG MAN SITS AT A PINE TABLE playing solitaire with a worn pack of cards. His son, three years old, stands by the chair, his small hand clenched upon his father's knee. The boy doesn't look at his brother, who sits in a wooden highchair with a smile on his round face. Fat, with his first year barely behind him, the baby paddles his hand in a pool of spilled food and milk.

Standing at the sink with her back to them all, her thin hands deep in soapy water, the young man's wife washes diapers. The ammonic smell of bleach and urine lifts with the steam into her nose and eyes. Her belly is already pushing her back from the counter and she has to lean slightly forward, a seven-month foetus high up against her heart.

She lifts a strand of hair, leaving a film of soap on the curve of her cheek. The baby raises his pudgy hand and brings it down in the puddle of soiled milk and mashed carrot on the board before him, yellow drops splashing upon his bare chest. The older boy grips the hard blue cotton seam of his father's pantleg.

The child's eyes barely reach the table. What he sees are the curled edges of cards, an ashtray with a rolled cigarette in it, and a cup of cold coffee. His eyes follow the blue smoke that spirals upward from the cigarette to where it flattens against the air.

In a moment the woman will ask the man to give the diapers a final wringing. Her hands and arms are tired from dishes and diapers and

How Do You Spell Beautiful?

lifting her sons from whatever griefs they have fallen into over the long cold day.

Outside snow falls from darkness. The wet flakes drift down on the aluminum roof of their narrow trailer. It's snowed for a night and a day and shows no sign of slowing. There is more than a foot on the gravel reach in front of the trailer. Months ago it was their garden. Now only withered corn stalks lean muffled in the drifts.

If there were a radio the young man and the woman would know the storm will last for another day or two, but there is no radio. They are living between two mountains three miles below Blue River Canyon. There is no radio here. The mountains are too high, the valley too narrow. The weather that surrounds them has its own life and the five of them live inside it.

The snow will stop when it stops. They are used to this, snow or rain, or the slowness of the sun when it at last moves above the mountain at ten in the morning. Half their day is spent in shadow.

The woman squeezes out what water she can from the last diapers and looks into the window above the sink. She can't see the snow through the grey glass, though she knows it's there. What she sees is her face and for a moment it seems as if a ghost stares at her from the night. Steam has covered the window and as it drips down the glass it cuts the ice, creasing her image with crooked vertical lines, the high cheeks and the eyes that stare back at her.

The child inside her moves, striking out with its hard heels, and the woman steps back, placing her wet hand upon her belly, feeling the body within her. She presses down and the heels push back.

Two more months.

It seems to her she's been pregnant all her life. This child, like the two before, is an accident. It's something that has happened to her in the way a leg gets broken or a hand burned.

Each time has been like a blow, as if someone has punched her hard in that place just below the ribs where her heart sits.

She's willed herself to bleed but nothing has happened. She's asked God to stop it, but her tired body is obdurate. It is separate from her. It grows what it grows.

The woman thinks what is between her legs is an enemy, something with a life of its own, a mouth with a terrible "yes" that is not affirmation but affliction.

The man goes through the deck one last time, lifting the cards off in threes and laying them down. He's unaware of the boy and the hand that grips his leg. It's his seventh game and he isn't winning again. He

2

Mill-Cry

feels a victory in the loss. It rises in him, a perversion, a kind of pleasure. He could cheat if he wanted but he doesn't. Instead, he lays what is left of the pack on the scratched table and pulls the other cards into it.

He's had enough. Soon it will be time to put the children down.

In a moment his wife will ask. When she does he will rise, lift diapers from the puddles on the counter and twist them violently in his hard hands. She will take them from him and hang them on the lines he's strung across their living room. The diapers will hang all night and into the next day until they dry stiff and hard, only to be taken down and replaced by others.

The man is tired. He has worked all day at the mill office adding columns of log scale on a hand-cranked adding machine. He is numb from repeating the same action thousands of times over nine hours.

But at least he's off the mill floor. He isn't just a worker like the rest of them. Not any more. He's on salary now. One hundred and seventy-two dollars a month. He could make more working shifts but he knows that's no answer.

A strike could destroy them.

Welfare or worse.

He's the first-aid man at the mill. Even though he's at home he's on call, and while he sits there gazing at the stack of cards there's a part of him listening to the scream of whistles crying into the night.

The whistles go all the time. If there are six in a row he has to go down through the snow to the mill because six whistles mean an accident, six whistles mean someone's made a mistake and broken something or lost something—a finger, a hand, a bone in a chest or leg— or it could be simply the flesh, a muscle opened up to the air, an ear torn partly off, an eye cut across the cornea by a slash of splinter.

The whistles seem to happen far away.

He's been a first-aid man for barely six months. The course lasted five weeks. Twenty hours of practical and suddenly he had a ticket and ten dollars more a month. The nearest hospital is six hours away in Kamloops. It's only one hundred and eighty miles south but the road is narrow, a thin track of shattered stone. Even driving at night as fast as he can it takes hours, the truck crawling over the mountains and through the canyons.

For a moment, far back in his mind, he glimpses the heavy blue arms of spruce and cedar reaching for him as he pushes a pickup south, a man beside him close to death, in shock or past it and crying out, talking gibberish, or worse, saying nothing, that steady glazed stillness of the badly injured.

How Do You Spell Beautiful?

He glances out the window and sees through the falling snow a faint red glow. It seems as if the snow is burning somewhere, as if there were a cold fire hanging far off in the night.

It's the mill burner a quarter mile away. The scream of metal on metal is all around them, dulled by the falling snow.

And the whistles?

The whistles cry out every few minutes, sometimes reaching all the way to five, and when they do the young man stops and waits through silence until it stretches past the sound he waits for, the sixth whistle, the one that means shock and blood and helplessness, a man lying in sawdust and grease staring stupidly at some part of his body disappeared, severed from himself.

~

None of them can remember a time when the diapers weren't there. It's been two months since winter began but they don't try to remember the fall or the brief summer before that. The past doesn't live inside them. What they have surrounds them, a narrow room eight feet wide and eleven feet long.

Beyond the tight lines of sodden grey diapers is a small couch set against the front of the trailer. The woman has scrubbed the stained fabric arms so many times she's worn through to the brown stuffing below.

There is nothing else in the room, only the table with three chairs and the wooden highchair where the baby sits splashing his hand in the last of his food. A coarse dribble of curdled milk and carrot seeps out of the corner of the baby's mouth and the man, without thinking, reaches and wipes it away with his fingers. The baby gurgles and tries to grab the hand that touches him, but the huge fingers elude his awkward grasp and he flutters his short arm in the suddenly empty air.

Behind a thin plywood door is the rest of the trailer, a tiny room with two narrow bunks against the wall, the lower boarded for a crib, then another door and a bathroom, and beyond that a bedroom at the end where the man and woman sleep. The bed takes up the whole space. It's too short for the man. His feet hang off the end. When he sleeps he wears heavy socks to protect them from the wall and the ice.

The woman who sleeps beside him there curls tightly into a ball each night, though now, with the baby growing larger and larger inside her, she has to stretch out her legs. She's a small woman, barely five foot two, and, pregnant, weighs only a hundred pounds.

4

Mill–Cry

What they have is here. The day they've lived through is gone. What is in the room is the present minute, the present hour. It lives in their lives, a small trapped animal without shape or substance that's given up struggling against what holds it in its place.

It's been like this for three years, since the first child was born, the one who stands beside his father with his hand gripping fiercely the pantleg beside him. He's not a noisy child just as his brother isn't. The world around the little boy is a silent world with once in a while, each month or so, a violence—abrupt, full of screaming and tears—and then silence again, deeper, more protracted.

The silence weighs heavily upon him, upon them all.

The diapers wrung and hung on the lines, the woman watches her husband go into the night. The door closes and she listens to him shovelling, the soft crunch of ice beneath the wet snow. The boys are in bed now. A moment ago she stood by the upper bunk singing the oldest a song from her childhood.

When she finished, the boy lay there on his back and she covered him and told him to sleep tight. He looked at her gravely and told her he would.

It's only nine o'clock but she is deeply tired.

She stands naked in the bathroom, her clothes on a hook beside her. There is barely room to turn around. The bathtub behind her is four feet long and a foot deep. The new one will sleep there.

Taking a washcloth from a nail, she dips it in cold water. The tank is empty, the hot water used up on the diapers.

She cleans herself slowly, her armpits, the creases below her heavy breasts, the veins and the nipples already swelling, her shoulders, face, and arms. Then she reaches between her legs and washes there. She lifts the cloth and looks at it. She's been doing this for months, hoping the cloth will come away with blood as it had when she was fifteen and miscarried.

She pulls on a heavy flannel gown and steps to the bed.

It's cold at the back of the trailer. The heat doesn't reach here and the walls are covered with thin sheets of ice. It's been weeks since the windows were clear. The bed is piled with blankets and towels and coats. She gets in and lies for a moment under the heavy covers and then rolls to her side. Down the hall through the thin doors she hears her husband come in, the front door banging shut, his boots falling to the floor, and then the long moment of quiet before a match is struck.

Silence.

He will come to bed eventually. She closes her eyes and falls

How Do You Spell Beautiful?

instantly into deep sleep, her mouth sagging, her breath heavy and thick.

The man sits at the table staring at the cigarette he's rolled. Like the boy earlier in the evening, he watches the smoke rise and flatten against the air. The afternoon shift is almost over. After the last whistle he will go to bed. The graveyard shift will start up after cleanup. If there's an accident someone will come to wake him. If there's no trouble he will sleep as he always does, fitfully, turning and moving beside his wife's slack body.

He follows the blue spiral up to where it stops and then he takes a deep drag and blows a ring into the quiet. It moves away from him, a sluggish hole that falls to the table and changes shape, becoming a thin stream that tries to find a place to fall from, an edge, somewhere to go other than the surface it's trapped on.

He waits, and when the shutdown whistle blows he snubs the end off his cigarette with his thumbnail and puts the butt beside the ashtray. There is only a bit of tobacco left in the can and payday isn't till Friday.

Everything has to be saved. There's no waste in his world, only a watchfulness, a husbanding of things around him.

He thinks he could go to his wife and wake her. They could talk, but about what?

Talking is the most dangerous thing they can do. All their words are traps. Talk turns from the moment—the children's day, an owl seen, or a bear—into other things, the maybe, the what if, or worse, the how and why.

It's a place they no longer go.

It leads to tears and argument and, if it goes far enough, to the other silence, the cold one he moves into. To go anywhere else is to release a violence waiting just beyond his life.

He can't go there.

He can't risk that.

The last time they tried to talk was a week ago. After the yelling and screaming he had stood in the centre of the room as she flailed him with her hands. She had slapped him across the face until, weeping with rage and frustration, her arms grew tired and she could no longer lift them. He stood there, eyes closed, waiting for her to finish, a familiar numbness in his body, barely hearing his flesh turn into sound, feeling the blood in his mouth where his teeth had torn his lips and the inside of his cheeks, the way the blood tasted thick on his tongue.

He can't tell her about Yaneck.

Mill–Cry

Yaneck, the sawyer on the graveyard shift who'd moved into town five months ago with his young wife.

The mill values Yaneck. A good sawyer is hard to find at the best of times and Yaneck is one of the best. The mill pays him well. The mill wants him to be happy. That's what Claude, the boss, told him that afternoon when Yaneck had asked the first-aid man to come to his house.

Months ago Yaneck moved into one of the houses reserved for sawyers, and after that first day no one had seen his wife. There were some in town who said she wasn't real at all. No one, they said, had seen her come down off the train.

He'd seen her.

He'd helped load the sawyer's things into the company pickup when the train arrived, and he'd helped the dark woman climb into the truck. She hadn't spoken. Yaneck told him she didn't speak and he wondered at the time what the man had meant.

Did he mean she was mute or that she didn't speak English, or what? He'd only nodded when Yaneck said it and didn't look at the woman again except when she'd walked to the house. She'd been swaddled in a shapeless coat with a black kerchief pulled tight around her face and knotted at her chin. Yaneck had followed her down the path, closed the door, and that was it.

No one but Yaneck had gone in or out since. The curtains were always pulled, the front door closed.

He'd spoken about her to Claude but the boss told him to leave it alone. The woman's his wife, he'd said. It's his business. Claude had told him Yaneck was his best sawyer and he didn't want anyone interfering with him. Did he understand?

He could wake his wife, he thinks. He could try to talk to her.

He could say he'd done one hundred and forty-three stitches, the woman sitting rigid and trembling only a little while the curved steel needle went in and out of her flesh, the stitches like small black insects climbing across her wounds. He could tell his wife the woman wasn't mute, that she'd made mewling noises in a language he couldn't understand.

But he can't tell his wife.

What would he say?

That he didn't yell at Yaneck and didn't insist she go out to hospital? Should he say he'd begged Claude to do something about it? Should he tell her he left the woman sitting in the bathroom while Yaneck yelled at him?

7

How Do You Spell Beautiful?

She's a crazy, this one. A crazy woman. That's what Yaneck had yelled. Damn her, he'd said, damn her.

And then he'd gone, leaving Yaneck and his wife inside their house.

~

The oldest child cries out in his sleep and the man goes to him, rolling the small body over and stroking until the child's eyes close. The small forehead below the red hair is creased with worry. The little one below has kicked his covers off and he tucks him back in. This one never makes a sound, never cries.

He walks back to the front of the trailer and strips to his underwear, throwing his clothes over a chair in front of the stove. He keeps his socks on. He is going to walk down the hall through the bathroom and to the bed, but he doesn't. Instead he sits at the table again, picks up the deck of cards and begins laying out another hand of solitaire.

As the cards lie down in their ordered rows in front of him the sawyer goes from his mind. The image of Yaneck's wife goes away as well. Just before she does he thinks of how clean her house was, how everything in it shone, the pine floors, the tables and chairs, everything. He remembers how strange he'd thought that was as he went into the bathroom and found her in her blood.

In the distance the mill starts up again. He hopes it will be a quiet night. He lays out the cards and turns the stock over three at a time. Three on the four. Ace of clubs up. Seven on the eight.

The trailer is silent and he thinks of his wife in the bed at the end of the hall. He lays down the cards and then, without thinking, pulls his underwear aside, releasing his cock. He looks down at himself, the cock hard in his rough hand, and, turning sideways on the chair, pumps himself, spreading his white legs and curving his back forward until he ejaculates into the cup of his left hand. He straightens then, stripping the last semen into the pool on his palm. With his free hand he pushes himself back into his underwear, glancing briefly down the hall.

He sits for a moment, shudders, and goes to the sink to wash his hand. Leaning against the counter, he stares at the pale fronds of ice climbing alive across the window.

Part of him knows he should sleep, but he's unaware of it. The mind he thinks with is blank, full of something he has come to know as waiting.

He moves into it.

The mill fills the night, the chains clanking heavily across metal and

Mill–Cry

the shriek of the saws moving sharp and high through the falling, muffling snow.

He doesn't hear them. There are only the whistles and his counting of them, one, and then two, and then three.

Silence.

Only three.

A millwright is needed.

He's heard the mill-cry for years. It's a part of him. It's who he is, his wife in the icy room at the end of the hall, his children, his son who looks out from his small thin body with a grave seriousness at what world there is, and his other son, the little one who won't talk, who never cries.

Somewhere in the room where his wife sleeps is another child. He felt it once while she was sleeping. He placed his hand on her belly and felt the child move. What was in there was alive. For a moment his hand felt protective and then he'd wanted to reach inside her, take the child out and kill it.

When the child comes it will cost one hundred dollars at the hospital in Kamloops. He doesn't have that money. He's still paying for the last one at three dollars a month. That debt and the debt to come stretches out in a long impossible line.

Beyond him, inside the red glow in the falling snow, a thirty-foot spruce slams down on the headrig, the dogs are set, and the log is rammed into the saws. Cants crash onto the gang-saws and edger-feed as men pull and push raw lumber through the mill. Someone swears at nothing, at everything. It is a man on the trimsaws or a man pulling two-by-twelves off the chain.

The young man sits at the table, picks up the deck of cards, then puts it down.

A whistle blows.

He counts until it stops.

Survival Kit

THE SUN WAS LOW IN THE SKY AND A light wind was kicking up the usual dust along the road. Jim's boots were covered with it. The leather was worn and cracked and the corrugated bottoms were almost completely worn off. He had dubbined the boots that morning, adding the thick paste of oil in the hope it would soften them enough to last a few more paycheques. He could feel the gravel right through his soles. He kicked a rock down the road in front of him.

Christ, he thought, if it's not one thing it's another. And Martha was pregnant again.

Nothing was fair. The doctors with their money and big cars, the lawyers, the businessmen, the mill-owners flying in from the States in their airplanes, everyone who had more than anyone else. He tried to think it all the way through but his mind seemed to stop somewhere before he could find an answer. It was the way it was and that was that.

Like the Bomb.

It wasn't as if there was nothing else to worry about what with money and debts and another child, but now, suddenly, he had to worry about *it* as well, the threat of a nuclear war and everything ending just as he was struggling to work it out.

He swung the two ten-gallon cans and smashed them together. The hollow metal sound boomed down the road, reverberated off the

Survival Kit

willow trees, and came back at him in an echo grown deeper and heavier.

What the hell could you do?

He hefted the cans for the twentieth time. They were light and empty. He'd washed them out with detergent down at the mill, making sure there was no oil left in them. He didn't want the water polluted with oil. You couldn't drink it if it was. At least they'd have that, Martha and the boys. Fresh water for a few days.

He had read the "Nuclear Circular" carefully and they'd talked it over late at night after the boys were down and their words wouldn't scare them. They'd need fresh water and food enough to last for a week before it would be safe to go outside.

If the Bomb fell.

When the Bomb fell.

He didn't want to think about how safe it would be inside a forty-foot aluminum trailer with nuclear fallout all around them. He just knew he had to provide them all with enough food and water to last. At least it was something he could prepare for, not like the bank or Martha's pregnancy.

The cans had cost him a dollar apiece. He'd almost had to beg for them at the mill. He knew Art had no business selling them, that they belonged to the mill, but at the same time it didn't make any difference. The foreman sold the cans to whoever wanted them.

He could've gone to the office and asked for them and probably got them too, but you didn't go around people like Art. And a dollar each when he knew the going rate was fifty cents. But Art knew he wanted them badly and when you want something that bad then you have to pay extra. There went his cigarette money for a week. He'd have to roll his smokes thinner and smoke fewer of them. At least they'd have fresh water. It was the price you paid.

As he walked slowly on the shoulder of the road, a blue pickup passed him. It was Bill Makeluk, the edgerman at the mill. Makeluk didn't bother slowing down to offer him a ride, even though he could see he was carrying two ten-gallon cans. He just hit the horn a couple of times and went on by. It was only a few hundred yards more to the Little River Trailer Court, but Jim felt he could at least have offered.

Bill Makeluk.

How come he had an almost new truck? He knew Bill had more money than he did and he was single on top of that, but it still rankled. Jim squinted his eyes at the dust the truck had raised on the road.

Christ, it was almost a main highway and it still wasn't paved in spite

How Do You Spell Beautiful?

of what the Socreds and Wacky Bennett had said last year during the election. So much for politicians. So much for all of it, the road, the fucking Bomb, Bill Makeluk's blue pickup, and the baby. He only made a buck sixty-five an hour, but at least he wasn't pulling lumber.

After begging and bitching he'd finally got a job on the trimmer and didn't have to work with the Sikhs and Portugese on the chain. No more smelling all that garlic and curry and listening to them butcher the language during coffeebreak.

Money. Jesus, money.

He banged the cans together again and turned in the road at the trailer court.

Alfred was lying on the ground beside his tricycle pretending he was fixing it while Timothy looked on. Timothy's diaper was hanging past his knees. The rear end of it was black but Timothy didn't seem to mind. He was trying to help Alfred and Alfred was telling him to go away. They both looked up when Jim crossed over from the road and walked through the thin brown grass to the trailer. He put the cans down and caught Timothy as the boy threw himself at his knees.

He lifted the boy to his hip, making sure the diaper didn't touch his shirt. He looked down at Alfred.

"What's the problem with the bike?" he asked in mock seriousness.

Alfred frowned. "It's the brakes," he said. "They're slipping."

"Are they all right now?"

"Yup," Alfred said, but he wasn't paying attention any more. He had seen the cans and he was already kicking one of them.

Jim put Timothy down and rescued the cans. "Don't do that," he said.

"Why?"

"Never mind, just don't do it." He looked at the little blonde boy standing in the dust. "Play with Timothy," he said. "I'm going to clean up and then we'll have supper." Before Alfred could argue with him about always having to play with his younger brother, Jim stepped around them and carried the cans into the trailer.

The aluminum door banged behind him as he stepped into the kitchen. Martha stood at the sink washing dishes. He put the cans down on the floor and sat at his chair by the table. Martha didn't turn around. "I got the cans," he said.

Martha held her hands out of the water.

"What cans?"

"You know," Jim said, "the ones for water. The ones in case of the Bomb."

She put her hands back in the water. "Oh," she said. "Those ones."

Survival Kit

He nodded at her back and then got up to get a cup of coffee. It was black and oily but he drank it anyway. He'd long ago given up asking if she'd have fresh coffee on when he got home. He sipped the coffee slowly, tasting its bitterness while he watched her at the sink. His eyes couldn't seem to get away from her waist. Already it seemed thicker, fuller, as if the child inside her was growing at a pound a day. He knew he wasn't being rational, but it seemed to be. He felt like getting up and putting his arms around her, but he didn't. The fight they'd had that morning was still too fresh.

The boys came in then and he picked up Timothy before he could spread wet dirt all over the floor. He carried the child down the hall into the tiny bathroom and laid him on the floor, stripped the dirty diaper off, and put on a clean one. The diapers were old and thin and Martha had begun to use three at once. They were hard and dry and the pins barely went through the fabric. Timothy twisted below him and finally, to stop him from getting a dull pin in the leg, Jim smacked him. Timothy lay still and cried. He clipped the last pin and lifted the boy to his feet. "Stop it," he said, but Timothy didn't. He pulled himself loose and ran down the narrow alley to the kitchen. Jim heard Martha say something comforting.

He sat back on the floor and rested his spine against the toilet. He took off his hard hat and ran his fingers through his hair. He was still sitting there when Martha called him for supper.

~

The trailer was dark except for the kitchen light, and Jim looked out the window at the faint glow of the moon on the willows by the river. Tomorrow was Saturday, a day off, and then Sunday, and then back to the mill. He thought of the poem scribbled on the wall in the coffee room at the mill. He said it quietly to himself, tasting the words.

Blue Monday.
Bitter Tuesday.
Long Wednesday.
Everlasting Thursday.
Friday, will you never go?
Sweet silver Saturday in the afternoon.
Sunday, may you last forever.
Amen.
Two nights in the straw and three meals ahead.

13

How Do You Spell Beautiful?

He looked at the night and then got up off the couch and went to the cupboard beside the stove. There was only a little whisky left in the bottle and he knew he should save it for another time. He reached for it, held it in his hand, and then put it back on the shelf above his rifle.

The rifle leaned in the corner behind the broom and the mop. Beside it the two cans of water sat like Buddhas he had seen once in a *National Geographic* magazine at the barbershop. They sat there side by side, shining and clean, looking like they held some mysterious magic inside them.

He squatted on the floor and touched them with his hands. He'd brought them home two months earlier and he looked at them every day. They were cool to his touch. On top of them sat the case of Campbell's Tomato Soup he'd bought that afternoon on his way home from work. Sixty-four cans of soup. There was that and the water. That was their survival kit. He'd bought the soup because it was the cheapest, though he'd hesitated before a case of creamed corn and one of green beans. Somehow that much corn or beans made him feel sick. Soup was more of a meal.

It isn't much, he thought. It isn't really anything at all.

How in hell were they going to make it with only soup and water? He knew it was crazy but it made him feel safe, almost as if he had a kind of treasure stored there in the closet.

He ran his hands over the brown cardboard and the smooth metal cans, and then stood up and took his rifle from behind the broom.

The house was silent except for the occasional moan from Timothy as the boy turned uneasily in his sleep. He glanced down the hall at the two bunks in the middle room. It's like living in a railway car, he thought. Alfred was lying on his back with the covers at his feet, and Timothy was below him with his blankets pulled out and wrapped across his shoulders and neck. Jim leaned the Lee Enfield against the stove and tucked the boys back in. Neither of them woke. He looked at them both for a long time and then, instead of returning to the kitchen, he walked through the bathroom and slid back the door leading into his and Martha's bedroom at the back of the trailer.

She was sleeping on her side with her legs pulled up under her breasts and her arms wrapped around her legs. Like a child, he thought, like a child outside a child, the two of them sleeping like wooden dolls he'd seen once, the ones with other dolls inside, each one becoming smaller and smaller and smaller. He had taken them apart. Where had he seen them, somebody's house, some place he'd been once in a town where he'd worked?

Survival Kit

He'd been sitting at a table and taking the dolls apart, lifting one out of another until he got to the last, the one that didn't come apart. He had held it in his hand and imagined the millions of dolls inside it until they became smaller than atoms. He suddenly thought of a math class he'd taken the last year he went to school, when Martha got pregnant and he'd quit to get married and go to work.

Who had the teacher been? Mr. Anderson? Mr. Craig? Whoever it was had talked that day about minus quantities of numbers. It had always stayed with him, that idea, although he hadn't thought of it for a long time. The numbers were like the dolls. It had never occurred to him before that there could be a negative world made up only of minuses.

He stared down at Martha. The child would be a girl. When Ellen and Bev and the others had hung the ring on a hair and swung it over Martha's naked belly to sex the child, he'd known it would swing in circles and the ring would say it was a girl.

He leaned against the door. It was all more than he could handle, more than he could understand or conceive, this woman who lived with him and was the mother of his children, who seemed to him as he looked at her to be a complete stranger, just as his sons in the other room were strangers.

He was a stranger. Suddenly and with a terrible need he wanted to climb into the bed and enter this strange woman's body and become a child within the child she was carrying. When he was there he knew a child would grow inside him, and another and another, and it would go on forever until they all became a negative thing, a minus child of unbelievable smallness. He shook his head and closed his eyes. When he opened them everything was exactly the same except now he knew who she was, his wife, pregnant with their child, the woman he loved and wanted more than anything in the world to leave.

But go where? Do what?

What was the point of leaving where you were if there was nowhere else to go? He turned and walked back into the living room. He carried the rifle with him. Sitting on the couch he removed the bolt and sighted through the empty barrel at the slim line of new moon above the trees. The barrel was clean. He knew it would be. He got up and took the gun-cleaning kit off the shelf in the closet, touched the carton of soup like a talisman, and returned to the couch.

He cleaned the rifle carefully, oiling the barrel, the breech, and the bolt, and then put it back together and laid it across his knees. The six bright brass shells clicked on the cushion beside him as he shifted his

How Do You Spell Beautiful?

weight. Something had to be done. There was no way they were going to make it. There wasn't enough money and there was never going to be. The trailer was going to take five more years to pay off and already it was too small for them.

His hands were shaking. He wrapped his fingers around the rifle and held it tightly. He didn't know who or what he was angry at. There wasn't anywhere he could aim his feelings. It wasn't Martha's fault and it wasn't his. It was no one's fault. It just was. That was it, a wasness, a wasness that sat on his shoulders like a mountain.

He stood up, carrying the rifle, went to the cupboard, and poured himself two fingers of whisky. He had saved the bottle from their last Christmas at home. There were only three inches left. He set it on the kitchen counter beside the dirty supper dishes and stood there with the glass in one hand and the rifle in the other. A case of Campbell's Tomato Soup and two cans of water, a Lee Enfield and six bright shells.

He decided to kill Bill Makeluk. They'd need a truck to get away when the Bomb fell and Bill had one. Bill was free. He didn't have to worry about anything. Jim knew he'd enjoy putting a bullet through his fat face, knew he'd enjoy seeing Bill Makeluk's head explode. He'd take the pickup then, after the fallout, and he'd drive his family north to the Chilcotin, where they could still make it. A place that didn't have radiation.

But that was far away, just like the birth of the child. Hunched there in the dark of the kitchen, he couldn't get his mind past Bill Makeluk. The sight of Bill's head exploding was stopped in his mind like a picture in a magazine. It gave him such a feeling of release that he shuddered. He took a drink, filling his mouth with whisky. Splashing what was left of the bottle into his glass, he went and sat down on the couch and looked out the window. He sat there a long time with one hand resting on the barrel of the gun and the other turning the glass around and around.

He wasn't sure how long he'd been sitting there when he saw a pickup with only its parking lights on glide into the trailer court. It pulled into the dirt in front of the trailer and stopped beside Alfred's tricycle. Damn, he thought. I told Alfred to put that bike away.

The truck's lights blinked off.

Makeluk.

Jim waited until the doors opened and two men got out. They talked for a moment and then one of them walked over to the trailer. It was Art Yastremski, the foreman. He stood in the light of the door, his large body framed on the torn screen. Jim lifted the barrel of his rifle in one

Survival Kit

hand and aimed it at Art. For a moment he thought of a bullet entering the foreman's body just below his rib cage, and then he laid the rifle on the couch and walked over to the door. He nodded at Art and then walked with him to the truck. No one spoke and Jim said, "Kinda late, isn't it?"

Art rested his boot on the corner of the front bumper and pointed at the running board. Jim sat down and Bill sat beside him.

Jim could feel the cold steel through his shirt. He imagined the truck as his own, with Martha and the kids on the seat beside him, and all of them driving north with the two cans of water and the case of soup in the back. The road in front of him was clear and on the hood of the truck, like some mad ornament, was Bill Makeluk's head, or what was left of it. He rubbed his hands through his short hair and then leaned forward and picked at a bit of dry grass by his boot.

"We wanted to talk," Art said.

"Yeah, what about?"

"We figured it was time some of us talked to you about the way things are right now." Art spoke slowly and carefully. Bill Makeluk nodded his head. "You know," Art continued, "the Bomb and all that."

Jim didn't say anything.

"Anyway," Art said, "I guess you read in the *Vancouver Sun* about all the refugees there's going to be and how they figure, after the Bomb, most of them are going to be coming up here into the Interior to live. You read about that, didn't you?"

"Yeah."

Art looked at him intently. Jim suddenly hated Art as much as he did Bill Makeluk. He hated him for charging him two bucks for the cans, for his better job, for everything that was going on everywhere.

"Look, Jim," Bill said, "we think we can trust you, but before we say anything we want you to promise us no matter what, you'll keep what we say quiet." When he just nodded, Bill went on. "Is it a deal?"

Jim nodded again and crushed the grass in his hand.

"This's how it is," Bill said. "It's like we know there ain't no room in Little River for any refugees from the Coast. Hell, there's barely enough in the stores to feed us when it comes down to it, and that's in spite of how much a guy can squirrel away for the day when it comes. And it's coming, the way Khrushchev and Kennedy are going at it. Anyway, we figure we'll stop them long before they get here. You know, blow the bridges, a rock slide here and there, that sort of thing. What that doesn't stop, then the rest of us will get. You know what I mean?"

How Do You Spell Beautiful?

"You mean kill them, murder them when they're coming up the canyon?"

Art dropped his foot off the bumper and kicked a rock. It bounced off the wheel of Alfred's tricycle. "Well, I don't know that murder is the right word for it. It's more like dog-eat-dog in a way. There's only so much. Winter's coming and you can't grow potatoes in the snow."

When Jim didn't say anything, Bill said, "You get our meaning, don't you?"

"What do you need me for?" Jim asked. "Sounds like you guys got it all figured out." He didn't know what else to say. All he could think of was the truck and them heading north, north and away from Little River and the bank and the mill and men like Art and Bill. He knew, if it came down to it, the two men would kill him just as easily as they'd kill the people from the Coast. He sat there and all the strength seemed to sink out of him into the ground. He could see it, that was the trouble, and they'd been making plans for it, better plans, while he was filling cans with water and buying cases of soup that he couldn't afford no matter how cheap they were.

"We don't really need you," Art said, "but we can use you. I heard how you might know a little about powder, and even if you don't, you got a gun."

"Well, what do you think?" Bill asked.

He stood up and walked over to Alfred's tricycle lying in front of the pickup. He lifted the bike by the handlebars and stood there with his back to them. "Well?" Bill asked again. Jim didn't turn around.

"I don't know," he said. "I don't know. I'll have to think about it."

Art walked over and touched him on the shoulder. "Don't think too long. You're either with us or you're not. There's lots are, with us, I mean."

"You got a nice pickup," Jim said.

"What?"

"That pickup," he repeated. "That's a nice truck."

"You mean Bill's truck?"

"Yeah." He shrugged off Art's hand. "I'll think about it, I guess." He started walking back toward the trailer with the tricycle in his hand.

"Oh, and them cans," Art called out.

He stopped. "What do you mean?"

"I just wanted to say you shouldn't put water in them 'cause it'll go bad."

Jim turned his head and looked at Art standing in front of the truck with Bill beside him. "I don't understand," he said.

18

Survival Kit

"They'll rust out in no time at all. They ain't lined or anything."

"I didn't want them for water."

"I just wanted to say. I mean, in case you did."

"I didn't," Jim replied, and started walking again. He pushed the tricycle under the trailer and opened the screen door. In the kitchen he picked up the empty bottle and held it to his mouth, allowing the few drops of whisky to dribble onto his tongue. He watched the truck pull away and drive with its lights out down the road to another trailer. That's Middleton's place, he thought. They want him too. They're all in it.

He dropped the bottle into the garbage and opened the closet door. Tipping the case of soup onto the floor, he hoisted a can of water to the sink. Even in the thin light from the moon he could tell as it poured out that the water was rotten. Art knew it, he thought. He knew what I wanted them for even when he was charging me a dollar a can. That's how come he knew I was thinking about the Bomb.

The water gurgled into the sink. He emptied the can, dropped it on the floor, and then lifted the other one and did the same. When it was empty he dropped it as well. It boomed against the other one and rolled under the table. He kicked the can across the room and leaned against the sink with the sick smell of rust rising into his face. Then he ripped open the cardboard box of soup and began opening the cans one at a time, his hands trembling.

"What is it? What's wrong?" Martha asked, standing by the door. Her hair was limp from sleep and she held Timothy on her hip, his leg curled above her swollen belly. Alfred stood beside her, his hand holding the edge of her bathrobe. "What was all the noise?" she asked.

"Nothing," he said. "There's nothing wrong."

"What are you doing?"

He looked at the empty soup cans scattered across the counter. The sink was full of thick pink soup. His hands shook as he took another can from the case and began cutting off the top with a can opener.

"What happened? What's wrong?" she asked again. She moved back from him and shifted Timothy on her hip. His small face was buried in her shoulder. "That's our survival kit. Why are you throwing it away?"

"Nothing, nothing, nothing," he said, shaking and trying to turn the small metal handle of the opener. It slipped and he cut his hand on the sharp metal lid. He didn't want to look at her. He wanted to disappear. He looked down at the blood dripping onto the soup in the sink. She

19

How Do You Spell Beautiful?

stood there holding tightly to Timothy. Alfred had left her and was kneeling by the couch. "Can I play with it?" he asked. "Can I play with the gun?"

"Get away from there," Martha said. Alfred looked at her, scared, and then walked quickly past his father and stood beside her in the doorway. "You're crazy," she said. "You do such crazy things. I don't understand. I don't understand anything."

When he looked up she was gone. He reached for another can but his hand, slippery now, couldn't hold onto it. The can dropped into the sink. He watched the soup part around it and then slide slowly back over the hole it had made.

It was quiet. He knew they were sitting on the edge of the bed. Martha and Alfred and Timothy. He wanted to go and sit beside them. He wanted to put his arms around all of them and say it was all right, that he wasn't crazy, that it was just a bad night, but he couldn't. There wasn't room for all of them inside his arms.

Rabbits

He was getting mad again. she was standing at the window ironing a shirt and he could hear the iron clicking against the buttons. Each time she lifted it a small cloud of steam shot out. She moved the shirt and pushed the iron back and forth. "But why rabbits?" he asked.

She shrugged her shoulders and went on ironing. She wasn't looking at him again. Why did she ignore him like that? He watched her finish the shirt. Picking up one of Mary's little dresses, she laid it across the board. He hated it when she wouldn't answer him. He never understood her when she was like this. Maybe it was her period or something. She was always strange around that time. "Is it your period?"

She looked out the window. "I just had my period. Last week, remember?"

Why should he remember? It was like trying to remember the last time they'd made love. When was that, a month ago, two months ago? Her period, that was a laugh. It used to be she liked to make love when she menstruated. He never did. He'd keep on thinking of the blood. It wasn't unclean or anything, but it made him feel uneasy.

Just after they moved they'd made love on the table in front of the window, and all the time he kept looking out, thinking someone was watching. That was right around the time he'd had to tell Dion to stay

How Do You Spell Beautiful?

away. "Someone might've seen," he said afterwards. "Like Dion or someone. He's always wandering the roads."

"We're way out in the country," she'd said. "Dion's place is miles away. Even he doesn't wander this far. Anyway," she'd said, "you told him not to come around here, remember? There's no one to see."

It had been crazy. He told her so and she laughed. "It excited you," she'd said. It had, but he still felt uncomfortable, her bleeding and them doing it.

But that was two years ago. He rubbed his hand on the side of the chair. The table looked so ordinary now. He found it hard to imagine them lying there on top of it, doing it for all the world to see. "But why rabbits?"

"Why not?"

"I don't know."

"There's just Mary and me here all day. You're off at the mill. You always said we should try and be more country. When we moved here you said that." She picked up another of Mary's dresses and began ironing again. "I want to, that's all."

"Never mind," he said, angry now. "I don't want to talk about it."

He'd been getting mad a lot lately. Maybe moving out to the country hadn't been such a good idea, but in the city they just seemed to be going around and around. Ever since they'd got here he'd been worried about her. She made him so mad. Her silences, her strangeness, their not making love any more. And now rabbits. Why rabbits? Why not pigs or something? He'd never eaten rabbit meat. The thought of it turned his stomach. What were they doing in the country anyway?

She was still looking out the window, ironing. It was like he wasn't even there. The discussion was over and they'd solved nothing. Lately all their arguments ended up that way, with him mad and her quiet. It had to be Dion. The Rabbit Man, Mary called him. Retarded Dion. "When did you talk to him?"

"Who?"

"Dion. You know who I mean. Who else would I be talking about?"

"I don't know," she said. "Last week, maybe. He showed me his rabbits. There's nothing wrong with that."

"Is that why?"

"What?"

"Rabbits, for Christ's sake! Stop the damned ironing and talk to me. I don't understand why you want to have rabbits. I could understand pigs or something, but not rabbits. The thought of eating a rabbit makes me sick."

22

Rabbits

"You shouldn't worry about Dion. He's a little slow is all."

"I don't give a shit about Dion."

"You know why."

"I don't know why!"

She wasn't making any sense.

"Yes, you do."

He was going to shout again or do something, but Mary came in the house crying. She'd fallen and hurt her hand. Diana picked her up and cuddled her as she walked into the bathroom.

"And I don't want that crazy Dion around here," he yelled after her.

He went outside and sat on the steps. He didn't understand, but it was better than fighting. Maybe she needed something else. He had the mill. She didn't have any friends to speak of and there really wasn't much to do around the place. He knew that. She said she liked living in the country, and maybe the rabbits would just be pets. What the hell did Dion do with his rabbits? Were they just pets or did he eat them? Why was *he* getting so upset? Her wanting them wasn't that strange. It was just that everything seemed a little off kilter lately. Like not making love. He couldn't figure it out and he always used to be able to.

~

He built the cages the next day.

Diana had drawn him a picture of what they were supposed to be like. He put them up behind the house near the old shed, nine of them. They were off the ground, each one separate and each one with a smaller box inside for when they gave birth. She told him they needed solitude and quiet when they were pregnant and even moreso after. If they were disturbed they'd go crazy. And you had to keep the buck away or it'd eat the babies.

He never knew that about rabbits before.

And then there was Dion. How old was he, twenty-five or so? Sometimes with people like that you couldn't tell. They didn't age like normal people. A big stupid kid, really. He didn't want him around Mary and Diana when he wasn't there.

Christ, only in the country would they let a guy like that live by himself without someone there to keep an eye on him. Dion might be harmless, but he didn't want him hanging around.

Diana said she'd take Mary and go get the rabbits, that he didn't have to come, but he did. He didn't want them going down there without him. She dressed Mary in one of her prettiest outfits, the yellow one with the flowers on it. "For Christ's sake, we're just going to

23

How Do You Spell Beautiful?

get some rabbits," he said when they came out and got in the car.

"It's special," Diana said. "Don't you understand?"

Mary sat between them as he drove down the road to Dion's place. The child was becoming strange too. He worried sometimes that living in the country wasn't good for her. There was no one to play with. She was only three, still a couple of years away from school.

"We're going to the Rabbit Man's," said Mary.

"Sure we are," he said. "But don't start thinking they're pets, okay? They're like pigs or cows. We're going to eat them." He waited for Diana to object, but she didn't say anything. Mary didn't either. She sat between them with her hands folded on her lap. "Do you understand?" Why wouldn't Diana say something? He wanted her to explain to the child. None of this was his idea. "They're your mother's rabbits," he said. "Why don't you ask her?"

"I guess I understand," Mary said. She sat very still. "But we don't really eat pigs, do we?"

At that moment he hated Diana, sitting there looking out the window ignoring him. He gripped the wheel in his hands and tried to speak lightly, easily, as if none of it mattered. "Sure we do. You like pork chops and bacon, don't you?" She moved over and climbed into Diana's lap. "Well," he said carefully, "pork chops come from pigs. That's what pork means. It means pig."

Mary looked at him oddly and then gazed out the window with her mother. "They don't call them pork in my books," she said. "They call them pigs."

"For Christ's sake, Diana. Didn't you explain all this to her?"

"She understands," Diana said, laughing. "Don't worry about it."

"I wish *I* did. I wish to God you'd explain it to me."

He kept on driving. They were almost at Dion's place and he felt awkward, especially since he'd told the guy to stay away. The guy was kind of crazy, but then a lot of country people were. Maybe it was just him. Retarded people had rights. Anyway, maybe Dion wasn't really retarded. Maybe he was just slow like Diana said. "We're going to see the Rabbit Man," he said, wanting to make a joke out of it all.

Diana held onto Mary and didn't say anything.

The hell with it.

He stopped the car by the open gate and set the emergency brake. The driveway was full of grass and the yard was a mess, broken bits of machinery everywhere, piles of rotting lumber, and old tractor tires with grass and ferns growing out of them. He held onto Mary's hand as Dion came around the corner of his shack. Diana walked over and

24

Rabbits

he followed slowly with Mary. The child tried to pull away and finally he lifted her up and held her.

Diana was wearing her blue dress and she had on her good shoes. "We've come for the rabbits," he heard her say. "Remember?" Dion grinned and nodded, and then he looked past her at him. "It's okay," she said. "He wanted to come." Dion stopped grinning and walked around the back of the shack.

Diana stopped. "Why don't you just let me get them?" she said. "You can wait in the car."

He walked toward her. Mary squirmed in his arms and he squeezed her hard and told her to be quiet. Diana stared at him for a moment and then walked on ahead.

Dion's hutches were nailed against the wall of a small tumbledown barn. There were dozens of them piled and nailed in staggered rows, all full of large white rabbits with pink eyes. He put Mary down and held her as he watched Diana help put the does in a large plywood box. Dion put a buck in a separate container, but before he did, he lifted the rabbit up to show them. His thin lopsided face broke into a grin. "This's the important one," he said, slurring the words. Diana laughed and so did Mary.

Dion held the buck by the ears in one hand and the hind legs in the other. Stretching the animal, he exposed its belly to them, gesturing for them to take a look. Mary tried to go forward to see better, but he held onto her hand and wouldn't let her go. "Are you really the Rabbit Man?" she asked. Dion looked at her, bewildered.

"Put him in the box," he said to Dion.

"It's only a rabbit," Diana said.

He picked Mary up again and carried her back to the car. They sat in the front seat and waited. Dion appeared first carrying the large box, followed by Diana with the buck. They put them in the trunk and, as soon as the lid closed, he started the car and put it in gear. Diana looked through the rear windshield at him. He could tell she was upset as she walked around and got in, but she closed the door quietly. Dion came around to the passenger side and pressed his thin face against the glass. "Goodbye, little girl," he said. "Goodbye."

"Goodbye, Rabbit Man," Mary said as her father released the clutch and pulled roughly out of the driveway.

No one said anything on the way home. He parked the car and carried the does to the back and put them in the cages he'd made. Diana carried the box with the buck. It gave off a rank musty odour. He hadn't realized they smelled like that. Diana put the box down and

How Do You Spell Beautiful?

opened it. She didn't get a very good grip on the animal and it almost got away. He grabbed for it, but the buck's jerking legs raked his arm. "Let him alone," she said. "I'll do it." He struggled with her, trying to get both legs in his free hand, but not before it scratched him again.

"Jesus," he said, and pushed her away, holding the rabbit tightly. Diana was breathing heavily as she opened the last cage. He threw the buck inside and told Mary to go to the house. "Never mind," he said when she complained. "Just go." She walked away and sat under the vine maples beside the driveway, where the salal brush grew in a heavy green wall.

He stood beside Diana and watched. At first the buck just squatted and stared at the doe huddling against the back of the cage. Then it thumped its back paws on the floor. The doe shivered and laid her ears flat across her back. The buck crowded her into a corner, grabbed her nape in his yellow teeth and mounted her. The doe screamed when he entered.

The cry shocked him. The sound was almost human. It was over in less than a minute, the buck lifting as he came and falling back off the doe to lie half-conscious on the wooden floor. The doe stood above the buck and smelled him, her pink eyes bright as she pushed her nose into the damp fur. The buck jerked twice and got back up. The doe moved away into a corner.

He went back to the house. Before he reached the porch he heard the doe scream again. He went in and closed the door behind him. Standing at the window, he watched Diana get Mary and take her back up to the rabbits. They held hands and watched, both of them in their best dresses. He poured himself a cup of coffee and sat at the table. What was the matter with him? It was natural for Mary to see them do that. Wasn't that why they were in the country? He started shaking and spilled coffee on his shirt. There was blood on his forearm and he wiped it across his pantleg, the long scratches burning as he rubbed the blood into his jeans.

He tried to talk to Diana that night after Mary went to bed, but she told him she didn't want to. And she didn't want to make love either. He put on some of the Dylan tapes, the early ones, and listened to them for a while. Diana went to bed after the first song. Two hours later he shut the machine off and put the tapes away. He checked on Mary. She was fast asleep. Her yellow dress with the flowers was on the floor and he picked it up and hung it in the closet. He didn't look in on Diana. Instead, he went to the couch and slept there. In the morning he got up early and went to work. Both of them were sleeping when he left.

Rabbits

All day he sorted lumber, but he couldn't stop thinking. He knew he shouldn't be worried. He had slept on the couch a few times before and they had always laughed about it later, but that was when they were living in the city. Something wasn't right. He didn't know what. Twice he almost told the foreman he was sick so he could go home, but he stopped himself.

It was crazy to do that.

Maybe they'd talk about it that night and everything would be all right again. They could talk about living in the country and having rabbits, and Mary going to school in Little River in another year or so, and how they were changing, and how probably that was okay because that's why they'd left the city in the first place, to get back to the land, to make their lives more real. All the things they'd talked about before they moved. And he would try to explain why he'd got so mad lately, and Diana would explain why she was acting so different the last few months, and they would end up laughing about it. And she would want to make love to him and they would. It was almost five o'clock and he was turning the lumber over on the chain, and he was crying and he didn't know why he was crying. He wanted to go home. He wanted to tell Diana he loved her and that he was afraid and didn't know what he was afraid of.

When the whistle blew he punched his time card and ran out to the car. The drive seemed to take forever. He tried to slow down, but he took the curves on the hills faster than he ever had before, the tires squealing, the car almost out of control. There's nothing to worry about, he kept telling himself. I love you.

As he passed Dion's place he slowed almost to a stop and hit the horn with his fist. He didn't know why. When the horn sounded, a rabbit jumped out of an old tire. It hopped twice along the driveway and then rose up on its hind legs and looked at him. He hadn't seen it before he hit the horn. He yelled but it didn't move.

Pushing his foot down hard on the gas, he drove the last mile. He kept looking around for Dion, but there was no one on the road.

He pulled into the yard and skidded to a stop on the gravel. As he turned the motor off, he saw the rabbits. They were out. He looked up at the cages but the doors were all open. As he ran toward the house, three rabbits scattered in front of him, two going around the porch and the other into the trees. He took the steps three at a time as he ran into the house.

"Diana?"

Mary was at the table. She was holding a pair of blunt-nosed scissors

How Do You Spell Beautiful?

and cutting a picture out of an old *Life* magazine. She seemed okay. "Diana?" he called, louder, as he looked around. Then he smelled something. The buck rabbit was on the kitchen counter. He picked it up. The neck was broken and the head hung awkwardly off his hand. It smelled terrible. He put the body in the garbage bag under the sink and went over and sat beside Mary at the table. He tried to be calm. "Where's your Mommy?" he asked.

"I don't know," she said. She didn't look at him as she worked her scissors in the paper.

Maybe Diana had just gone out for a walk. She did that sometimes. "Why are the rabbits out?" he asked as quietly as he could.

"I don't know," Mary said. "I'm not supposed to go out there any more. Look at the pig," she said, holding the picture up to him. It was a picture of a pig on top of a barn roof, one of the funny ones from the last pages of *Life*. He watched as her scissors worked slowly around the edge of the barn.

"Do you like it here? Do you like it here in the country?"

It was all he could think of to say. He waited for her to answer. She was holding her lip in her teeth. The scissors cut very carefully along the top of the barn and then, with sudden excitement, she cut the pig off the top of the roof. "See," she said. And then she began to sing. "The pork's off the roof. The pork's off the roof!" She stood up in her chair and danced up and down, her yellow dress with the flowers on it lifting and falling around her legs.

"Who killed the rabbit?" he asked. "Was it the Rabbit Man?"

She stopped dancing. "No. It was Mommy. Mommy did it."

He picked her up and began to shake her. "Where's your Mommy?" he yelled.

"I don't know," she said, starting to cry. He stopped shaking her and held onto her as tightly as he could, but she wouldn't stop crying. He held her and held her, wanting her to stop, wanting her to tell him everything was all right, that Mommy would be home soon, that she loved him, really loved him, and she didn't want rabbits any more.

Honey

JOHNNY AND CARL WERE FRIENDS AND SO were their wives, Madge and Mabel. Mabel and Madge. They all used to laugh at that, the way the names sounded together. Carl even made a little poem about it. One Friday night when they'd been drinking and playing cards, he tipped his head back and said in that crazy way:

Madge and Mabel,
they're both able.

He and Johnny nearly killed themselves laughing. Madge and Mabel, they're both able. They repeated it like it was some kind of chant, their voices saying it together, Carl pounding on the table with his fist and Johnny sagging against the chair he was laughing so hard. Madge said she didn't think it was that funny, which made them both laugh even harder.

Mabel didn't say anything. She just sat there with her cards in her hand and a funny look on her face. The cat, who'd been sitting on her lap, jumped off and went over to the couch. It climbed up and sat on the back of it, hunched over its white paws.

"Look," Madge said, "you even scared the cat."

Carl said, "C'mon, honey, it's just a joke. "

"Well," Madge said, "it may be funny to you two, but it makes us both sound, oh, I don't know, loose or something."

Carl and Johnny started laughing again, Carl saying the word loose

How Do You Spell Beautiful?

between his laughing and Johnny finally slipping off his chair and lying on the floor saying, "Stop it, you're killing me."

Madge looked at Mabel and said, "C'mon, why don't you give me a hand in the kitchen. I think it's time we made some coffee for these two."

Mable nodded her head and they left the room, Johnny lying on the floor, his face all red, and Carl with his fist making the glasses on the table bounce around. Finally he stopped pounding and reached for the bottle of Seagram's and poured himself another drink. "Hey, Johnny," he said, still gulping for air, "get up and have a drink."

Johnny groaned and then uncurled himself and crawled back into his chair. He watched Carl pour him a drink and said, "Carl, you've got to be the funniest guy I ever met. I mean it. There isn't anybody who can make me laugh as hard as you."

Carl agreed, saying he didn't know how he did it. "They just come out of me," he said. He reached out and picked up his cards. They'd been lying in the spilled drinks. "Jesus," he said. "Look at the mess." He started wiping the cards off on the sleeve of his shirt.

Johnny yelled, "Hey, Mabel, bring a cloth or something. There's drinks spilled in here and the cards are all wet."

"Who was your slave last year?" Madge hollered back.

"Women," Carl said to that. "What're you supposed to do?"

"Well, I'll be go to hell," Johnny said. He was pouring more whisky into his glass while he said it. "She's your old lady, isn't she?"

Carl said, "It's just a fucking joke. Can't they take a joke for Christ's sake?"

Johnny took a drink from his glass. "Jesus, I'm getting drunk. Where the hell are they? I'd like to play some more cards. Hell, I was winning until you broke us all up."

When Carl just kept wiping the cards on his shirt, Johnny got up and went into the kitchen. The girls were standing by the stove waiting for the coffee to start perking. "Hey," he said.

He went over to his wife and put his arms around her, and she tried to push him away. She said, "I agree with Madge, you know. It wasn't all that funny once you think of it."

Johnny fought her arms away and picked her up off the floor. He swirled her around the kitchen. "Who's my pretty girl?" he said. "Let's dance. You know I like dancing."

Mabel put her arms around his neck, trying to hold on as her feet swept in circles about a foot off the floor. Johnny looked over her small dark head at Madge and told her to go out and be nice to Carl. "We

30

Honey

didn't mean it," he said. "Go on. Be nice to him. Hell, we're friends and this's a party, isn't it?"

The coffee had started burping on the stove and Madge turned it down so it wouldn't boil over. "Go on," she heard Johnny say again, and so she did. On the way past the fridge she jerked a dish towel from the handle.

"It never ends," she said.

By the time she was out of the room, Johnny had stopped swinging Mabel. They stood in the middle of the kitchen and Johnny held her up so she wouldn't fall down.

"I think I'm going to be sick," Mabel said.

"No, you're not," Johnny said. "The best thing to stop yourself being sick is to have another drink." While he was saying this he was trying to slip his hand inside the back of Mabel's skirt.

"Don't," Mabel said. "I mean it, Johnny. I really think I might be sick."

Johnny just laughed and kept trying to get his hand in. When he finally did, Mabel twisted away and two of the buttons on her skirt popped off and bounced crazily across the floor.

"Now see what you did," Mabel said. She got down on her hands and knees and tried to find the buttons. One of them she found right away, but the other had rolled under the fridge and she couldn't reach it. "It's under the fridge," she said to Johnny. "Help me get it. I'll never find a matching button anywhere else."

"What did you say?"

Mabel looked up over her shoulder. "Under the fridge," she said.

"Hey," Johnny said.

He was grinning when he stepped over to the fridge. Mabel was on her hands and knees on the floor and Johnny put his legs on either side of her and, bracing himself, pushed the fridge so it was tilted up on its side. "Reach under and get it," he said.

Mabel hesitated. "You won't drop it, will you?"

Johnny grunted. "For Christ's sake," he said. "What do you think?"

She looked up at him for a moment and then she leaned her head down and peered under.

"It's way at the back," she said.

"Well, get it," said Johnny. "Hurry up. I can't hold this fridge here all night."

Mabel put her arm under and reached for the button, but it was still too far, so she eased her head under. As she did, Johnny lowered the fridge, bracing it with one shoulder so it rested lightly on the top of her head.

31

How Do You Spell Beautiful?

Mabel screamed.

When Carl and Madge ran into the room, Johnny was slapping Mabel on the rear end with his free hand. Not hard, just regular little slaps so it sounded like someone playing patty-cake. "Jesus, Johnny," Madge said. She punched him on the arm and told him to lift the fridge so Mabel could get out from under it.

"Don't bump me," he said, "or I might drop it." When Madge hesitated, he flipped Mabel's skirt up.

Madge reached out and pulled the skirt down. She got down on her knees and, putting her arms around Mabel, pulled her out from under. Johnny lowered the fridge back onto the floor. "Whoof," he said. "That bugger was heavy." Carl grinned as if he didn't know what else to do, then followed Johnny into the living room.

Madge and Mabel sat on the floor beside each other. Mabel had her hand open in her lap and was looking at the button in it. "At least I got my button," she said.

Madge said, "That Johnny."

"He scares me," said Mabel. "He could've dropped it on me."

Madge giggled. "You sure looked funny with your bum up in the air."

"It didn't feel funny," Mabel said, and then she started to cry. She was trying to hitch her skirt around so she could see if it was ripped.

"Don't cry," Madge said. "He didn't mean it. He was just having fun." She put her arm around Mabel's shoulder. "C'mon," she said, "we've just got ourselves two really crazy guys, that's all. He wouldn't have dropped that fridge on your head. You know that." But Mabel kept on crying and trying to turn her skirt around so she could see it.

"Now what's the matter?" Johnny yelled from the living room. "Is Mabel crying, for Christ's sake? Hey, Mabel," he called, "quit that and c'mon in here and play some cards. You're being a real party-pooper."

Madge finally got Mabel up off the floor. She got a safety pin from the windowsill and pinned Mabel's skirt together. The waist was torn. "Now don't worry," Madge said. "It isn't torn too badly. You can fix it easy." Mabel had stopped crying by this time. She was holding a dish towel up to her face.

"You go on to the bathroom and fix up your face," Madge said. "After, we can go and play some more cards. It'll be fun, honest. You know Johnny. You know how he likes to fool around. He's just like Carl," she said.

~

Carl had his arm around Johnny's shoulder, trying to hold him up

Honey

as they walked home. Mabel was behind them. It was dark with heavy clouds and a strong hard wind. Johnny was staggering and Carl was having trouble holding him up. Every few steps Johnny would stop and sway on the side of the dirt road leading back to their cabin. When he did, Carl swayed with him, the two of them weaving back and forth, almost falling together. "Don't let him fall down," she said to Carl. "He hates falling down."

Johnny sang, "Madge and Mabel, they're both able."

"If you fall down I'll just leave you there," Carl said to Johnny. "I'll just leave you in the ditch if you do, so don't." He was laughing as he said it. "I mean it, you bugger. I'll just leave you right there in the ditch and I'll take Mabel home instead of you."

"Don't say that," Mabel said behind him.

Johnny stopped again and spread his arms in the air. "Carl's my best friend," he slurred. "Did you know that? 'Cause that's what he is. He's my best friend in the whole fucking world."

"I know, I know," Mabel said. "Please, Carl," she said. "Let's go. We're almost home."

"My best friend," Johnny kept mumbling as Carl steered him up the road. "That Carl. He's my best friend."

When they got him into the cabin, Carl took him to the back and let him fall on the bed. He looked down the hall to the living room. "Do you want me to help get him undressed?" he called to Mabel.

She didn't answer him.

Carl undid Johnny's shoes, took them off, and then stripped off his socks. He tried to get the pants off. He got them to where they were just below the knees and then they got tangled in the blankets. "Shit," Carl said, and fell sideways, landing on the floor. He looked across the bed at his friend. Johnny's arms were folded across his chest, his hands clenched into fists. He looks like he's ready to fight or something, Carl thought.

The heavy gold ring on Johnny's left hand shone dully in the light reflecting from the hall. Carl decided he should try to take off Johnny's shirt. He got up off the floor and, balancing himself, tried to undo the top button. Johnny jerked his arm and hit Carl hard on the chest.

"Fuck it," Carl said. His chest hurt where Johnny had hit him. "You bugger," Carl said, and then realized he was talking to himself. "Hey, I'm talking to myself," he said. "Hey Johnny, can you hear me? I'm talking to myself." He got up and leaned heavily against the wall. "Take her easy, buddy," he said.

While Carl was trying to get Johnny undressed and into bed, Mabel

33

How Do You Spell Beautiful?

stood by the stove. She turned the front element on and turned it off again. She pulled her skirt around, undoing the safety pin Madge had loaned her, and dropped her skirt and slip to the floor. She stepped out of them and then rolled her stockings down and off. She walked unsteadily over to the long mirror beside the kitchen table and looked at herself. She started at her toes and worked herself all the way up to her face and then back down again. Taking her face in her hands, she moved it from side to side and looked at it. "You're too damned pretty," she said to the mirror. "Nobody should be as pretty as you."

She dropped her hands away from her face and, twisting her arms behind her, undid the buttons on her blouse and slowly peeled it off as if she were a stripper in a bar. She mumbled a song to herself and did an awkward bump-and-grind in front of the mirror.

When she heard Carl behind her, she didn't turn around. She kept moving slowly, looking out of the mirror. Carl just stood there, swaying in the doorway.

Carl felt a little bewildered. He shook his head and tried to smile. "Well, looky here," he said.

Mabel didn't say anything for a moment. She just kept moving. After she'd done another bump or two she said, "I'm practising. It's Johnny's dance. I don't do it very well. I try. But I don't."

"I got Johnny into bed," Carl said.

"Where's Johnny?" she asked suddenly.

Her eyes were very wide and her voice sounded funny. Carl stared. He couldn't keep his eyes off her. She's almost totally naked, he thought.

Mabel put her hands on her hips and did another bump-and-grind, falling against the table and then onto the floor. She sprawled there with her hands between her legs, her palms flat on the floor.

"I'm his pretty girl, Johnny says."

"Johnny's my best friend," Carl finally said. He looked at the dark bruises on her breasts and sides. There were bruises on her legs as well. Some were almost black while others were blue, fading at the edges to a soft yellowy green.

"I'm the prettiest girl in this whole town, that's what Johnny says. Only sometimes I don't dance just right." She put her hands up to her face and turned it from side to side. "Johnny's sleeping, isn't he?"

"Yeah," Carl said.

"I want him to be sleeping," Mabel said. "Will you stay here until he's for sure sleeping? I don't want you to go if he isn't. He's sleeping, isn't he? Is he?"

Honey

"I gotta be going," Carl said.

When Mabel said, "Please stay," Carl put his hands into his pockets. "So, I guess I'd better go," he said. "I guess we got Johnny home all right." Mabel sat on the floor and kept touching her skin. Carl turned around and went out the door, leaving her sitting there in front of the mirror.

Carl fell down twice while he was walking home. The second time he fell he looked up at the sky. There weren't any stars. As he lay there he could see her again with her head under the fridge and Johnny standing there slapping her. He thought of the sounds Johnny's hands made. He couldn't seem to get them out of his mind.

He lay there and held up his hands and looked at them. He clapped them together, loud in the night. He did it again and then again. He liked his hands clapping hard against each other. "Madge and Mabel, they're both able," he sang out loud. He smacked his hands to the rhythm of the words, repeating them over and over. Then he felt sick.

He got as far as the doorstep before he threw up. When he was finished he staggered into the house. Madge had gone to bed and the house was quiet. He walked into the living room. The table was still covered with glasses and cards. The cat stared at him from under a chair and Carl said, "Hey, cat." The cat didn't move, just looked at him warily as he tried pouring himself a whisky. Some of the liquor spilled on the floor and some into his glass. He lifted what was there and drank it. The next one was harder, most of the liquor spilling onto the floor. He went down the hall into the bedroom, balancing himself by leaning against the wall, the glass held far out in front of him.

It took a long time to get there.

Standing in the doorway, he looked at Madge lying in their bed. "Honey," he said. "Honey? There's something crazy."

Madge stirred and pulled the blankets around her shoulders.

Carl sat heavily on the edge of the bed. Madge's brown hair had fallen across her face so all he could see was her arm where it stuck out from under the blanket. It looked white. He stared at it. It didn't look like it belonged to anybody. It just looked like an arm somebody had left in his bed, an arm with some brown hair beside it.

He wanted to reach out and pull the blanket down a bit to see if Madge was really there. His drink was spilling and he tried to put it down on the night table. He couldn't reach, so he dropped the glass on the floor.

"Madge," he said. "Madge, are you there?"

When he didn't get an answer, he lifted the blanket and crawled

How Do You Spell Beautiful?

under. He reached out and touched her and then he pulled himself closer and put his arms around her, pulling her to him, her body folded into his, his arms around her holding her there.

Madge groaned. "What is it?" she asked, struggling in his arms. "What's the matter?" She rolled over and faced him. "Carl," she said, "you've still got your clothes on."

He put his face in her hair and kept it there. "Put your arms around me, honey," he said. "Hold onto me."

"You," she said. She wrapped her arms around him. "Between you and Johnny, a girl's got her hands full."

"Hold on," he said. It was all he could think of to say, so he said it again. "Hold on."

"I'm holding you," Madge said. "I've got you."

He lay there with her arms around him and his face in her hair. "I saw your arm," he said. "Everything's so crazy. Everything's crazy."

She stroked his head as he stared into the darkness of her hair. "I know, I know," he heard her say.

The bed began to turn slowly.

He closed his eyes, the bed turning, and Madge murmuring something he couldn't hear. This's what we're doing, he thought, his eyes wet, his body shaking. "You've got me," he said.

"Oh, honey," said Madge. "What is it? What's the matter? Is it Johnny and Mabel? Is it our friends?"

"Hold on," Carl said, the bed turning faster and faster until it felt like he was in the centre of a big dark wheel with the only thing saving him, Madge. "Hold on," he yelled. He pulled her body to him, wrapping his legs with hers, his arms around her, her skin in his hands.

He lay there in the centre of the dark world of their bed, the two of them getting smaller and smaller. Both of them were falling somewhere. "Carl," he heard her say. "What is it? What's gone wrong?"

"I don't know where we're going, honey," he called out, hoping she would hear him over the sound of the wheel as it kept spinning and they kept falling, faster and faster.

Irene Good Night

WE LIVE AT THE LITTLE RIVER Trailer Court, Jim and Irene and me. It's a nice place. There's a creek running just behind where our trailer is. I guess it's called Little River just like the town.

It's only a creek really but it's nice. Nice and cool with lots of willow trees. Mother always said willow trees were like women. I like that. If I was something else I guess I'd be a willow tree. I like to sit under them with my baby and sing to her.

Sometimes she goes to sleep there even if it's hot, like now. When she's sleeping I sit and watch the water, where the willow branches float. They look like hair floating and moving the way they do. It's real peaceful and quiet.

It would be nice to swim in it but Jim says I can't. He says he doesn't want other men looking at me. He says the water's dirty too and I guess he's right. Still, it would be nice to swim there when it's hot. I'd like to carry my baby right into the water. It would cool her off sometimes. It's been so hot here lately.

I miss my mother. She's dead now, just like my dad.

She died right after I married Jim. I don't know what from. She had a hard life. Life is hard, she always said to me. But it don't have to be, she said. I think she died from that, from living hard. She'd a lot harder life than I do.

How Do You Spell Beautiful?

I remember when I was little and my dad lost his arm down at the mill. That was hard.

He never got over that. And then he died.

I hadn't met Jim then. I met him after.

Mother didn't like Jim and Jim didn't like her. She always said he was a bad one and I guess he is sometimes. But he's a good worker. It's not easy down at the mill. That's real work, he says, and I bet it is.

Someday I'd like to go down there and see where he works. I wouldn't want to stand in the sun all day and pull lumber off the chain. It's no wonder sometimes he gets mad.

It's not easy feeding a family and working all the time. He gets headaches. I was sorry my mother never got along with him. Jim tried for my sake. They put up with each other. She'd be nice but it was never good with them. I'm sorry about that now.

I miss her all right, but we have our baby. I named her after my mother. Irene.

It's a nice name. Just like in that song, "Irene Good Night." I don't know all the words. I just know part of it and that's the part I sing.

Irene Good Night.

I sing that to Irene when she's cranky and sometimes she goes to sleep.

My name is Rhonda, Rhonda Berngarten. That's Jim's last name. When we got married I was proud to take his name. I'm still proud of it. Jim and Rhonda Berngarten and their daughter, Irene. Doesn't that sound nice?

That's our trailer over there, the silver one with the blue stripe along the bottom. Jim says he's going to get some paint one day and paint it where it's all flaked off. It's not one of the big ones but it's nice.

It's only got just the one bedroom, but there's a bathroom and a kitchen and a little living room. That's lots for us right now. Irene sleeps in the bathtub. I don't know what we'll do when she gets older. It gets so hot during the day but it's better than a lot of people have. There's worse trailers than ours, that's for sure.

Poor Alice Macassy and that baby of hers. Her trailer was just a little one. There was only one room. Maybe that was the problem, I don't know. But he didn't have to run off like that and leave her with nothing but waiting. I'm glad I didn't have to go in there. I'm glad it was the men who did. I wouldn't have wanted to see that after all those weeks, and with it hot.

Poor Alice. I watched from the window when they took her away in the truck. And that little baby.

Irene Good Night

They hauled the trailer away. I don't know where. I guess somebody bought it.

Jim bought ours with the money Mother left us after she died. It wasn't much. Not enough to anywhere near buy it outright, but Jim makes the payments every month. It'll be ours in five more years.

Two thousand dollars. That's a lot of money.

I wish my mother had liked Jim a bit more. He isn't mean to me, not really. Jim isn't a mean man. Sometimes he hits me but I understand. It's working in the mill all day in the sun and then he gets those terrible headaches.

He doesn't beat Irene though. There's lots of fathers beat on their kids. I know a few, some right here in the trailer court.

Tommy Macassy did that.

And theirs was only a baby, not really a kid at all. I could hear it from our trailer, and Alice crying. Jim never does that.

It hurts when he hits me. I wish he didn't. Every time he does I think of my mother, but he's not as bad as she thought he was.

She told me not to marry him. But I loved him. What else was I supposed to do? You got to marry the man you love. And he's not like my dad. He doesn't do any of the things he used to do.

I don't like talking about my dad. He did lots of bad things, things you shouldn't talk about. Don't get me wrong. I'm not glad he's dead. You shouldn't be glad anyone's dead. But I'm glad I'm not living at home no more like I used to. Sometimes it was really bad. I used to be afraid to go to sleep at night. I used to dream the night would hurt me.

Mother always said Jim was just like him, but she didn't know Jim like I do. Jim's different. He'd never touch Irene. He hits me sometimes but it's because I've burned the supper or something.

The worst is when Irene cries.

It's so hot now. It'll be better in the fall when it's cooler. Irene's got a rash. I put lard on it but it doesn't seem to help. The rash is what makes her cry and if Jim has one of his headaches, well, I guess I don't blame him. It's hard enough sleeping without a baby crying all night.

Jim's not a drinking man. He has a few when he's with the men from the mill but, like he says, he has to. It wouldn't do if he didn't have a few when they're drinking after work.

He doesn't have many, just a few.

And no hard stuff. Just beer.

That's okay. Like Jim says, if he didn't drink with them they'd think there was something wrong with him. It's not like he's a Jesus freak, he says.

How Do You Spell Beautiful?

I wish he believed a little more. We don't go to church. Jim won't have it. He says all they do is steal from people like us. He says they just confuse people and make them think about things they've got no business thinking about, so I don't go. I pray when he's at work but I don't tell him. I prayed for Alice and that baby of hers. I prayed and prayed. Jim wouldn't like it if he knew that.

He never told me he wasn't a church person before we got married. But I didn't ask him either. Maybe I knew, I don't know. But we had a real church wedding at The Friends of the Rising Light. That's where my mother used to go. Irene was baptised there. Jim let me do that. He's not all bad, far from it.

I like it when he plays with Irene, but I wish he wouldn't throw her so high in the air. It scares me. She always cries when he does. It starts out so good though. He'll hold her on his knees and play with her. She laughs then.

It's when he throws her up in the air she cries. That's when he gives her back to me. He always asks what's wrong with her and I tell him she just doesn't like being thrown so high in the air. He says kids are supposed to like it. He keeps trying and Irene keeps crying. I wish she didn't. It always makes him mad and then he gets one of his headaches.

Maybe if I have another one it'll be a boy and then Jim can throw him in the air. He'd leave Irene alone then. Boys like being thrown, I think. And Irene isn't well. I don't know what's wrong with her. I put lard on her rash and wrap her so tight but nothing seems to work. It's the heat. It'll be better in the fall when it's cool. She won't cry so much then.

I wish and wish she wouldn't cry at night.

I lie in bed and pray she'll stop crying. I stare up at the ceiling, and there are times I can see right through the roof and up into the sky with my eyes open. And I pray that Irene will be quiet.

It works sometimes.

I don't go out much. It's best if I stay home. It's a woman's place, that's what Jim says. He worries about me and other men. I don't know where he gets his ideas from. I wouldn't let another man touch me. I let Jim touch me. I like it when he touches me. I wish sometimes he'd touch me with the lights on but he won't. He thinks that's wrong. I told him once there was nothing to be ashamed of, that God gave us our bodies. What could be wrong with seeing the way God made them? Jim didn't like that. I never said it to him again.

Sometimes, when I know he's asleep, I turn the little light on and I

Irene Good Night

look at him. He's just like a boy then, so beautiful. I like the hair down at the small of his back, the little black ones that go under his underwear. They're beautiful, so soft. Just like Irene's hair. She got her hair from him.

I would never tell him I look at him like that though. He wouldn't like it. I remember the time I told him about us being all God's body. It was the first time he hit me. It hurt but I understood. He thought I was shaming him. A woman shouldn't ever shame her husband. It's not right.

I like it when it's dark out like now. I like to come out at night after Jim's gone to sleep. It's because it's so hot. That's why he hit me tonight. I know it's just the heat and the mill and those terrible headaches. He had one tonight when he came home from work. He was late and I got some ice in a dishtowel and tried to cool his head, but I didn't tie the towel just right. I get so nervous sometimes. I want to do right for him. I don't want to make him mad. It was the ice slipping out and all down inside his shirt. I was careless and I shouldn't have been.

I don't know how many times he hit me.

I worry so much they'll hear over at the other trailers. I'd hate it if they knew. Jim's liked by pretty near everybody and I wouldn't want them not to like him. I tell him not to hit me but he just keeps doing it. Like when I made him mad with the ice.

There's so many times when it's good. That's what I try to think of when he's hitting me. The good times when Irene's sleeping and he's okay.

I'll only be able to come outside now when it's dark. I don't want the neighbours to see. It's why I'm out here now. Irene was crying and Jim was trying to sleep. I said I'd just hold her in the kitchen but I took her outside here by the creek.

It's such a little creek really.

Little River. It's funny they call it that.

Jim didn't hear me go. I've learned to be real quiet. He's sleeping now and so is Irene. She's fast asleep. I wish I could see the willow leaves better. If there was a good moon I could see them. They're so beautiful the way they move on the water. I think there isn't a more beautiful tree anywhere.

Irene's sleeping. So is Jim. I wish my mother was alive so she could see how beautiful Irene is sleeping on my lap. I took her clothes off and she's cool now. I think if I pray my mother will be able to see her.

She's so beautiful.

Dear God, let my mother come down and see how beautiful Irene is. Let her,

41

How Do You Spell Beautiful?

when she's in heaven, look after the babies. Let Jim sleep. Let him be happy.
Don't give him no more headaches. I want us all to be happy like I used to
dream we'd be.

~

There.

I know she's watching now. I know she can see Irene sleeping.

Irene Good Night.

That's such a beautiful song. I wish I knew all the words. I can almost hear my mother singing it. I can see her leaning over the woodstove putting up the food for winter and singing that song so soft and quiet. Irene will love it in the water with the willow leaves. When she's floating there I'll sit and watch her, and I'll sing the song and she'll hear it and she'll sleep and sleep and sleep. And Jim will sleep and so will I.

I haven't had a sleep for such a long time.

Sleeping Annie

ANNIE'S LYING BESIDE ME ON THE couch. She won't go to bed unless I go with her, but she understands how I like to sit late at night in the dark. She'll stay up and read and then she'll lie down on the couch and go to sleep beside me.

I like that. I like her here, the coals glowing in the fireplace, the night outside.

I lift my hands and hold them over her. I turn them and look where the skin's grown back, and then I touch her cheeks and the smooth skin beside her eyes. It's like the skin of my hands are made of drifted snow and they're protecting her. For a while I thought they were ugly but Annie told me how beautiful they were.

I like to touch Annie. When I do I can see things. It can be anything, a book, a table, some flowers, anything. It doesn't matter what. First there's a clear pure fire and then I go inside.

She knows. She understands.

Annie and me, we're good now. We have been for a long time. I'm working steady and I'm not drinking any more. Liquor and drugs. I put them behind me.

I tell her that. She likes me to tell her. She knows what changed me. Tell me, she says. Tell me how you came back.

I tell her she doesn't want to hear about that again, but I know she does. She knows I like telling it. She's curled up beside me on the couch

How Do You Spell Beautiful?

and her head is in my lap. I watch her close her eyes. I know she'll be asleep long before I finish, but it doesn't matter.

It was Prince George, I tell her.

Yes, she says.

That morning I beat you up so bad I went north. I wanted to get as far away from the Coast as I could. Far away from you and what I'd done. I got in trouble up there. It didn't take long. It never did in those days. When you're putting the things I was into my body it doesn't take long before everything screws up. The upshot of it all was I was running, only this time the people who wanted me were serious.

Oh, Annie says, and I tell her it's okay now. Everything's okay.

When Annie quiets, I continue.

So, I say, the next I knew I was climbing over a chain-link fence down by the rail yards looking for a way out. I couldn't go near the highway. I knew they'd be looking for me there.

I was passing a long line of sealed boxcars and loaded gondolas when it started to snow. This's January remember. My hands were pushed into the pockets of my jeans as far as they could go, but it didn't help. Without a coat I was freezing.

Annie just says yes.

The tracks went on forever. I thought if I followed them to the end of the yards I'd at least know whatever train came along was going south. I hoped it was south and I hadn't got confused and gone north instead. I didn't know Prince George outside of hotels and bars. In those days that's all I ever knew about.

I remember, Annie says.

A switcher passed me two tracks over and some guy yelled at me to get the hell outa there. I yelled back and said that's what I was trying to do. He went the other way. I watched him till he disappeared, those red lights hollowing the snow.

North of summer.

Whoever said that knew what he was talking about.

Huge flakes were coming down on my head and shoulders. It was way after midnight and the snow was coming down heavy with a wind. I couldn't feel my hands or feet. By then I must've walked five miles and the yards long gone. I think I'd forgotten about the trains. I was just walking. I kept promising myself I'd straighten out if ever I got outa there, but I'd said that before.

That's when I saw the fire. It was way ahead of me, glimmering through the snow. It looked like it was off to the side in a little coulee. When I started running it was just a round red glow, like something

Sleeping Annie

you see that isn't there. I can still see it. It's clear as a bell, that fire, and the snow falling through it.

All I wanted was warm. I was stumbling and falling in the snow. There were six or eight inches of fresh and the wind was drifting it over the old. I wanted to pick up that fire and stuff it inside my clothes, swallow it whole so I'd never be cold again.

I broke into the light and stopped dead. There was an old guy sitting by that fire under a piece of corrugated iron propped up on boxes. He peered out at me from under a grey army blanket. I hadn't seen a blanket like that since I was a kid. His eyes didn't move. They just looked out and past me. I squatted on my haunches away from the fire. I could barely feel it from where I was.

I saw your fire, I said to him. He just kept looking. Can I come in? I'm cold is all. Real cold.

This's the part where Annie always interrupts and wants me to tell her his name. She's heard me tell this I don't know how many times, but she always interrupts right here. I tell her to wait and she always gets quiet and puts her head back down and closes her eyes.

I stop telling the story. I'm waiting for it.

What was his name? she asks.

Just like that, the same every time.

You remember his name, I say.

Annie's quiet for a minute and then she says, It must've been terrible.

Well, it was, I tell her.

Anyway, I say, he finally blinked a couple of times and pulled the blanket tighter round his shoulders. He was a little guy. He pushed his head out like it was on a stick and looked me over. Sit down, he said. It's a bad night to be without a coat.

I swear I jumped into that cave he'd made there in the night. I don't know what I would've done if he'd said no. I used to think I was pretty tough back then, but walking all those miles had taken that out of me. I think now I'd have just wandered off and probably died out there. I know what that sounds like, but it's true. You'd have to have been me to know. That country up there isn't like a city. When you're up there in the bush and snow and wind you're not a person any more.

I got in and sat under the iron. The heat reflected off it onto my back. I leaned toward the flames and stuck my hands in. They were like two bags filled with bones. I squeezed and rubbed them until they started to hurt.

Don't let them get too close, he said. Take it easy until the blood gets used to running again.

How Do You Spell Beautiful?

I pulled them away, but it was a hard thing to do. I couldn't feel my feet at all. The old guy turned his head under that blanket. I looked at him. He was small with a little crooked face and stringy beard.

It's okay, he said.

Annie opens her eyes then. Bill, she says. That was his name. Bill.

That's right, I say to her. His name was Bill.

That's such an ordinary name, she says, and then she closes her eyes again.

You sleep, I say. I'll keep on with the story.

Annie gets quiet and I start again.

So the old guy reached out a skinny hand from under the blanket and tapped my shoe. Take them off, he said. Rub your feet, but not too hard. If your hands are bad, your feet are worse. When it's cold like this the most important thing you got is your feet. That's all you got to get you where you're going. You can't walk on your hands. Not very far.

He stopped talking and so did I. I took my shoes off and put them by the fire. They started steaming as soon as I put them down. That's when I really tried to get some life back in my body. As the pains in my hands went away they started in my feet, only worse. I had pain everywhere. I was better than five hundred miles from the Coast and for the first time in my life I had a fear in me.

I rubbed my feet for about ten minutes and then I felt my face. My ears were hard. They're froze, he said. You'll feel the cold in them from now on. I know. I got two ears that feel it too.

What can I do? I asked.

Just hold your hands over them until they start to hurt. That's the trouble with freezing. You can't feel it until after. All that pain you got in you right now is your body coming back to life.

He reached out and put some wood on the fire.

You looking for a freight?

I'm trying to get to the Coast, I told him. I got a woman down there. Annie. She'll look after me.

Ever jumped a freight before?

I was going to lie and say I had, but I didn't. I told him the truth and after that I started to tell him everything.

I spilled it out. I didn't even know him but I knew it was time to tell it. I knew this was somehow what I was there for, that everything was a leading up to this. I even told him how I'd beat on you but how I figured it was the booze. And then I said, That's a lie. It wasn't the drinking. It was me. It was me wanting to.

Sleeping Annie

He just listened until I was done.

Jumping a freight isn't easy, you know. There's a trick to it.

I was glad he said that instead of talking about what I'd told him. I didn't want him to.

I don't understand, I said.

There's ways of doing it.

I never did it before, I told him. I thought maybe you just kind of climbed on when it went by, so long as it was going slow enough.

He didn't look at me. Every once in a while when I was talking he'd take a chunk of wood from the pile beside him and put it on the fire. It was a careful fire. Not too big and not too small. He'd built fires before, that's for sure. The wood was old ties, broken up. He must've hauled them from the grade. As for the iron and boxes, I don't know where he got them. There was junk like that scattered all over the north. Stuff left behind. The north's a place you leave things in. That's what people have been doing for years. Old trucks, barrels, everything, all the junk it isn't worth carrying back.

I started to shiver and he shook his arm loose from his blanket.

Climb under, he said. It'll be warmer.

When I didn't, he said, Don't worry. I ain't that kind. Might've been once. Might've been a lot of things once, but not any more.

I moved over and pulled the blanket around my shoulders until I was almost touching him, and then I did. I was still shaking, but the heat he was throwing off under that blanket felt good. We both stared at the fire.

I saw a lot of men die because they didn't know how to jump a freight. A lot of men.

Where? I asked. I wasn't afraid any more. We were talking like we'd known each other a long time.

Everywhere, he said. He was rocking himself while he was talking and I was rocking along with him. Everywhere there was a train going anywhere, men died. Fell under. Slipped. He poked my knee with his finger. You ever seen a man with his legs pinched off? Or a arm? Did you ever see that?

I shook my head. The snow was coming down and you couldn't see five feet. We were sitting inside a glowing ball. All there was was his voice and us rocking and the fire snapping in front of us.

I seen it.

Legs.

Arms.

I found a head once on the ties. No body. Just a head. The eyes were

47

How Do You Spell Beautiful?

wide open and staring straight up into the sky. What they were seeing was all of it.

You know how much a head weighs? he asked me.

I told him I didn't.

About thirty pounds. You wouldn't think so, would you? You carry it around but you don't know how heavy it is. I picked up that head and stuck it in a poplar crutch out on the prairie. About ten or fifteen miles east of the Winnipeg yards on the CP line. There's a little slough there with some poplar trees. I put it in the crutch of a tree so it was staring straight ahead west where I was going. I'd seen those eyes and I knew what they were knowing. I wanted them watching me when I left. I wanted them on my back. I knew that if they were, then I'd be all right.

I sat there keeping warm and listening to him. I'd never thought about my body. It was just something that moved me around, that was all.

I miss Annie, I said when he finished. Her last name's Gotobed. Isn't that a strange name?

When I say that, Annie stirs and looks at me. She says, You didn't tell him that, did you?

I tell her I did. I told him everything, I say. I wanted him to know it all. I wanted him to know about you and me.

There's lots teased her, I said to that old guy, but she never once thought of changing it. I loved her and maybe that's why I laughed at her, why I made fun of her. I didn't want her to know I loved her, so I laughed.

While I was saying this I was holding onto my hands. I was holding them as hard as I could.

Why did I do that, Bill? I don't know why I did that?

Yes, you do.

~

Annie's sleeping now. I can tell by her face. I touch her hair real soft so's not to wake her. It's like we're on this couch and the couch is a boat going down a river. It's quiet and we're floating. I look at her sleeping and then I go on. I keep telling the story.

I looked into the fire with him, I say to sleeping Annie.

She's hearing me. She knows.

Annie, I say, the flames took on every shape of everything I'd never known. For a long time I saw a face in the coals under the blue flames coming out of the creosote. It wasn't anyone's face I knew. It was just there, smiling at me, and all around were flames. The flames were birds

Sleeping Annie

and animals and crazy things, but the face didn't pay any attention to them. It just sat there in the middle of the fire. I stared at it until it was gone and the fire had changed into people and cities, whole worlds being born and dying in the fire.

You can see a lot of things in a fire, the old guy finally said. If you watch it long enough you can see it all. I've looked into a lot of fires in my life. Sometimes I think that's all I've ever done. What you see is who you are.

Hold onto it, he said. The fire's talking to you.

We were quiet then a long time.

There'll be a freight through in a few minutes, he finally said. It slows down here. There's a big curve back there and a grade. You must've seen it when you were walking. Right around here it'll start to pick up speed. It doesn't stop till it gets to Vancouver. You wait till you see a gondola. There won't be no empty boxes on a through freight from the north. You jump a gondola. If you ever jump a box, you run along beside it and then you put your hands on the ledge of the open door and jump up. Don't ever try to pull yourself in. You jump with your legs and your arms and you turn as you go up so you land backwards, and then you roll. You try it frontwards you'll end up under the car. Not always, but it only takes once. You jump a gondola. You grab the first ladder as it comes up beside you. That way there's a few seconds before the next set of wheels goes by. Grab the ladder high and don't let go.

I pulled my shoes on. They were stiff and hard.

She's coming. Can you feel it?

Where?

Put your hand flat on the ground. Feel it?

I put my palm on the warm dirt beside the fire and felt a tremble run up out of the ground and into my shoulder.

Remember, he said. When you get in, cover yourself with snow. It's like a different kind of fire. It'll keep you warm.

I saw the engine's light then. The train was coming slow. I could hear it too, the steady breathing of a diesel pulling grade. I got up and moved over to the other side of the fire. My muscles felt like my shoes, stiff and sore from sitting. I stamped my feet to get the blood moving. The engine was almost even with us. The old guy hadn't moved.

Aren't you coming? I asked.

Nope.

I didn't ask why. Maybe he lived under that iron. Maybe he was waiting for someone else, a friend or someone.

How Do You Spell Beautiful?

A second or two later I was running through the snow to the tracks. I was running beside the train.

The cars lifted above me, snow drifting off their backs. They were black like animals, beasts leaning over me who didn't know or didn't care if I was there. They were passing me, box after box picking up speed, and then there was a gondola and then another.

I ran.

I ran as hard as I could.

Another gondola came up. It was streaked with sulphur and coal along the sides. I tried for the ladder, but all I could see was the wheels, and I let it go. I kept running until I felt the breath going out of me, falling out in thick white clouds. I couldn't get enough back in. The iron wheels were grinding beside me, creaking and groaning as they cut the snow.

I looked beside me and a ladder was there. I jumped and grabbed as high as I could. The iron was frozen and I felt my skin stick to it, but I didn't let go. My feet stepped and bounced off the snow and the frozen shale. I could feel them still trying to run.

I lifted my knees. They thumped into the side of the gondola, and then I felt my shoes touching a rung. They found their place, the heels hooked there.

I hung off that iron. My eyes were closed. I knew I had to climb up and get into the car but I couldn't, not yet. I didn't have any breath left. I hung there, and I could see the bodies.

They were under the train and they were reaching up. I thought they were trying to pull me under, but all they wanted to do was touch me, touch my shoes and pants, my legs, their bodies touching me.

I opened my eyes, the wind blasting, scouring my face. My hands were frozen hard to the iron rung. I looked at them stuck there and it was like I was in the silent world. My hands had a million lights.

There was a hole in the air. My hands were in it and they started moving, pulling me through. I could feel the skin coming off but I didn't care. We were going through the hole. We looked at each other as we went. We didn't let go.

50

All of Their Hearts

HE TAKES THE SAVAGE FROM THE wall, walks over to his leather chair and sits down, the rifle resting on his bare legs. It's an old rifle, one that belonged to his father before he died.

It feels cold in his hands.

His mother gave it to him when his father died. When his father was killed. When his father was shot in the heart. He always thinks of it like that. First he died, then he was killed, and then he was shot in the heart. It's backwards, but that's how it seems to him.

When she gave him the rifle they'd been sitting at the kitchen table. "These flies," she'd said, waving her hand in front of her face. "I hate these flies." Then she got up and went to the back of the house, returning with the rifle. "Here," she'd said, "you can have this."

When he took it from her she asked if there was anything else he wanted. "No," he said.

It hadn't occurred to him there was anything. What he wanted was something all right, but what it was he didn't know.

Whatever it was, it hadn't been the Savage.

He didn't like killing any more. When he'd been a boy he'd done his share. He'd killed things until he was sick of it. One day he'd taken his rifle

How Do You Spell Beautiful?

and shot three robins in a nest out in the orchard. He ran away afterwards, ashamed, not wanting anyone to know. But at the same time he'd felt exultant. There were other things too. But he'd only been a boy.

It's what boys did, kill things.

The day his mother gave him the rifle he'd gone out on the back porch and killed the flies. While he was smashing them with the swatter, he'd thought of killing flies with his brothers one summer when they were all still young. His sister had wanted to play but they wouldn't let her. They'd made a competition out of it, just like everything else. He'd won, though they'd argued about it at the time.

You can just spray them, his mother had called out, but he didn't answer her. He just kept hitting them methodically until they were all dead. He thinks his mother and he talked after that but he's not sure. What he remembers is killing the flies and then taking the rifle and leaving.

He looks at it resting across his knees. It's all he has from that time.

The rifle is a 22/410, over and under, the thin 22 resting precisely on top of the shotgun barrel. A small brush gun for birds. The shotgun part isn't accurate after thirty feet. The 22 is. A 22 Long will kill a bird at five hundred feet if the shot's true.

He's killed a lot of birds with this gun. But not for a long time. It's been fifteen years since he took a rifle out hunting. His heart just isn't in it. He wonders for a moment what his heart is in these days, but he's not sure.

He lifts the rifle to his shoulder, aiming at the wall. The wall's blank but he centres on a hole where a nail used to be and presses the trigger.

Softly.

A rifle is like a woman, his father always told him. He was still a boy then and he was learning how to shoot. *Softly, softly,* his father said, and he'd try not to jerk the trigger so the barrel moved and he missed. It was the first idea he had of what a woman might be. Those words of his father's telling him something he didn't understand, the word *soft* staying with him for a long time.

He remembers being in cadets and the CO teaching them about rifles. The CO was built like his father, short and stocky with a heavy chest. He'd been in his father's outfit in Europe. The CO told him over and over again what a man his father had been. He was a real sonufabitch, the CO had said. Toughest man there.

This is your rifle, this is your gun. This is for fighting and this is for fun.

The CO taught him that. He taught him other things too. How to strip a rifle, how to march, how to sneak through the brush at night

All of Their Hearts

without a sound. How to kill somebody if there was a real war.

The CO taught him many things, things he didn't want to remember. Like the times in the car when the CO insisted on driving him home every Tuesday night after cadets. The times they stopped in the dark along Pleasant Valley Road.

But his father's words were the first he knew about women.

Sex.

He moves the rifle slowly across the wall at chest height, and then down the angle. He stops where the walls and the floor meet in the corner. The rifle rests easily in his arms, the butt tucked into his shoulder. He holds it there, not moving, the bead of the sight precisely on that confluence of lines where everything comes together. Lifting his thumb he pulls the hammer back and brings his thumb down, curling it over the stock. He squeezes very very softly, as if it really were a woman, and hears the hammer fall on the chamber with a sharp click.

Pow.

He almost says the word out loud.

He doesn't. It's inside his head. He shifts to the other chamber, the one where the 22 Long is. The sound of the word *pow* expands inside him until it fills his mind like a ball of soft feathers.

He doesn't move.

He knows his arms will ache soon but they haven't yet, not yet.

Marlene is sleeping in the room beyond the wall. She's lying on her side, facing away from him. It's the way she sleeps when he's in bed with her.

But he isn't in bed with her. He's in the room she calls his study, his brown study, and he's holding the rifle very still.

She's on the other side of the wall, her body stretched out and her long blonde hair pushed away from her face.

She hates her hair.

She thinks it will come alive and strangle her while she sleeps. She tells him that but she doesn't really believe it. She says, I know it won't but that doesn't mean it can't. It's just a thing I have inside my head, she tells him.

There are a lot of things inside Marlene's head. Some she tells him about and some she doesn't. What she hasn't told him he doesn't want to know. Not really.

He's been with Marlene for thirty years. That's how old Jesus was when he died. I've been with Marlene for as long as Jesus.

Thirty years.

It seems a long time. There was a picture he saw once of a statue in

53

How Do You Spell Beautiful?

Italy somewhere. It was Mary Magdalene, or maybe it wasn't. Maybe it was Mary the Mother. It was one of them. The statue was covered in hair. The woman looked like an animal or something. He'd showed it to Marlene but she didn't say anything. She never did when he showed her things.

Their kids are gone. They aren't here any more.

Marlene and he are the only couple he knows who've stayed in one place. Except for his mother and father. But his father is dead so it isn't the same.

It's not like him and Marlene.

There aren't any couples around any more. Friends have come and gone just like the boys. He hasn't seen the boys for years. Or his friends.

Marlene gets letters from some of the wives. Myrtle Scambaugh. Edwina Marcott. Other ones.

He doesn't. He's not a letter writer, he tells Marlene. Men don't write letters, he says. Marlene says that's too bad. She says if men only talked to each other the way women do it would be better all around.

All around what? The mulberry bush? The house?

He used to see some of the friends on holidays, but none of them has come back for a long time. They've got other lives now. Not like him. His life has been all one thing.

Maybe that's what he's doing in his study? Maybe he's doing the one thing he's always done? But if he is, what is it?

His arms are getting cramps, small fluttering tremors in his forearms and across his shoulders. The rifle is still steady though. The bead hasn't moved from that corner. For a moment he thinks he should lift it up and aim it through the wall at Marlene.

He tries to think just exactly where her heart is on the other side of the wall. He tries to measure with his eyes to the precise spot where her heart must be, and then he moves the rifle to where he thinks it is.

He trembles.

A bullet could leave the barrel of the 22 and go through the thin gyprock walls and tumble over and over until it reaches her and enters her heart.

That's what happened to his father only it wasn't a 22, it was a 303. It only took one shot.

Pow.

That's all it takes if the shooter's accurate.

He's accurate. His father taught him that. They'd practised for hours out in the country at Black Rock, using a cardboard target he'd made with his crayons.

54

Softly, softly, his father would say. A rifle is just like a woman.

His mother didn't want him to learn, but his father had come back from the war and thought it was important.

Was that it? Was that the reason?

It's what his mother said it was. "You and that war," she'd say to his father. "You and that damned war."

He tries to remember what else his father said about women. He can only remember one thing. *"Keep yourself clean."* They were in the bathroom. *"A woman likes a man to be clean."* His father was standing at the toilet and he was at the sink.

It was the only time he'd seen his father's penis. It was huge. He remembers looking at it hanging there from his father's hand, the piss leaving it in a thick strong stream. It had scared him. His own was smaller then, just a kid's. He'd wondered then if his would ever be that big. It scared him to think of something that big growing out of his body.

He didn't ask what his father meant when he'd told him to be clean. He'd washed his hands very carefully as he watched his father finish and then put his penis back inside his pyjamas.

He practised holding his just like his father did. Shaking it to get the last drops off.

Always lift the seat.

That was another thing. Women don't like to sit on a wet seat. It was years before he understood what that meant.

He knows now his father had the hard-on you get sometimes when you wake up. Now his penis is probably as big as his father's. He'll never know for sure. Maybe it isn't. Maybe his father's was bigger. And he knows now what his father meant by being clean. It's one thing he's always done. He's always kept himself clean.

For a moment he tries to imagine his father pushing his penis into his mother, but somehow he can't. He thinks of himself and Marlene when they do it. They don't do it much any more. He wonders why. It's not like they don't like it. He likes it and Marlene says she still likes it.

He tries not to think but it doesn't do any good.

He imagines getting up from the chair and going into the bedroom where Marlene is. He can see himself getting into bed with the Savage and lying there with it between them, the smell of gun oil, the heavy blue barrel on the pillow beside him.

That little girl in The Lucky Seven store. She wasn't so little. She'd been buying a popsicle and he was standing beside her waiting for her to pay so he could go through. He was buying razor blades. He wasn't in a hurry like he usually was. The girl gave the money to the big blonde

How Do You Spell Beautiful?

woman at the checkout, and he looked down at the girl and saw her breast.

Just one of them.

It wasn't very big, just a kind of swelling at the nipple, a small soft lump where her breast was going to be one day. She couldn't have been more than eleven or twelve. Right around the age he'd been when his father told him about being clean. Right around his age that first year in army cadets.

He got hard right there at the counter. Just because he'd seen a little girl's nipple.

It'd taken him a minute to get his head clear, and he fumbled with his money for a while until he felt it go down. He hadn't wanted the woman at the counter to see him like that. Not anyone. He'd fumbled around as if he was confused or something, but he couldn't take his eyes off the little girl as she walked out of The Lucky Seven.

For a moment he was going to follow her to see where she lived, but he hadn't. He'd wanted to though. He'd thought about hiding near her house and watching when she came home from school or wherever. And then he thought that was crazy, thinking things like that.

Marlene had little girl nipples once. But that was before he'd ever met her. They aren't like that now. They aren't small and pink like soft buds on her chest. They're big and brown now, hard, like nuts hanging off the end of her breasts. He doesn't like putting them in his mouth, but Marlene likes it so he does it whenever they make love.

Making love. As if it was a statue you were building or a house you were making with all kinds of rooms in it, each one separate. Some of them were bedrooms and some of them living rooms. He wondered why they called only one room a living room. It's like all the other rooms are something else, dead rooms. Is that what the other rooms are when you're making them?

He doesn't know. It isn't something he's ever thought of before.

His arms are really shaking now, the sweat dripping off his face and down onto the worn stock. He can feel it, the wetness and the shaking. He knows he has to put the rifle down soon. He has to. The little girl is standing there and he can see her small nipple that's going to become a breast someday. He can see it growing there in his head and then he takes it and puts it somewhere else.

He wishes his father were alive so he could talk to him about what he's feeling. He wonders what his father would say. He wonders if his father ever thought about things when he was alive. Before he died. Before he was killed. Before he was shot in the heart. Maybe all his father thought about was being clean.

All of Their Hearts

Maybe that's all there is to know.

He wonders that and then he pulls as much of himself together as he can and puts it all into his arms and shoulders so they stop hurting him for one clear moment.

There's something in him and he doesn't know what it is. He wants Marlene to wake up from her dream. He wants her to come out of the room where she's sleeping and come into this room where only he ever is. He wants her to stand beside him and say something like: "For God's sake, Ron, it's late. Why don't you come to bed?"

If she did then he could put the rifle down.

He could laugh and say something to Marlene like: "Jesus, Marlene, it's been a day." Then he'd just follow her out of his study and into the bedroom and get into bed with her, and that would be the end of it. He'd put his arms around her and she'd say, "Don't, you're too hot." And he'd let her go like he always does. "Good night," he'd say, and she'd say nothing, and that would be it.

But she won't. She's sleeping with her hair all around her and something, he doesn't know what, in her heart. Just like his father was really only sleeping, except he had a bullet in his.

All of their hearts.

His body hurts. His whole body hurts but he's perfectly still, perfectly steady. He can feel his heart beating all the way from his feet through to the ends of his fingers. If he could have said something to the little girl with her breast just beginning he would have said: "Take heart, little girl."

Something like that.

Yes. He'd say that to her and she'd smile at him and he'd feel clean and good because of her smile and because he was going home.

He wishes he'd said that.

Then everything in the room stops and he gazes down the long blue line of the barrel of his father's rifle to the sight and beyond it to the wall. There were the flies and then his mother giving him the rifle.

Why had she done that?

He thinks of Marlene and thirty years. And then the CO in the car. His father.

Oh Jesus.

He thinks of everything he can think of and then he starts to think of nothing.

"*Softly, softly,* " he says.

Apple Peels and Knives

Sнe picks up an apple and slides the knife under the red skin, turning the apple carefully so the peeling doesn't break. She tries to do this with every apple and today she hasn't succeeded. If she can do it she'll hold the peel at one end in her left hand and swing it around her head three times with her eyes closed.

Each time the peel makes a complete circle she'll say, Who is my true love? If the peel doesn't break as she swings it, and if she succeeds in saying the words without anything intruding on her mind, she will drop it on the floor. The shape it takes will be the initial of her true love.

The apple turns slowly in her hand and just as she gets to the hard part, the part near the end where the blossom used to be, the peeling breaks. It drops into the sink on top of the others, and she slices off the last bit and cuts the apple into the third pie shell. There are only two apples left. She picks up the smallest one and begins again. There is one large red apple left in the sink. She noticed it when she began making the pies and she has left it to the last. Maybe it will be the one to tell her.

She learned about apples when she was a little girl. Her mother had

Apple Peels and Knives

been full of superstitions, things you had to do and things you must never do. Like putting new shoes on the table. She doesn't remember exactly what it means to put new shoes on the table. Does it mean a death? Strange, but she can't remember. She only remembers she shouldn't do it, so she doesn't.

And dropping a knife on the floor, or a fork or a spoon. She remembers only what the knife means. Wherever it points it means an unwelcome guest, a visitor, someone who will come and bring bad luck to the house.

Most of the things she remembers are about bad luck. The knife and the shoes. Other things.

She picks up the last apple. She will peel this one with the knife in her left hand as she always does, her woman's hand. If you're a woman, her mother told her, then the left is the hand where your power is. It's the evil hand if you're a man.

She had to train herself to use her left hand for things like peeling apples, and now the hand is sure of itself. The knife feels safe, almost as if it knows this is the precise moment when everything will become clear. The apple will peel itself and then she will push the knife into the pale flesh, lift the peel in her left hand, and swing it around her head. As she does she'll say, Who is my true love? three times.

As she's thinking this, the apple is turning and the knife is slicing through the skin, the peel coming away from the flesh and settling in the sink. The apple turns and the knife moves with it, both of them moving together, each knowing exactly what it must do in order for the peel to be perfect.

It's Carl's birthday today. She hasn't made apple pies for years. When she asked him in the morning what he wanted for his birthday, he said apple pie and kissed her goodbye.

She's making three pies because one isn't enough. It used to be, but the twins can eat a whole pie between them at one sitting if she lets them, and she usually does.

It was cute seventeen years ago when she named them. Carl, Cam, and Craig. Her three boys, her men. She doesn't think it's cute any more. The names make her uneasy now. All they did was confuse everyone and make them look at her in that way people have and say, Isn't that cute.

Her daughter's name is Carla, which is even worse. Did she ever teach her about apples? She doesn't think so. Carla was never interested in making pies. Carla wanted to make something out of herself and sometimes she wonders what it is Carla made. Her daughter is

How Do You Spell Beautiful?

different. She guesses that's what Carla was making all those years when she was growing up, something different.

Carla's away at university. She's studying to be a psychiatrist, like her father. Maybe that's what she wanted to make out of herself.

She wants there to be enough pie so Carl will be able to have a second piece. The boys will finish one pie at supper and the second pie before they go to bed. They're still growing. They're much taller than she is. They've been taller for what seems like years. She wonders how they could ever have been inside her body, the two of them together, growing there.

She's half-way around the apple. She tries not to think of it breaking. If she does, it will. That's what her mother told her. Her mother used to say, Don't think of it and it will happen. She didn't understand what that meant until she was older. Now she understands, but she can't explain it either. Even if someone asked, she couldn't.

And it doesn't matter. No one is going to ask.

She thought Carl was going to say chocolate cake but he didn't. He said apple pie. That's why she's peeling this last apple, why there are two full pie shells and another one almost full, and a sink full of broken peelings. She turns the apple and the knife moves.

In another year or two the boys will leave and then there will be only her and Carl for the rest of her life. In a few years the boys will be the same age Carl was when she married him. Carla is already past the age she was when she got married. Carla says she'll never get married and she isn't going to have any children. She says she doesn't want to have a life like her mother's.

What's wrong with her life that Carla doesn't want it?

Cam and Craig don't want to be married either. When she asks them they look at each other and laugh. She wishes she knew what they laugh at when they laugh that way. They tell her things are different from when she was young and married their dad. She asked Carl about it once and he told her he didn't blame them. What did blame have to do with it?

The knife is nearing the end where the blossom used to be and she ignores it. This time the peel will be perfect. She knows the whole thing she's doing with the apple, the knife, and the peel is childish, something her mother did to entertain her when she was a little girl. But knowing that doesn't change anything.

She watches the knife slide under the last bit of peel and then the peel drops into the sink.

It doesn't break.

Apple Peels and Knives

She puts the apple down. Her hands are shaking. She reaches for the peel and drops the knife on the floor. For a moment she's frightened. She almost wishes her mother hadn't filled her head with superstitions, but she did. She put them into her head and they stayed there.

She picks up the apple peel with her left hand and lifts it out of the sink. It's long and red and it curls down from her outstretched arm like a snake. You're very beautiful, she says out loud, and is surprised at her voice. She closes her eyes and begins to swing the peel slowly around her head. Each time it passes in front of her she says, Who is my true love? She says it the three times and then drops it on the floor. She hears it fall, the wet slap on the white linoleum.

She stands with her eyes closed, her arm outstretched, her left hand open in the air. The peel is on the floor in front of her. It's formed a letter there, the initial of her true love, the one who truly loves her. She's going to open her eyes in a moment and look at it and then she will know.

Your eyes must be clear, her mother told her. She didn't know what her mother meant. Now she does. In a moment she'll lower her arm, her hand, and her eyes will open and see the initial on the floor, and when they do, she'll know. Then she'll pick up the peel and throw it into the garbage under the sink, and put the pies into the oven and cook them until the crusts are a golden brown.

If Carla were here she would tell her about apple peels and knives.

But the others will be here. They'll all arrive together. They'll be laughing and excited and Carl will put his arms around her and say he loves her, and she'll say Happy Birthday and the boys will say it too.

But first she has to stop thinking.

Her eyes have to be perfectly clear, and right now they aren't. She knows they have to be when she looks at the apple peel. Her eyes will be wide open and she will see, and then she'll pick up the knife.

Jack on the Queen

WHAT?" HE ASKED. HE WAS STANDING at the stove pouring his first cup of coffee. The heat from the blackened iron rolled up his chest and over his face and he turned away.

It was only seven in the morning and it was already hot. He wished they at least had an electric stove instead of the old woodburner. He'd meant to buy her one. God knows they'd talked about it enough. Now it was high summer and hot as hell.

He carried his coffee over to the kitchen table and sat down. She was sitting where she always sat, staring out the window, the stub of a rolled cigarette stuck in the corner of her mouth like a cricket living there. He sipped at the coffee and then reached for the tobacco can. He rolled two, placed the first one by her mug and put the other in his mouth, lighting it with a match from the egg-cup.

"What did you say?" he asked.

She lighted the cigarette he'd rolled for her, placing her dead butt in the saucer between them. "He's coming home," she said.

"What?"

"Bobby," she said. "I can feel it."

He put the mug of coffee down carefully so he wouldn't spill it. He looked at her narrow face staring out the window, the small dark eyes and the grey hair pushed up under her yellow bandana. Her babushka as she called it. She liked that word. She'd learned it from Mrs.

Jack on the Queen

Urbanowski, the Ukrainian lady who'd lived down by the river. But that was years ago. *Why am I thinking of that now?*

"Ma," he said, "you know that's not true. Bobby's not coming home."

"Your Grandmother Rainford knew those things. You know I got the same gift."

"Jesus, Ma."

"I felt him all night. Closer and closer."

The ash from her cigarette fell off and landed in front of her. It trembled slightly. He brushed it off onto the floor. Her hands were hanging off the edge of the table with just the fingertips holding on. It was the way she always sat, her shoulders sharp and low under her print dress and her head, with the babushka on, peering forward and looking out the window at the fields and the road beyond, and the brown hills beyond that.

She's so small, he thought.

Turning to him, she smiled. "I talked to your father last night. He's fine, you know." Her smile was small and quick as a wren moving through leaves. "Did you sleep all right?"

He nodded his head.

"That Bobby was a wild one, especially when it was hot like this. Not like you were."

He nodded again, thinking, *She's just like a bird. A little thing made out of bones and air and not much else. How old was she now? Ninety? She must be ninety. She was born in the last century, he knew, but exactly when, he didn't know. God, all this was still a territory then. She's only old because she's always been here. She was old even when I was a kid. She never stopped being that. But now, right now, right at this very moment, she looks like she's old.*

She was talking to him but he wasn't listening. He was thinking of Bobby, how sometimes he'd thought he knew him but mostly didn't.

"We got to move," she said. "It's the war."

Then his father was lying on the kitchen table again. He could see him lying there even though his eyes were wide open. It was as if there were two pictures in front of him. The other was his mother, peering at him out of her small dark eyes, the stove behind her with the coffee pot on it, steam rising out of its spout in thin wisps. Beside the stove was the screen door and outside, the dog, lying on the porch staring in at them with her wet tongue hanging out, breathing heavily in the bright early shade.

"You're not to be dreaming. You stop that."

How Do You Spell Beautiful?

He was helping her again. He'd undone the buttons on the shirt and was trying to bend his father's arm so he could get it out of the sleeve, but the arm was heavy and didn't want to move. He stood there holding it, looking down at the hand. The fingers were as large as sausages, the colour of spilled wine on wood, the nails cracked and yellow. There were bits of sawdust under them and sawdust in the pale red hair on his wrist.

His mother was at the other end undoing his boots. His father's legs were hanging over the end of the table, bent at the knees, and she was squatting on her haunches pulling at the knots in the laces. He could see the top of her head and that was all.

Cut it, she said. Get the scissors from my room and cut it.

And he did. He cut through the thick stained denim from the wrist up to the neck, severing the collar, and then cut the other sleeve the same. By then she had the boots and socks off, and she took the scissors from him and cut off the pants. They were her sewing scissors. Her good ones, the ones she'd never let him play with. The blades followed the inside seam carefully and she said, These can be saved.

She wasn't talking to him.

She came around then and lifted his father's head in her small hard arms, the shoulders rising with it so he could pull the shirt out from underneath. Then she put the head back down, her hands in his father's hair, thin fingers lost inside that immense red.

"Where are you?"

He blinked his eyes. "Nowhere, I guess."

"The owl is back. She's hunting out of the old cottonwood just like she always does. She's got a little one this year. She's teaching him to hunt."

"Him?"

"I think so. It's early to tell but I'm pretty sure. Your father never believes me but I know. They hunt different from the females. Somehow their spirit's not in it. They don't have the same need."

In the far cottonwood beside the dugout he thought he could make out a single owl on a dead branch, perched high above pale wavering leaves.

"The crows will find them," she said. "They always do." She laughed. "But at night it's the other way around."

He got up and put his empty mug in the sink with the other dishes. He stood beside her a moment as she shuffled the cards and laid out a hand of patience. "Jack on the queen," he said when all the cards were down. Then he walked out on the porch, the screen door slapping behind him. The dog looked up.

Jack on the Queen

"I know," he said. The grey boards under his bare feet burned even though the porch was shaded. He sat on the top step and pulled on his socks and boots. The dog whined. "It's all right," he said. "It's okay." He tied the last lace and stood up.

"I'm going into town later," he called to the door. "Don't worry. I'll get my own supper."

~

It was early evening before he started back from Little River. The electric stove sat in the back of the pickup. It was braced against the cab by a block of fir and the spare tire. It wasn't new. The oven door was scratched and one of the back burners didn't work. Cranford guaranteed what was left worked or he could have his fifteen dollars back. "What's wrong with your old one?" Cranford had asked. He didn't tell him the old one was a woodstove. He just said it stopped working. "They do that," Cranford said.

He drove slowly, not hurrying, not wanting the stove to bang around in the back. The light was almost gone but there was a glow in the western hills, the earth turning the narrow valley slowly away from its light. As he passed along the dusty road by the river he saw the crows flying low toward the scrub spruce by Sandy Flats. He slowed down even more and squinted his eyes as he got closer, trying to find the lookout bird. The bird was a kind of charm to him, a crow with a single white feather in its tail. It was the one who watched out for hawks and owls and hunters. As he pulled around the last curve where the road broke away from the river, he thought he saw it perched on the dry top of a widow-maker. The crow shuffled its wings at him as he went by. The last of the flock settled out of the sky and found their way into the branches below as his truck moved slowly north.

The light wasn't on in the house but he knew she was there at the table looking out the window. He parked the pickup by the porch, picked up the case of beer in one hand and the groceries in the other and pushed the cab door shut with his boot. The dog looked at him from the porch, her ears up. She lifted herself to her front legs and then fell back down, her tail thumping on the boards. Small whispers of dust breathed from the cracks.

"Hey," he said. "Take it easy. I'm home."

Putting the groceries down on the counter, he opened the fridge and put in the case of beer. The cupboard door was open and he took out the bottle of Teacher's and poured two fingers into a glass and

65

How Do You Spell Beautiful?

then added a teaspoon of the white powder the doctor had given him three months before. It was almost gone. He'd have to get some more. He took the glass of whisky and a beer over to the table and sat down in his chair.

"He'll be here soon," she said. "I was going to make him some supper but decided to wait. He wouldn't like it cold."

For a moment it came back to him again. The wound and the huge hands tied together just below it with a piece of binder twine so they wouldn't slip and fall off the table. Bobby and Maryellen were standing by the screen door watching, Maryellen holding Bobby so he wouldn't run. His mother was washing his father and he was beside her holding the basin of warm water. She cleaned his father's thighs, wiping away the smears. "They do that," she said. "Most of them. Someday maybe you'll have to do this for me. Maryellen should be the one but it'll probably have to be you."

He stared at his father's penis. It was long and red and partly swollen. She reached into the basin with the cloth, ignoring him, and went back to his father's white legs, cleaning them all the way down to the ankles. Then the feet, washing the toes and scrubbing the soles with her nails until they came up a pale wrinkled yellow. "You go now," she said, "and take Bobby and Maryellen with you. There's things now I've got to do."

"The owl is back," she said. "She's got a little one."

He set the glass in front of her, rolled a cigarette, lighted it for her, and then another for himself.

"Where's that Maryellen? She should be home now. She'll want to be here when Bobby comes."

"There was no knowing them," he said to her at last. "They were brother and sister but I didn't know them. They were blood, you always said. You'd say, Know your own. That's all you've got in this world."

"He's a big one," she said.

"What?"

"That baby she's got."

He put his hand up to his face and looked away from her.

"I know," she said. "There's a certain kind of blood in a family and it always ends up in just one. In our family it's Bobby. You've got to understand that. He's just like your Uncle Joe. You know, the one none of you's met yet. He's just like him, your wild Uncle Joe."

Her eyes were bright in the new dark. He looked down at the cards laid out in front of her. The tableau hadn't been touched. He

Jack on the Queen

wondered if it was the same hand she'd laid out hours ago when he left the house. "Jack on the queen," he said stupidly, but if she heard him she gave no sign.

"We carry it in us. The women, I mean. It gets passed on and it's the women who pass it. It's like the blood's in a silver cup inside them and when the time comes they pour it all into one child. Grandmother Rainford gave that blood to your Uncle Joe and when it was my turn I gave it to Bobby. I don't know why I picked him but I did. I knew it too. I knew it the night I made him. You and Maryellen were sleeping in that little room at the back. It was just winter. I knew before ever we got into that bed I was going to make a child. Your father didn't know. I don't think men know that kind of thing, but women do."

He drank his beer and looked out the window as she talked. He thought of his Uncle Joe dying in the war, his father, Bobby, Maryellen, all of them. The moon had begun its rise over the hills, a heavy golden ball that paled as it rose into the night sky, putting out the stars with its light. She had stopped and was sipping her drink.

It isn't like she's thinking what to say, but more like she's not. She's slipped away from me, he thought. She's gone back into herself. Everyone's alive in there. Maryellen had the same way to her. She used to go away like that.

Maryellen. Her golden red hair. Gone away, God knows where, God knows how many years ago. And Bobby too.

His mother pushed a strand of hair up over her ear. She picked up her glass again and the hair fell like a feather, slow and grey across her cheek.

She said, "When your father was at last asleep I came downstairs and sat right here at this table. I had his seed in me. It was winter and it was cold but I didn't care. I remember I thought I should go and make sure you and Maryellen were covered up, but I didn't. I sat here the whole night with that boy inside me. And I didn't cry. I didn't want to. It wasn't tears I felt. I cried for you and your sister but I never cried for him. Not for Bobby."

She turned her face to him but he didn't look back at her.

"Your sister's got a daughter," she said. "Oh, she's a pretty one. A little girl with red, red hair. And that little girl will do it. This family's always had a Bobby or a Joe. It's the women who make them. The men don't have anything to do with it. They throw their seed into the world but it's the woman who's the vessel. The men are just the ones who get made. Your father never understands that."

"I don't want to talk," he said.

How Do You Spell Beautiful?

"It'll be all right," she said. "It's the war and him working so hard at that mill."

They were quiet then for a long time. Once he got up and turned on the light to get a beer and another whisky for her. He switched the light back out before he sat down. The dog shifted once or twice on the porch. He watched, loving the way the light glimmered in the dog's thick coat, the long hairs glistening with dust and moon. Everything can be beautiful, he thought. Everything. He waited while his mother sipped her whisky, her tiny mouth pulling the last drops from the glass one at a time so they would last.

"I wanted to," he said. "But I never understood any of it. Not him, not Maryellen, and most of all not Bobby."

"You know," she said, "I've been playing this game of patience all day and I still haven't won."

"Put the jack on the queen."

"You come," she said, her voice sudden. She took his hand in hers and he followed her out the door and across the porch. The dog rose out of sleep and went with them, her paws moving softly behind them, her tongue hanging out, almost touching the dust.

She held him with her tiny fingers and drew him along beside her. Her head with the yellow babushka barely came up to his chest. She walked quickly, holding his hand, not pulling him but as if he were blind, holding and guiding him all at the same time.

They crossed the yard and entered the dry yellow grass beyond. It crackled and broke under their feet as crickets cried and fireflies lifted around them. She stopped for a moment and put her hand on the dog, who sat and looked up at her. Then they went on.

"Look," she said, and sank slowly and carefully into the grass.

He stared up into the old cottonwood, where an owl was perched on a high dry branch. It cowled its wings at them and cried. The dog answered with a long howl from the far field. He felt his mother below him as he waited, his eyes moving across the fields and the distant trees. Finally the female came riding out of the pale light and dropped down on the branch. In her beak was a mouse. She held it for the young one. He was as big as she was. The young owl took it from her and placed it under one of his talons, ripping awkwardly at the body with his beak and then swallowing it whole.

He sat down beside his mother, looking out over the night, the stars and the quiet rustling of creatures everywhere around them. After a while she began to lean and he put his arm around her, pulling her into his shoulder.

68

Jack on the Queen

She rested there. Then he picked her up and carried her over the field to where the dog waited. The three of them went to the house. The dog lay down again on the porch, and he opened the door and carried her up the stairs to her room.

Laying her gently on the bed, he removed her dress and stockings and pulled the summer quilt over her. The babushka had slipped back on her head and he carefully removed it, her thin grey hair falling onto the pillow. She looked up at him with her dark eyes.

"I forgot to tell you," he said. "I finally got that stove. The electric one."

She smiled her smile then. "The owl is back. She's got a little one this year." Her voice was bright.

"Yes, I know."

"When Bobby comes you make sure he eats," she said. "And you finish that game for me. You put the jack on the queen. I'm tired now."

He looked down at her, her body small in the bed.

She went on, her voice quiet beside him. He sat on the low stool beside her bed and waited for her to finish. From where he was he could see nothing but sky and the stars coming back one by one as the moon went down.

Blue

I'LL GO DOWN SOON. I KNOW THEY'RE waiting there, for me or for themselves, the five of them ranged round the table talking, or some of them, or none. The boy won't talk. He's barely here at all. Maybe they're only sitting without words to say, but that's not likely. They'll be going round and round, even the ones that never talked too much will yammer, will throw whatever words are needed on the cloth, will spill and splutter, each of them convinced that talk will tell it all.

They talk too much. It's all they've got is words. Remember this, remember that, the time, the time, the time. The oldest one has got the albums out from where I packed them. She'll be flipping through the lives.

Remember this, remember that?

When I was a boy I thought if only I could stand in the right spot I could see around the edges, and I'd move to the seat in the farthest corner of the picture show and try to see what was happening outside the screen.

I don't remember being young.

But I'd do that, try to peer around the edge to see what wasn't there. I still catch myself doing it, my eyes turning to the margins as if what wasn't there was more than was. All black and white back then and not a word.

I haven't been a boy for years and think I never was one. It's what

Blue

she did, those albums, all those shots of kids and trees and cars. Great piles of albums stacked beside her chair so she could find the years. Look, she'd say, remember that?

I don't want to remember, never did. I think she loved the past, and I hated the way she'd take her hand and hold it flat upon some photograph, just lay it flat as if whatever thing was there could climb into her bones and make a living there inside her. She had them all, even the ones that came before our time, old boyfriends, girls, the child she was before I met her, her mother and her father.

That damned man.

I proved him wrong who said I wasn't man enough for her. How's more than fifty years?

They can have them all. I put them in a box, even the ones in frames she had on the bureau there. The one of me and her when we were young back then before the kids were born. She was perched up on the fender of that Ford, all beads and shining, and I was by the door with my hand inside the window on the wheel. And real silk stockings that cost me a day's pay.

Why I was doing that I'll never know. And why weren't we together? It was her brother-in-law took that. He was a drunk even then. Only a drunk would take a shot like that. And there she was, all shining, with her back against the light, her one arm cocked up on her hip and that still face. She hated being taken. Almost all the pictures were of everyone but her.

~

Look at this room. It's where we slept for more than fifty years. There were other rooms before it. Different rooms, but all the same at last. She painted it a thousand times. You could take a knife and scrape her life from off these walls. Layer by layer, every one a colour she'd a mind to make. The time she painted every wall dull black and made the ceiling red. There was no talking to her. I let her alone when she did that.

I hated sleeping then. The walls would climb all over me. Dull black and everything above me hanging red. And once she painted every wall a different colour. That one there was green and this one yellow. I don't remember now the ceiling's colour. Purple, orange. And then there were the other rooms. The house a craziness, just like her mind.

God knows what she was thinking at the best of times.

You could take a knife and if you took a care could walk through half an inch of paint, go year by year and year until you got to the

71

How Do You Spell Beautiful?

beginning, the plaster I lay down like skin. I built it for her the first year I was back. Her father said she'd never have a roof over her head if she married me. I proved him wrong. Every nail in every wall is mine. She said she wanted a room that looked into the north. Why not the south? That's where the sun was. The north was always only cold. She even planted Virginia creeper so the windows were obscured. I hated not being able to see out, that creeper climbing there. In winter it was worse. The leaves would fall with everything a spider web of vines.

And the furniture. I never knew what every room would be from week to week. Couches would be turned and tables tried in corners where you least expected them. Bedrooms would be moved. She would've moved the bathroom if she could. I'd come home late at night and trip on things. But not this room. This room stayed as it was except the walls. The bed was here, the head of it due west.

This was my side, that was hers.

What was it made her want to be away from things?

It's like this room was where she hid. Like all the rooms. I never left our bed, though she did twice. I told her it was where I slept and that was that, and then she left.

The children never knew. She was always up before them, fires raging in the stove, the coffee hot, and they'd come down the stairs still half-asleep, as kids are when they wake, and there she'd be with toast for them or cocoa, milk, and eggs.

Who was to know she'd slept out by the tree?

What will I do with all the things?

The kids will clear them out. I'll have them sent down to the Sally Ann. I'd burn them if I could. The kids would think that strange. I can see me walking in the town and meeting some strange woman wearing her coat or dress or blouse. I couldn't stand the sight. I know I'd think the woman her. I'd smell her smell.

And they're all down there waiting.

What'll I say?

They'll want a word from me. They'll want me to be the kind who grieves. You haven't cried, my daughter said. I said I would in time. You have to cry, she said.

Well, let her cry. It's hers to do so if she wants.

It's not as if I think a man can't cry.

They've got my clothes laid out. My shirt is hanging there and the suit the boys have bought. Are they ashamed of me? They'd food enough to eat the years they grew. God knows I'm just their father. Did they think I'd go with grease on my hands? And if I did, at least it would

Blue

be honest dirt. What I brought home I worked for, every grain of dust.

It's a good suit. Anyone could see that. And the shoes all polished. I did that, but then my shoes were always polished. You can tell a man by his shoes. A bit of rag and spit. I learned that and still wouldn't hire a man whose shoes were scuffed. Even a bum can have a little class if he's a mind to.

I never left her. She did me.

But I went to her that night. I could've stayed inside. She made the choice to leave. The night was mostly gone when I went out. There were the stars and her in that blanket on the lawn. The dew was on her. I could see it glimmer from the step and thought her dying from the wet and cold. There wasn't much of her at best. There's not an ounce of fat on me, she told me many times. I'm mostly skin and bones. Yet I loved holding her. Her bones were mine.

Who knows why she went out?

I lay down there beside her. I never said a word, just lay out on the lawn. I felt her stiffen when she heard me there and knew it would be right again, that she'd some feeling left.

She looked like something thrown there. A little pile of white out on the lawn, as if a child had dropped a blanket there, the willow tree above her swinging slow. There was no wind. That tree just seemed to breathe. She stuck a wand into the ground and made a tree. A thumb as green as any woman had. Just took a broken branch and stabbed it there. It's like she ordered it to grow.

The other time I didn't go at all. I might've but I didn't. Perhaps I should. I probably should have gone just like the time before, but I was mad. A man's a right to that. When a woman leaves his bed a man has every right to say the hell with her. It's what I said when she went out the door. The hell with you, I said.

And then the toast and jam and cocoa, all the things for them, still sleepy-eyed and stumbling like small kids will do who haven't left their dreams. The boys were worst for that. The girls seemed more awake. It's like they saw the day the moment that the light walked on their eyes. All bright and shining. But she had coffee on for me before I went to work.

We never talked about that time and there's no talking now. What's done is done and she came back to me. She walked into this room and lay her body down.

I could take a knife and scrape her life from these walls. If I'd a mind to I could do that. I could be an archaeologist of her, could say that this was 1945 and tell the year from winter into spring. That year the walls were blue and she was happy.

How Do You Spell Beautiful?

Did someone die that year?

A lot of us had died. They never made the bullet that was meant for me. I knew I'd get back home.

I'll go down soon. I'll walk into the room and one of them will straighten out my tie or comb my hair from where it falls across my eyes. Oh Dad, someone will say, and some will look at me and some will not.

The boy will look away.

He'll never change from that. The others will. The wives and husbands will be wandering about. The ones who married in. And the ones who aren't there any more. I could line them up, the ones they've left behind. And all the kids. She was a grandmother twenty times. They're all there too. The kids in running shoes and jeans.

We held for fifty years.

If you count back there's only forty lifetimes between then and now. That's all there is. They think time's forever but it's not. At half a century there's only forty to where it all begins. That's something they'll learn if they've got time. There's no telling of it though. Oh Dad, they'd say. Oh Dad.

I'll go down soon. I will.

I went to her that night and felt her stiffen there. And so we lay, me looking at the stars and her with that long back away from me. Looking at what?

The dark was there.

Maybe she stared at that. Or maybe there was some animal she saw, some thing that shared her sight, a mouse half-caught by night in her still eyes. Or even just a spider with a moth all rolled and ready. Something, or nothing, or just what she could see inside her mind. Who knew what she could see? I never knew what looked at me.

And then she cried inside my arms and that was where we stayed until I carried her to bed as light as cotton, her head right here, her arms around my neck. I could have carried her a hundred miles that night.

But not the second time.

Oh, we were older then. If she'd a mind to go then she'd a right, and so had I.

She'd pick an album and stare for hours at some picture that she'd taken. The boy who died. I cried for him. That's one I cried for if they want to know. Just once. I could've eaten the dark that night. I tried.

When will I ever wear this suit again? They'll have me lying in it someday soon, a flower in my buttonhole and a smile some

Blue

undertaker's put there, wax and cotton in my mouth to hold a smile I wouldn't want to have. I think a face should be what it should be. I'll throw it out when they're all gone.

Look at my feet, my hands.

I built a house with these. No one believed I could. Her father said I was a bum. I proved that bastard wrong. His little girl. When she ran off with me he almost died. I think he wanted her to be another wife. A cook and housemaid, entertainer, all of that. His girl, he said. He met me at the gate and closed it there. Said he'd follow me to the ends of the earth and shoot me down like a dog if ever I hurt a hair on her head.

Imagine that? It's like he came out of a book. The ends of the earth. No one talked like that. That's all he had was books. Old Dickens, Shakespeare, and the rest. A damned American was all he was. My family walked away from that and came up north to live. Good Loyalists. We chose a colder place for pride.

I touched her and she rolled back into me, the blanket soaking wet. I held her in the night, with stars as many as a mind could want to see, the willow moving round us. A summer night so still the moths refused to fly. The room was blue that year. I'm sure it was, can see her standing on that stool stroking out the colour that she'd picked. Long strokes, the colour laying down.

You could take a knife.

One of them will come for me, a daughter or a son.

They always knocked. The door was always closed. It wouldn't do to have them see me naked as a child. All knees and elbows. Boney knees. Even the hair has gone from off my legs. I still could walk them into the ground. There's muscle here though looking wouldn't see it.

Christ, my skin is old. It hangs off me in rags. My hands are knuckles, bones, and liver spots. I know each scar. The one there on my knee when the saw slipped in the rain. I worked the shift right through. There's no one ever said I shirked a job. There was blood in my shoe and her so mad when I got home.

There was the time the boy took my arm and bent it down. God, he was proud that day. I tried to take him too. But that's what sons will do. I did the same to my old man and would have broken his arm if I could, I hated him that bad.

I used to watch the mountains as a boy and knew before I walked I'd find a hiding there he'd never know. Close enough to touch, that long blue reaching.

Pincher Creek. The sweetest place this side of love. The chinooks would roll on me all warm and wet. If he were still alive I'd break more

How Do You Spell Beautiful?

than his arm. I never gave an inch. I wish sometimes the boys knew what to hate. Instead they stand apart. Well, let them stand. As if a suit was honour to a man. I'd rather they'd bought nothing.

Why did I have my hand on the wheel? I should have been with her. It was the drunk took that. He's long gone, rolled into a canyon with a bottle in his arms. I liked him well enough. She was pretty with her back against the light. The room was blue.

She'd put her palm on a picture, place it there so that I thought at times the picture would come off upon her skin. I'd look at her hands sometimes as if the years were tattooed there. She'd a touch that lifted off what life there was.

I loved to watch her.

This was mine and that was hers. I'd wait a minute till she went to bed. I'd say, Five minutes, I'll be there, and then she'd go ahead of me and do whatever women do before they sleep, rub cream into their skin or brush their hair. I loved her lying there ahead of me. She'd always turn away and I would reach for her.

I never went the last time.

What did she know out in the dark? We never talked of it.

We never talked.

That's what they do. It's like they want to make their lives with words. As if there wasn't a life already there. They talk of everything too much. There's nothing private in their world.

She stood there at the station with the kids. One I never saw except the picture, the one she sent me when I was first in England. That's years ago. Me leaning out the window of the train, her reaching up, a child inside her arms. Which one was that?

She wouldn't forgive that.

The war. And why should I have stayed when all the others went? Each man has got his war. My family fought in every one. My father in the First and his father before that in Africa.

She lay right there. I knew she was gone. I woke to her and felt her go from me. It's what it was, a fading and a gone and nothing left but what I still could touch. I put my hand upon her face. Her eyes were closed. I lay there all that night. It was her breathing that I missed. I lay there in her stillness.

I'd go somewhere if there was a place to go. I'll sell this place. Who's to do the garden now? I never knew a flower from a weed. I'd wear the grease I wore but they'd be shamed by that. A suit. I can hear the girls tell them to buy a suit for me. Think of our mother, the oldest one would say, and down the boys went to Skinner's store.

76

Blue

Old Skinner's dead. His kid still runs the place.

She always loved the creek behind the house, the hill with its old pear tree standing there. She wouldn't let me cut it down. It flowers still each spring and grows spare fruit. She loved its flowering. You'd think a tree would simply die, yet still it shoots a branch or two each year and blossoms white.

I should have stood by her. My hand on the wheel and her just looking past me with her back against the light. Her face would brighten when she looked at that. Was that what it was, me reaching for the wheel and her just sitting there?

It's almost time. A thousand cakes and sandwiches. The neighbours brought them all. They'll all be over. The five of them and fifty more besides, and all of them with smiles. The sorry this and that.

I'll put the damned thing on and tie the tie. They think I don't know how. I'll tie a Windsor knot to show them what I know. Could do it blind. Can even tie a bow. There's damn few left can do it, in and out, the double fold. My father taught me that. My shoes are shined.

Look at these hands.

I hear them coming now. Just one or maybe two. Can hear them saying to each other, It's high time, and sending both the girls.

Go get him now, it's time.

I'll go when I've a mind to go. I'll go down soon. I'll put the damned suit on. I will. I'll do it now.

Oh, she was cotton in my arms the night I carried her across the lawn, her head right here, her arm around my neck. I never went the second time. She would've come to me. Did she lie there waiting for my touch? I could have gone, but we were older then. I left her to herself. I think she wanted that.

And I'll not tell them how I carried her out there. They've got no right to know. Oh, she was light as cotton in my arms. I put her by the willow and held her there all wrapped inside my arms.

We never talked.

I watched the stars and woke with her to dew, our bodies wet as morning when the sun has heated them. She wasn't cold. I should've gone to her that other night. I told her so when we were lying there.

I told her everything that night.

I carried her inside and called them all, and she was gone away and now they're here. I'll go down soon.

This suit's too big for me.

I think they see me as I used to be. I look a child in this. I'm half the size I was.

How Do You Spell Beautiful?

I'll put a stone beneath that pear tree. She'd like that. There's one that's in the flower bed she wanted out. She asked a thousand times for me to dig it up. I'll do it now. It's right for her. It's blue. If I put my hand upon that wall I'd feel the years. You look a fright, she'd say. I should've got my hair cut.

Should've this and should've that.

I should've gone to her, but we were old.

I think I should've died before she did. I think a woman's better at a death. I always thought I'd go before she did. Isn't that the way it's supposed to be? A man's not suited for it. Who'll look after me? This garden and this house. You could take a knife and scrape her life from off these walls.

A stone will do, that pear tree shooting white.

There were so many stars. I kept her warm right through until she died. I felt her go at dawn. It's funny how she stayed that long with me, all crouched inside, as curled as all the nights she slept, so that I had to straighten her to hold her.

I would've held her longer if I could.

What Is It You Want, Exactly?

"HE ISN'T GOING TO MARRY ME," Elaine said when she opened the door. Then she started crying.

John guided her to the living room, stepping over scattered toys and dishes, newspapers and books, and bits of food. He sat her down in her nightgown on the couch in front of the fireplace and wrapped her in a blanket he found in the corner by the dead fern.

"What happened to the fireplace?"

Of all the things he could see in the living room, it was the strangest. It looked as if someone had tried to burn the house down. The oak lintel was scorched and the wall above was stained with what looked like soot. There was a white rectangle where the painting of the ships had hung. He wondered where it was.

There were smoke marks on the ceiling too. Someone had thrown water on the wall because the soot was streaked, the wallpaper wrinkled and coming off in places.

"There was a fire," Elaine told him, continuing to cry, though not as hard as before.

That's when John started cleaning up. The kids, who'd been nowhere around when he arrived, came out of rooms, his five-year-old daughter lunging at him as he passed by the open door leading into

How Do You Spell Beautiful?

the basement. She screamed while he was picking things up.

All three were like wild animals.

Their hair was dirty, the pyjamas of the two boys covered in what looked like blood but was probably only ketchup or tomato sauce. He hoped that's all it was.

When he couldn't take it any more he spanked the three of them, put them all in the bathtub still crying, washed them, and packed them off to bed, the boys first and then the little girl.

When he pulled the blanket up over her she threw it off and snarled at him. It was the only way he could think of to describe what she did. Like an animal, he thought. Like a wild animal.

There are things here that need doing, he thought.

He left the girl in her bed and went into the other parts of the house, picking things up and putting them away, towels and clothing, dishes and food. He left the kitchen as it was. It seemed to him he could attack all that in the morning after they had a chance to sleep. I'll get to it. I'll clean this place up till it shines.

It made him feel good to be straightening things out.

Things have gotten out of hand here, he thought, as he walked through the living room. He smiled at Elaine when he passed. She was still on the couch. Her feet were tucked up, the blanket wrapped tightly around her. She didn't look at him when he smiled at her. She was staring at the fireplace.

When he packed the third load of pots and silverware into the kitchen he found a vodka bottle behind a bowl of smashed, blackened bananas.

It was full.

John thought about it for a moment and then he washed a glass, poured some vodka into it, and carried it back to the living room. He gave it to Elaine. "Here," he said. "Drink this. It'll make you feel better."

"Christ, John."

It was the first time she'd looked at him directly since he got home. He grinned and then, because he felt foolish, tried to stop and couldn't.

Elaine's hand came out from under the blanket and she took the glass from him and pulled it under. The glass reappeared at her throat. She bent her head and took a drink.

The last thing he did after picking up the obvious stuff was to vacuum the carpet in the hall and the living room. He began to sing to himself and for a moment he thought Elaine looked at him strangely.

80

What Is It You Want, Exactly?

As he sang he tried to figure out what it meant. It was a look he hadn't seen before.

He shook his head. He knew who she was. That Elaine, he thought as he vacuumed around the couch, the spilled cigarette butts and ashes disappearing into the end of the tube he held in his hand.

"This carpet's going to need cleaning," he said.

Elaine gave him the look again. He tried to figure what it meant as he sang, and then gave up. She's tired out, he thought. That's all it is. As he stood there figuring and singing quietly, she held out the glass from under the blanket and he took it to the kitchen. When he came back he brought the bottle with him and another glass.

"I'm going to need a drink too," he said, "just as soon as I've got things in order around here."

He put the empty glass on the coffee table and then refilled Elaine's and gave it to her. Her hand and arm came out from under the blanket and took it away from him. "I'll join you in a minute," he said. "I'll just finish this vacuuming. Things have been pretty crazy around here, haven't they?"

Her look had changed a little, John thought. It wasn't quite as strange as before.

~

He poured himself a drink and a fourth for Elaine. By this time she'd told him everything about the rich guy. He was someone called Peter she'd met shopping at Safeway. "It was kind of crazy," she said. "We were both buying oysters."

John had never met anyone at Safeway and he wondered how you went about meeting people there. Maybe the oyster section was where you did things like that. The seafood place.

But John *had* met the guy. Elaine had invited Peter and his then-wife Shirley over for drinks and dinner a month before Elaine had told him he had to leave. He hadn't known the guy was the rich man in question. The guy he'd met was an American from Florida. He'd had that going for him, John thought at the time. That and being rich.

They sat around that evening after dinner. Elaine cooked it. Seafood, John thought. That's what we had. Some kind of fish and clams.

The rich guy had some marijuana and they all smoked it and listened to The Beatles's White Album. The man told them the album was just out. "This is completely new," he'd said when he took off the cellophane. "It's the first copy in Vancouver. I ordered it from New York."

John hadn't smoked a lot of marijuana before. It made him dizzy.

How Do You Spell Beautiful?

Elaine seemed less dizzy than he was and he'd thought that was strange at the time.

He didn't now.

When they'd finished eating, the rich guy made a production about rolling the marijuana, the *grass* as he called it, and then suggested they all take off their shoes and lie on the floor to hear it. "This's the only way to listen to this kind of music," he'd said.

Taking off his shoes like that made John feel awkward, almost naked. They all lay down then in front of the fireplace and listened. The rich guy turned off the lights. He even made a fire. The light flickered across all of their faces as they lay there smoking. John hadn't liked the songs very much but the rich guy, Peter, liked the album a lot. So had Elaine.

Peter kept saying The Beatles were geniuses. "They're such fucking geniuses," he'd said. What John had thought, besides the songs being pretty ordinary, was that the album cover was going to get dirty easily, being completely white. He said so and Elaine and the rich guy and his wife had all laughed at him.

"Christ, John," Elaine had said. "Listen to the songs."

John didn't remember what the guy's wife thought about the songs. He didn't remember much about her at all. She had brown hair and white arms with almost no hair on them. She took up a lot of room on the carpet. That was about all he could remember of her. Her hair and her arms and how long her body was, stretched out. He'd thought at the time it was peculiar. She hadn't seemed so tall when she was standing up.

~

"The hell with him," Elaine said.

John thought she was pretty drunk. She acted like it. She'd had a lot of vodka. "Well," he said, and put his hands behind his head and leaned back against the couch.

"Fuck'm," said Elaine. She got up then and said she had to go to the bathroom. "I've gotta pee."

She staggered a little and leaned against the wall for a moment. "Take it easy," said John as she disappeared down the hall.

John thought he'd look for the painting of the ships tomorrow. It had to be around somewhere. Pictures don't just disappear.

He was still staring at the scorched wall and ceiling when Elaine returned. He'd been thinking it was going to be a major job to clean everything up. Professionals would have to do it.

What Is It You Want, Exactly?

Elaine came back wrapped up in the blanket. She sat down on the couch and held out her hand for more vodka. Her leg sticking out from under the blanket was naked. John could see her foot and her toes. He hadn't noticed them before. That's her foot all right, he thought. That's Elaine.

Tipping the bottle, John noticed it was almost all gone. He wondered why it was vodka. Before, when he was still here, they drank rye.

Vodka's something new.

Elaine smiled at him. Her hair was combed now and she'd put lipstick on. It was a colour he recognized, a dark purple. She was the old Elaine now.

"We had some times, didn't we?" she said, looking at him through her glass.

"What?"

"Back then," said Elaine, taking a sip. "All the years and everything. Before, you know, Peter and everything."

"Well, yes," John said. He felt suddenly warm thinking about the years before Vancouver, up north, everything, how they'd been before all this. Suddenly he felt things were going to be all right.

We can do this, he thought. We've been together for almost nine years, not counting the last three and a half weeks. They could just forget. They could just put that part of their lives out of their minds.

"Nine years," he said, and raised his glass in what he thought was a toast.

Elaine lifted her glass too and smiled at him. It was more than just a smile, John thought. It was the kind someone gives you when they've got a secret. A smile that meant they were both in this together.

We are, he thought. We're together in this.

"Who wants to go first?"

"What?"

"C'mon," Elaine said. "All those years. You must have been a pretty busy boy." Her eyes were dancing.

"Well, I was," said John.

He thought about the years, the different jobs, the moving around from place to place. The ups and downs. Well, that's over, he thought. Things are going to be different now. Things are going to straighten out. We're going to put all this behind us, the *White Album* with its stupid songs, the rich guy with his marijuana, all of that. He'd get the house cleaned up, bring in some professionals, and then he'd get another job somewhere. Not with Charlie Tingle at the upholstery shop, but with someone.

83

How Do You Spell Beautiful?

"Well," Elaine said, "I was too," and she giggled at him.

John laughed too. It felt good to be laughing again.

"I'll go first," she said.

John waited for a second. He didn't know what she meant exactly.

"Jerry and Ed for starters."

She looked at him expectantly, and John laughed. "You mean my friends?" He hadn't thought of old Jerry for years. And Ed too. They'd all been friends back in the days when he and Elaine were first married.

When John didn't say anything, Elaine said, "I slept with them. You know. Both of them." She looked at him then as if she expected something, as if there were something she wanted but didn't know what exactly.

"You mean my friends?" John asked. Somehow it scared him to ask but he didn't know what else to say. "Jerry and Ed?"

"Oh, John," Elaine said, giggling into her glass. "Don't act so surprised. You knew that, didn't you?"

John knew what he'd just heard wasn't a confession. It was more like a clarification, as if for some reason Elaine thought they needed some clarity right now.

"We were pretty busy, weren't we?" she said. "Alice and Ed, Jerry and Sophie and the rest. You know."

"What?"

Then he said, "Yeah, well, I guess so."

He hadn't slept with anybody back then. Not anyone. There had been one woman in a little town somewhere they'd lived once, but he hadn't done it with her. Not exactly. Her name had been Gail and he didn't think Elaine had known her. She was a waitress at a little place he used to go to for coffee breaks. The Venice Cafe.

It was Gail who suggested they go to The Bluebird Motel. It was the place businessmen went on their lunch hours when they wanted to take someone, a secretary or customer. It was a first time for him. He'd almost done it with her, but when he tried he'd been impotent. It had never happened to him before. He remembered it scaring him, and then the apologies, her saying she understood and saying it was all right, that it happened sometimes like that.

He remembered after he couldn't do it holding her in his arms and singing her songs from records he'd listened to years ago when he was young. Show tunes from *Guys and Dolls*, musicals like that. His mother used to buy every long-play when it came out. She'd loved the Broadway shows.

What Is It You Want, Exactly?

Singing was all he could think of to do. Gail had listened right through to one o'clock.

She was the only one.

Gail told him she loved him when she got out of the bed and started to get dressed. He'd finished singing by then. "I really love you," she said when she got her clothes on. She said she understood why he couldn't.

"I understand," she'd said, "I really do." Then she told him she didn't want to see him any more. What they hadn't had was over.

He never went back to The Venice Cafe.

"Old Jerry," said Elaine.

John felt a little sick. It's the vodka, he thought. And the room, the walls and fireplace. The missing picture. Everything.

"C'mon," Elaine said, laughing now. "Let's go to bed."

She stood up and dropped the blanket.

She was naked.

This is my ex-wife, he thought. This is Elaine. I'm going to go to bed with her. He felt confused. He kept thinking of his old friends and how he hadn't seen them for a long time. For some reason he tried not to look at her.

Elaine leaned over and took him by the hand. "Good old John. This's all been so crazy, hasn't it?"

He closed his eyes.

She held onto his hand and drew him up, and he followed her down the hall. He looked into the rooms they passed, the dining room, the rooms where his children were sleeping.

These are my belongings, he thought.

When they got to the bedroom the same bed was there, a pale grey with wicker on the headboard. It was the bed they'd slept in before he'd left. He didn't know why it should seem so odd to him, but it did. Somehow he thought she would've changed it, what with Peter and everything.

He stood there and Elaine began undoing his shirt. She undid all the buttons and then she pinched one of his nipples. She'd never done anything like that before.

He kept his eyes closed as she got onto the bed, then he took off the rest of his clothes. He felt a little shy. He didn't know why, but he turned away from her anyway.

When he got his clothes off he pulled the covers back and started to climb in, but Elaine told him not to. "No," she said. "Let's do it on top so we can see."

85

How Do You Spell Beautiful?

He stopped where he was, half in and half out of the bed. He balanced there on one arm, embarrassed. He felt big and tried to hide his erection with his hand. It was as if she was Elaine, his old wife, and a stranger at the same time.

"What is it?" Elaine asked. And then she said, "Is there something you want me to do to you? We can stop pretending now, John. Anything. Just don't let conscience be your guide."

She lay back on the bed and opened her legs. "Go ahead," she said. "Whatever you want."

When he didn't move, she lifted her head off the pillow and looked at him. "Jesus, I'd forgotten. The Jolly Green Giant." John just leaned there, trying to keep his balance.

"C'mon," she said. "Hurry."

How Do You Spell Beautiful?

He WAS SITTING AT THE TABLE BY the front window. The light was changing and everything in the yard was beginning to take on a luminous quality. The grass, the trees, everything, seemed to expand with colour and get larger. Even the shadows, already long and stretched from the falling sun, became deeper. He looked out the window and saw the cat cross the thick lawn.

She looked heavy, her belly swinging as she moved. She didn't look like she was walking. She never did. Her black body seemed to float. Especially now, he thought, in this light. He watched her until she disappeared below him, under the house.

"There's the cat," he said.

Doreen didn't say anything. She was sitting on the couch writing in her notebook. She wrote in it every night. She never used to keep a journal, only now, since they retired. He asked her once what she wrote about. She told him but he hadn't paid any attention. That was the way it was with them, comfortable and quiet.

"Did you see it? The cat, I mean?"

Doreen didn't look up.

He sipped his tea. She never seemed to move lately, always sitting

How Do You Spell Beautiful?

on the couch, always writing, he thought. The way she was going at it you'd think she'd been writing forever.

The light was beautiful. He'd never looked at it quite this way before. He knew that wasn't true, but it seemed like it. It seemed like a completely different world from what it had been only an hour or so before.

"She's got kittens again," he said.

"What?"

"Kittens," he said. "Under the house."

She looked up briefly and then down at her journal. She started writing again. Every time he wanted to say something, like now, she had her head in the notebook. Writing what? What would she have to write about? Nothing much happened to her, to them. The days came and went just like they always had.

Retirement, doing nothing, enjoying doing nothing. He fished a little, less now than when they first moved here from Regina. He'd bought a boat and named it *The Doreen*, but she never came out in it with him. She said it always made her sick. He'd resented it at first, and then he began to get lonely out there. He didn't know anyone at the lake. Like most small places, it took a long time to get to know people, and they had only been there three years.

The weather was great out here most of the year except for two or three months in winter, and that was nothing compared to what it had been on the Prairies. He didn't miss the city or his job. As for the kids, they wrote regularly and visited in the summer. Doreen looked after that. He'd never been much for kids. He liked his, but he didn't miss them. Doreen liked it here too, or at least she never said she didn't.

It had been his idea to move. He'd dreamed about it all his life. A little place, a boat.

"How do you spell beautiful?"

He looked away from the window. He had been thinking of the cat and the kittens under the house. They'd had the cat in the city but she'd never had kittens there. She was a housecat back then. Not now. When they'd moved to the lake she'd littered right away. And then twice more. Each time it had been under the house.

The kittens were always wild. He'd been thinking he would like it if they were in the house and not outside. It would be nice to have them in the house, playing around. Cats were all right. Not like dogs. Not so messy. Not running after you all the time and getting underfoot.

He looked at Doreen. She was staring at him. There was no expression on her face. Her hair seemed damp, almost as if she were

How Do You Spell Beautiful?

sweating, but it wasn't that warm. It was actually cool in the house, not hot.

"What?"

"Beautiful. How do you spell beautiful?"

He spelled it for her.

She wrote it down after crossing something out. At least he thought she wrote it down. Maybe she was writing something else. He watched her. "You okay?" he asked. "You look hot or something."

She didn't answer. She crossed something else out and then stopped and looked at him again.

"I think I'll try to get those kittens from under the house," he said.

"What?"

"The kittens. The cat has kittens. They're under the house. I think I'll get them and bring them in the house. If I don't, they'll go wild."

"It's up to you," she said. "I always get it wrong."

"What?"

"Beautiful. I always get it wrong. Ever since I was a little girl I got it wrong."

"You mean spelling it?"

She didn't answer.

He walked out of the house and got down on his hands and knees where the cat always went in. It was dark and there didn't seem to be much room. The house was on a slope and it didn't have a basement. Most of the houses at the lake didn't have basements. Close to the lake there wasn't much soil. It was all rock mostly. Bedrock. The front of the house was off the ground about three feet and the back was level with the stones that had been moved when the place was built.

The light was getting dimmer. He got down on his stomach and began to crawl under. He wondered how many she had. He hoped there weren't many.

It was damp under the house and he could feel the wetness on his clean shirt.

He stopped crawling and listened. There was a slight scuffle ahead of him, the smallest of sounds toward the back. Sure as hell she'd be there. They always hid in the most difficult places where you couldn't find them. He almost backed out and then he heard the sound again. The floor above him was getting lower as he moved carefully forward.

He stopped again, breathing hard. I must be getting old, he thought. He could hear Doreen above him. She was walking quickly back and forth on the floor above his head. What the hell is she doing?

89

How Do You Spell Beautiful?

It sounds like she's almost running, he thought. She never moves when I'm there. He peered through the gloom and then hunched his shoulders forward, dragging his feet behind him.

There was no sound where he thought the cat was, but he knew he was getting closer. He could feel it.

He wished Doreen would stop walking on top of him. It was distracting. He put his hand out tentatively and felt around. There seemed to be a narrow space just in front of him. He felt it carefully. It was just wide enough for his body. The joists of the floor were scraping his back as he pulled himself another foot, another, and then he was in the narrow space between the rocks. He could feel the floor pressing against his back.

That was it.

It was as far as he could go. He reached out again. His hand brushed something and then the cat scratched him. He pulled his hand back. Jesus!

He tried to look at his hand. He could barely see it, but it hurt. He licked it and tasted blood. His blood. Reaching forward very slowly, he tried again and the cat suddenly screamed and tore at his hand. This time she used her teeth and her claws. He jerked back and then swung his fist through the air, trying to hit her. He didn't touch her. Instead he scraped his knuckles on a rock. "The hell with it," he said. "Stay there if you want. I don't care."

He started to back out, pushing against the damp stones with his hands, but he had barely moved an inch before he stopped. He was caught on something. A large spike coming down from the floor above him was caught in his belt. He moved forward again and then back, but he couldn't move far enough so it would let go. He tried to reach behind, but he couldn't get his hand anywhere near where he was caught. He pushed forward again, trying to go farther, and this time the cat yowled and raked his forehead. He stopped dead.

I'm stuck, for Christ's sake, he thought. He tried wriggling free, but there wasn't enough room. He couldn't even get his hand underneath to undo his belt. The stones were in the way. He lay there breathing heavily. It was dark. He thought a long moment and then he kicked with his foot, his heel banging against the floor above. He kicked until he was tired.

He could hear Doreen moving back and forth above him and then, far away, he heard the screen door slam.

"Doreen!"

He yelled as loud as he could. He yelled her name over and over.

How Do You Spell Beautiful?

His eyes were closed in case the cat attacked him again.

He never thought it would do that.

"Doreen!"

Her feet echoed faintly on the porch steps, and then he heard her crossing the lawn by the flowers, and finally her voice behind him.

"Yes, Richard?"

"Gimme a hand," he said. "I'm stuck and your damned cat attacked me."

She didn't say anything.

"Doreen?"

"Yes?"

"I'm stuck! Didn't you hear me. Give me a hand."

"I can't, Richard."

"What do you mean, you can't? I'm stuck here and your cat's gone crazy. She scratched me. She even bit me."

He could feel the air getting closer and closer. He was sweating and it was hard to breathe. He tried moving again, but this time the spike ripped through his slacks and shirt and stuck into the small of his back. He moved forward the inch or two he was allowed and the cat, just in front of him, growled.

"Doreen?"

"Yes, Richard?"

"Help me."

"I'm sorry, Richard. I can't. I just can't."

He was very quiet and still. He waited for almost a minute and then he asked her. He didn't want to, but he did. It was suddenly very important.

"Why?" he asked. "Why can't you help me?"

"I don't know," she said. "I just know I can't."

It was very dark now. He didn't move. He lay there with his face in the dirt and rocks, and his eyes closed. The cat had begun to purr. He didn't say anything. He could hear Doreen behind him, her breath slow and regular like a heart beating. He knew she was sitting there looking into the dark at him. He didn't know what she could see.

The Babysitter

WHO'S GOING TO BABYSIT?" RUTH asked, while everyone else watched Dana circling the almost-like-new arborite table Tom had brought. The legs were chrome and it had four chairs with it, three of them matching and one not. Two of the chair seats looked as if they'd been cut with a knife, the pale stuffing held in where Tom had tried to fix them with bits of green leatherette and tape.

He'd brought the table and chairs in his truck as a surprise for Martha. He was trying to tell Martha where he'd got them and what a deal it had been, but the kids were yelling. "Gawdammit," Tom said above the racket, "who can hear anything in this place?"

Dana was running and holding high the cracked blue plate with the last Dad's cookies on it, Billy and Little Sal circling after him and crying out how he had the cookies and wouldn't give them any. "Why won't he, Mom?" they cried.

"At the Sally Ann," Tom said. "Twenty bucks. Can you believe it?"

"For God's sake," Martha said, catching Dana with her outstretched arm as he rounded the table, striking him on the chest, the blue plate spinning out of his hands. It flew in the air, landing on the worn green linoleum near the stove. The plate broke and cookies scattered across the floor.

"Now see what you've done," she said, and tried to hit him again.

The Babysitter

Dana ducked under her arm, crying and trying to get some of what was left, as Little Sal and Billy crawled among the shards, stuffing broken bits of oatmeal cookie in their mouths.

Ruth's brown eyes watched from the door, where a bluebottle crawled across the screen, exhausted by its fight against the mesh. Her arms were crossed upon her chest. The hot summer air poured across her shoulders from the backyard.

"I didn't do nothing," Dana cried. "It's their fault."

"Oh for Christ's sake," Tom said as Martha grabbed Dana and held him struggling in her arms. She kissed him on the cheek as he raged against her, his sharp face pressed against her arm, his small teeth in her skin. As he bit her she yelled and slapped his face.

Tom said, "Look at how they race around like wild Indians. They need a stronger hand. I've told you that."

Martha pulled Dana's head away from her arm and then plucked the cigarette out of the corner of her mouth. The smoke was curling up around her face and her right eye was watering. While she was distracted, Dana slipped away from her and aimed a kick at Little Sal, who rolled under the table, stuffing the last bits of store-bought cookie into her mouth.

"Well," Ruth said again, "I want to know, that's all. I want to know."

"You just shut up." Martha wiped her eye with a knuckle and dropped the cigarette in her empty beer bottle, the butt hissing in the foam. "You always want to know," she said, and glared at Ruth, her oldest at eleven years.

"Uncle Charlie's babysitting," Tom said without turning around. He had an Old Style in his hand and turned it on the table, making circles with the sweated glass. "Well, and ain't this some table, eh?"

Martha rubbed her arm where Dana had bitten her. "Look," she said, pointing at the teeth marks on her bare arm. She chuckled. "The little bugger bit me, just like that." She looked across the room to where Dana stood against the archway, his hands tight fists, the knuckles white. "How come you bit your mother?" Martha asked, a new cigarette in the corner of her mouth. She sucked on it, blue smoke seeping from her nostrils.

"Fuck you," cried Dana and ran across the kitchen past his sister, striking the screen door with outstretched fists, the thin door flapping open as he fled. The bluebottle laboured after him, heavy in the thick air of early evening.

Ruth didn't stir as her brother went by. She lifted a brown hand and pushed her dark hair back from where it had fallen across her cheek.

How Do You Spell Beautiful?

She tried to hook it over her pink barrette. It was a running lamb with a bow around its neck and she'd treasured it ever since she found it on the sidewalk down the street. The hair didn't hold and fell again like a dusty wing across her face. "I'm almost old enough," she said. "You told me I could the next time you went dancing. We don't want Uncle Charlie here again."

"You're only eleven, for Christ's sake," Tom said.

"Don't sound so disgusted," said Martha. "She's just a girl." She turned to Ruth. "And what if there was a fire, eh? What would you do then, miss smarty-pants, tell me that? How would you get your brothers and sister out of the house?" When Ruth didn't answer, Martha went on, "They'd burn up in here, that's what'd happen. And you would too. Do you think your mom wants that? Do you?"

Ruth stared at her mother, her small hands white as they gripped her elbows.

"Ain't this some table," Tom said. He put his heavy hand on it and pressed down hard on the swirling red arborite. "You can put whatever you want on it and it won't burn. Hot pots, whatever. Look at this," he said, and butted out his cigarette on it. Smoke swirled up as he crushed it hard on the smooth surface, and there was a crackling noise. "Well, would you look at that." He brushed the ash away and stared at the spot where the arborite had bubbled under his cigarette. "I never knew it'd do that."

"Look at what you did," Martha said, starting to laugh. "Talk about setting fires."

"Well, it ain't so new any more," said Tom, grinning.

Billy slapped Little Sal and ran out the door after his brother. He could see Dana sitting in the old apple tree, swinging his skinny legs in the air and screaming at the German shepherd in the next yard. The dog was racing back and forth inside its pen, biting at the chicken wire. As Billy ran he saw Dana tear off a branch and throw it down across the fence. The dog raged against the wire, its sharp barks tearing at the air.

Ruth turned her head for a moment and watched her brothers. Billy was climbing the tree and Dana was pushing his bare foot in the younger boy's face. As Billy started to fall she turned back to the kitchen. Tom had opened another beer for her mother. He could barely stand as he handed it to her, he was laughing so hard. Her mother tried to take a drink from the bottle. The beer bubbled between her slack lips.

Martha put the bottle down and rubbed at her eyes with both hands

The Babysitter

while Tom went ga-hunk ga-hunk, trying to catch his breath. He was still gaping at the bubbled arborite. Martha suddenly stopped laughing and jerked her head at Ruth. "Look at Little Sal," she said, as if she'd just noticed the child on the floor crying. "You take her out to play right now and don't start whining again about Uncle Charlie. He likes to babysit, you know that. He loves kids and he don't have any of his own." She looked away from Ruth to Tom and started laughing again, the beer bottle rocking on the table.

Ruth grabbed Little Sal's arm and pulled her outside, the screen door flapping closed behind her and almost catching Little Sal's ankle. Little Sal cried as she went, her chafed legs blinkering. Her underpants were wet and stained with ash from where she'd been sitting on the floor by the stove.

"And change her panties," cried Martha as they went, but Ruth, if she'd heard her mother, didn't answer.

"Damn her," said Martha. "She never does anything she's told."

"Well, that's the truth," said Tom, getting up from the chair and going around the table to Martha. "God, wasn't that weird, the table exploding like that?" He got behind her, and as Martha said no, slipped his hand over her shoulder and down the front of her loose dress, his hand moving there under the scant fabric like a furtive animal.

"Now don't," said Martha, moving her head to the side as Tom nuzzled her neck. "The kids," she said, but didn't try to get away.

"God, I love your tits," said Tom.

"Don't call them that. You know I don't like it," said Martha, arching her head back at the same time, her red hands flat on the table and Tom's hand moving from one of her heavy breasts to the other, cupping them and pulling at her nipples. "Oh sweet loving Jesus," Martha said, and lifting up her arm, pulled Tom's face against her mouth.

"I see you," Billy screamed through the screen door, and Martha pulled awkwardly from under Tom's hanging face and yelled at him to get the hell away and what did he think he was doing spying on his own mother when she and Tom were only playing.

"Don't you know better than that?" she said, as Billy pulled back from the screen.

"I saw you, I saw you," he screamed.

"Those gawdam kids," she said, breathing hard, Tom's hand still inside her dress pulling at a nipple, his mouth at her neck, licking there. His stubbled beard scratched the skin below her ear.

"I love your smell," said Tom, "I just fucking love it."

95

How Do You Spell Beautiful?

The front door slammed in the distance and Martha jumped, Tom's hand sliding out and going to her shoulder. He was pressing against her through the slatted back of the chair and she could feel him there, hard between her shoulder blades.

"Now get away," she said. "That must be Charlie." And she lifted her hands to her hair as Tom pulled back.

"Hey, Charlie," yelled Tom. "We're in here. C'mon and have a cold beer before we go, you old bugger."

"I'm changing," said Martha, getting up and moving past Tom to the stairs. "Hey, Uncle Charlie," she said as she left. She didn't look at him, just kept on through the door, her feet in the fluffy pink slippers Tom had bought her the week before from Army and Navy slapping on the stairs as she went up. "Oh Jesus," she said, "Oh Jesus," her right hand moving on the worn rail, the other pressed against her belly, the fingers splayed there, holding herself.

Uncle Charlie came in and sat down heavily on the chair that didn't match. He lifted a beer from the case beside Tom, and holding the beer cap against the edge of the table, slammed his hand against it, snapping off the cap, the beer foaming.

"Jesus, Charlie, I swear you're fatter than ever," said Tom.

Charlie grinned, sucking on his beer.

"Lookit you," Tom said.

"It's honest fat," said Charlie, patting his stomach where it bellied out and sagged over his thick belt. "It took many a beer to grow this." He looked around and said, "Where's the kids anyway? Where're those little devils?"

"Guess," said Tom, the sounds of the dog barking and the children screaming coming through the door. "Listen to that, would ya?"

"That Ruth," said Charlie, shaking his head.

"She's got a problem, that one," said Tom.

"You can say that again, but it ain't nothing I can't handle. Hey, where're you and Martha going tonight?"

"Willy's Roadhouse," Tom said, "and we're going to be late. We're going to shut this town down tonight, we are."

Ruth opened the door, dragging Little Sal by the arm. Billy came in behind, crying about how Dana had kicked him right in the face. "He did it on purpose," he cried.

Ruth tried to move past the table to the stairs, but Charlie reached out and stopped her with his hand. "Hey," he said. "Ain't you going to say hello to your Uncle Charlie?"

Tom told her to say hello. "What's the matter with you anyway? You

The Babysitter

should be thankful Uncle Charlie's willing to come and look after you. And for nothing too."

"Ain't that the truth," said Charlie.

~

"You kids be good," Martha said. "You do as Uncle Charlie says, you hear me? You don't and I'll skin you alive when I get home. I mean it."

Tom stood beside her at the front door, the heat pouring in. A beer hung from one hand while the other unfolded the pack of Exports from his shoulder, where they were tucked into his T-shirt. Across his chest a banner of faded red letters with a blue python entwined among them said, "Born To Die." He gave his beer to Dana to hold for him, slipped out two cigarettes, and lighting them both, gave one to Martha, leaving the other in the corner of his mouth. "You hear your mother?" he said.

"They're always good for me, even that Ruth," said Uncle Charlie. He was sitting on the sofa with Little Sal on his knee, a bottle of beer tucked into the pillow beside him. It had tipped and beer was soaking into the faded design of purple roses, turning them black. Little Sal squirmed as he tickled her. Ruth stood in the kitchen doorway with Billy beside her as Dana lifted the beer bottle, drinking as fast as he could.

"You're looking good enough to eat," Uncle Charlie said to Martha.

Tom grabbed the beer bottle from Dana and held it up to the bare bulb above the door to see how much was left. "You little bastard," he said, and Dana laughed crazily as he jumped back from Tom, who tried to slap him. He bounced against the Lazy-boy rocker, falling into it, his white legs thrashing in the air.

"Well, I try," Martha said.

She was wearing her best dress, a blue sheath she'd let out the day before. It hid her belly enough so no one, she thought, would notice. Her hair was back-combed, frizzed, and high upon her head. Her lips were a bright orange.

"And them boots," said Uncle Charlie. "Lookit them boots."

The two men looked at Martha's feet and admired the white boots with the fringe of shivering leather around the tops. "C'mon," said Tom, "let's go, let's go. We don't get outa here the band'll be playing the last waltz before we get there."

He gave Martha a playful slap on the rear and Martha jumped, surprised, and then giggled. "Now Tom," she said. "The kids."

Tom guided her out the door into the darkness with his free hand,

How Do You Spell Beautiful?

the last thing she said drifting around the door as it closed, "You kids better do as you're told," and then Tom laughing as it swung shut.

Little Sal kept giggling as she leaned against Uncle Charlie. "Tickle me again," she said and screamed as he did, Uncle Charlie's thick fingers digging into her ribs.

"Well, I will, I will," he said, laughing out loud. The sound of Tom's truck starting up roared through the window, but no one except Ruth seemed to notice.

Ruth watched her sister squirming in Uncle Charlie's hands. "Dana," she said as she went to the kitchen, "you got to help like Mom said," but Dana just bounced in the Lazy-boy and ignored her.

"All right," Uncle Charlie said, "you kids go get your pyjamas on."

"I don't got pyjamas," Dana said. "I don't wear nothing to bed."

"Your sisters do," said Uncle Charlie.

"But not boys," Dana said.

Uncle Charlie lifted Little Sal off his lap and stood her between his legs on the floor, trapping her there with his thighs. "You get," he said, rubbing her chest with his huge hand. He laughed as she struggled to get away. "You too, Billy," and he let Little Sal go, both children going up the stairs together.

From the kitchen Dana and Uncle Charlie could hear Ruth doing the last supper dishes. "You go help her finish them dishes," Uncle Charlie said.

"I don't have to," said Dana. "They're macaroni and I never have to do them when they're that. It's her job anyway," he said, peering at Uncle Charlie from half-closed eyes. "I don't have to do nothing."

"You never mind about that," said Uncle Charlie.

"Gimme some money," Dana said.

Uncle Charlie pursed his lips, shifting his leg and reaching behind him to his hip pocket for his wallet. It was attached by a chrome-steel chain to his belt. He pulled it around in front of him and undid the snaps. "Here's a dollar," he said.

Dana slipped off the Lazy-boy and took the bill from Uncle Charlie's hand. As he did Uncle Charlie gripped him around the wrist and pulled him close. "You're going to be a good boy, ain't you," he said. He smiled into Dana's face and Dana could see the pores in his nose, clotted there, and the hairs.

Dana had his hand wrapped around the dollar. He grinned at Uncle Charlie and Uncle Charlie let him go. "You're not even a real uncle," Dana said, pushing the bill into the pocket of his shorts.

Upstairs they could hear the two youngest ones roughhousing, and

The Babysitter

Uncle Charlie let Dana go with a look and went to the stairs and told them to quiet down. "I'll be up there in a minute," he said. "I'll read you that story again if you're good."

Dana climbed back into the Lazy-boy, his bare back and shoulders lying across the seat sideways. He watched as his sister Ruth slipped under Uncle Charlie's arm and went up the stairs. Uncle Charlie stared after her. "You be good," Uncle Charlie said to Dana as he slowly went up after Ruth.

Dana said nothing to that. His hands were in his pants and he was playing with himself, a vacant look on his face. The red light from the leopard lamp bathed his face. The leopard's ruby eyes were missing. The lamp sat on the side table beside the broken TV Tom had said he was going to fix.

The dollar Uncle Charlie had given him burned in Dana's pocket. He felt inside his pants but he still didn't have hair and he wished he did. His stiff penis twitched in his hand. When he was older he would make it do what the older kids did in the shed by the creek. He rubbed it as hard as he could but nothing happened except it began to hurt. He didn't stop. The hurting felt strange and good to him.

Upstairs Uncle Charlie sat on Martha's bed and read *The Three Little Pigs* to Billy and Little Sal. Little Sal kept repeating everything, telling Uncle Charlie not to leave anything out. Billy said nothing. He lay on the other side of Little Sal.

Billy liked Uncle Charlie. Uncle Charlie was the only one to ever read them stories except for Ruth, and he didn't like it when she read because her voice was a girl's voice and didn't do the big bad wolf right, the way Uncle Charlie could.

Uncle Charlie stopped reading for a minute and shouted for Dana to get his ass upstairs to bed like he was supposed to. "Get up here," he yelled, and waited till Dana did. "You get in there with your sister," he said as Dana sidled by the door. "You go right to sleep, you hear. I'll be in there in a while as soon as I got this story finished."

"C'mon, Uncle Charlie," Little Sal said. "I wanna hear the part about the first little pig," and she began to chant, "I built my house of sticks, I built my house of sticks."

Dana scurried down the hall to the room where he and Ruth slept in cots, one on either side of the window. The room was dark but the street light outside shone through, a square of light upon the wall across from the cots. Ruth lay in one of them with the blankets pulled up to her chin. Her fists held the grey blankets tight. She stared at the wall and the shadows of the trees moving there.

How Do You Spell Beautiful?

Dana took off his shorts and turned toward his sister. "Look what I got," he said, but Ruth didn't move. Dana danced between the beds and then finally, laughing, fell onto his cot and climbed underneath his sheet. "You don't need no blankets," he said to his sister. "It's hot."

Ruth made no reply. In the other room she could hear Uncle Charlie reading to her brother and sister, Little Sal saying, "Read it again, Uncle Charlie." She hoped he would read it again. Please read it again, she said to herself. Read it and read it and read it. Little Sal screamed and she knew Uncle Charlie was tickling her again. Then Little Sal said ow, and started to cry, and she could hear Uncle Charlie whispering.

She couldn't hear Billy.

Dana whispered at her, "You just think I'm sleeping, but I'm not." When she didn't reply he said, "I hate you."

She tightened her fists on the blanket and pressed her legs tightly together. She was wearing the pyjamas Dana never wore. They were boy's pyjamas and she'd bound them around her waist with the roll of tape Tom had left in the kitchen. She'd stretched the tape as hard as she could, winding it around and around the pyjamas until it was gone. The black tape hurt her and she breathed shallowly, her mouth partly open.

The two of them lay still and listened to Uncle Charlie reading. He was at the part where the wolf was blowing down the house made of sticks. "And he huffed and he puffed and he blew the house down." There was no sound from Little Sal, and both Dana and Ruth knew their sister was almost asleep in their mother's bed. Billy would be. He always went to sleep as soon as he was read to.

Dana closed his eyes and thought of the dollar in his pants pocket. He'd buy candy with it tomorrow and he wouldn't give any to anybody else. It would be his candy, his and his alone.

He was glad he wasn't a girl, like Ruth. He put his hand on his chafed penis, but it hurt too much so he just held it lightly, moving the skin up and down. Pretty soon Uncle Charlie would come.

He knew his sister wasn't sleeping. He knew she was lying there wide awake. He rolled over on his side and curled his knees up against his chest and waited. He stared into the space between his cot and his sister's.

Later, thought Dana, when his mom got home, Tom and her would put his sister and brother in bed with him and Ruth, but not yet. First Uncle Charlie had to come.

A thin breeze pushed through the window and Dana could feel it

The Babysitter

like a tongue, hot and wet against his arms. He stared at his sister, the blanket pulled up tight against her chin. "I know you ain't sleeping," he whispered. He closed his eyes, listening for whatever sounds he could hear in the night outside.

A car went by, its muffler roaring, a voice screaming above the roar as it passed, the sound growing fainter and fainter as the car went down the block and turned in a screech at the corner. It was quiet for a moment and then he heard the door of his mother's room close softly and Uncle Charlie's footsteps in the hall. They stopped outside the door and he held his breath, waiting for the knob to turn and Uncle Charlie to come in to their night.

Whatever Was Going to Happen

HERE WAS A BEER BETWEEN ARTHUR'S hands, and in front of them, two blue five-dollar bills sitting side by side. Arthur didn't look at them. He looked at his hands. It seemed like he'd never quite looked at them before, though he knew he had.

Many times.

Maybe it's the light in here, he thought. Anyway, what can you tell by just looking at them?

He stared at his beer for a while. It was just a beer, a pale yellow with a bit of foam on the top. He rearranged his hands on the table on either side of it. First he put them palm down and then he turned them over. He didn't like that. They looked odd sitting there with the fingers curled, so he turned them on their sides, his thumbs bent and hidden inside his palms.

That's better.

He was going to take a drink out of the beer in a moment, but not right away. First he had to know if his hands were exactly right.

What's in front of me is a picture, Arthur thought.

He remembered the hands his mother used to have above her bed. Praying hands. He'd always wondered what it was those hands must have done, having to pray. He wished his own hands could

Whatever Was Going to Happen

have been like that instead of the way they were.

He brought his fingers around and pressed on his thumbs, forcing them down, the pain swelling hard in his knuckles. Then all by themselves, they stopped.

My hands have a life of their own, thought Arthur. They do things without my thinking. They wave at people or pick things up, like hammers or needles, or they can steer a car or do any damn thing.

He was trying not to think about them when the drunk woman sat down at his table. She had black hair tied in a pigtail, a red bit of dirty ribbon binding the end. Her lipstick was mostly chewed off and her cheek was swollen as if someone had hit her there. Her lip was split at the side and one of her eyes was puffed almost closed.

Arthur guessed she was probably an Indian and wondered why she'd picked his table. He thought he should say something but he wasn't sure what. She wasn't supposed to be there.

"You know how hard it is to keep your hands still for more than just a second or two?" he asked.

When she didn't reply, he said, "You should try it sometime. It isn't easy. It's something I have to learn how to do. If I can, then my hands will stop."

"You gonna buy me a beer?"

"Okay," he said, "but you'll have to get the waiter. For the moment I can't move these."

Arthur watched as she lifted her arm and waved at the waiter across the room. She had long arms for an Indian. She had long arms no matter who or what she was, he thought. They seemed to reach forever.

He'd never seen such a pair of arms.

"You've sure got long arms," he said.

He didn't know what else to say.

"I ain't drunk," the woman said, "so don't start thinking I am. I just want a beer and that's all. I don't do nothing with white bastards like you."

"That's okay," said Arthur. "I don't mind. Look," he said, thinking some kind of explanation was needed. "I don't have a wife. I'm all by myself if you really want to know. Women and me don't get along. I keep to myself. I have to."

Arthur stopped for a moment and then he said, "You want a beer? I don't mind buying you one I guess. But hey," he said, "take a look at these hands. Do they look strange or what?"

He smiled hopefully. "It's hard," he said. "These hands of mine

How Do You Spell Beautiful?

move all the time and I keep trying to stop them. It's hard work, I can tell you."

The waiter came by with a full tray and Arthur told him to leave a couple. The waiter took change out of one of the five-dollar bills, looked hard at the woman, and left.

"Have both of them," Arthur said when the waiter left. "I don't mind."

"What's all this shit? You white bastards are all the same. You're crazy if you ask me."

She said that and then she took a drink of her beer. Some of it spilled from the corner of her swollen mouth and she wiped at it with the back of her hand, wincing at the pain.

"You ever look at yourself real close?" said Arthur eagerly. "Take your arms. Take a look at them. They're the longest arms I've ever seen and I guess I've seen a lot of arms in my day. I guess I've seen millions come to think of it. But you take the record," he said. "You could send those arms of yours to *The Guinness Book of Records* and I'll bet they'd put them in. They'd put my hands in if they knew about them."

The woman ignored him. Her mouth had started to bleed and she was trying to wipe the blood off the lip of her glass with her fingers. It smeared and she put the glass to her mouth and tried to lick it clean. Her tongue looked purple.

She's an Indian all right, thought Arthur. There's no question about that. Here I am, looking at an Indian. I never really looked before, at least not this way, not this close. "Your people are great," he said. "They're just about the greatest people in the world when you come to think of it. Don't get me wrong now, I don't mean anything by it, but it's something I want you to know. If I could've been born an Indian I'd have been an Apache. Then I wouldn't have been afraid of my hands. They'd be Indian hands and they'd be allowed to do things."

"Fuck you," she said, and reached for the second beer.

Arthur watched her arm lift up from the table and put the hand at the end of it around the glass. It's really incredible, he thought.

"So what's an Apache?"

Her lip had stopped bleeding, the blood on her chin starting to cake.

"They were Indians," Arthur said. "They came from the States. The most famous was Geronimo. He killed a lot of white people before they got him."

She stared at him without saying anything and Arthur went on, sure she'd be interested when he explained it all. "They say he was the

104

Whatever Was Going to Happen

toughest Indian there ever was. And the smartest. That's about all I know. Indians were in the movies a lot when I was a kid. Oh yeah, there was another one called Cochise. He was a chief, I think. But it was Geronimo I liked. Maybe it was just his name. Did you know what Apache meant?"

When she didn't answer, he said, "Enemy. It meant enemy."

"I ain't no Apache," she said. "I'm Cree."

"The Cree too," said Arthur. "They're a great people. Big Bear and Poundmaker. They were great."

"You don't know nothing about Indians," she said. "Why don't you just shut up and buy some more beer."

"I guess you're right. I guess I don't know anything about Indians really."

"That's for sure. You people think just because you buy someone a beer you can do any damn thing you want. Isn't that right? It is, isn't it?"

"Look, don't get me wrong," said Arthur. "All I'm doing is trying to stop. That's all I'm doing."

"Well okay," she said. "Just don't start going on about Indians. I'm up to here with Indians. I've been an Indian all my life so if there's one thing I know it's Indians. The only worse thing is a white honky like you." She picked up her beer and drank half of it. The waiter went by and she told him to drop two more.

"You two okay?" the waiter asked. "She's not bothering you, is she?"

"No, no. It's all right," Arthur said.

"Don't you bother him," the waiter said to the woman.

When the waiter left, she said, "So what's so important about your hands anyway? They look like honky hands to me, all white with brown spots all over them. I hate white hands," she said. "I had white hands all over me. They're ugly hands. They're not beautiful like Indian hands."

"I guess I can agree with you there," Arthur said. "These hands have done things."

"Is that why you're going on about them all the time?"

"I don't know. I just decided to make them stop, so there they are. The longer they're still the harder it gets. It's like they aren't even mine."

She reached out and touched his hand. "It feels just like a hand to me."

"Does it?"

She took her fingernails and pressed them into his skin.

105

How Do You Spell Beautiful?

It's my hand, Arthur thought. It's my hand she's doing that to.

She pressed harder and Arthur watched her fingernails go right into his skin. Then she pulled and his skin lifted and curled away. She scraped at him until the blood started to come, and then she did it to his other hand. The blood came out of the back of his hands and ran slowly down his skin onto the table. He liked the pain. He liked the way it happened inside him.

"You're crazy," she said.

"I'm sorry."

"Look at you."

She took a drink. "I'd like to cut those hands right off," she said as she took another drink. "That's what I'd like to do. You and your stupid hands."

"They've done things," said Arthur.

"You think I care about those hands of yours? Look," she said, and she reached out and scraped at the torn skin on his right hand, making it bleed harder. "I can just sit here and pull all the skin off those hands of yours and you ain't going to do nothing about it, right?"

He didn't say anything, and she said, "That's right, isn't it? Isn't it?"

She lifted up her empty glass and brought it down hard on his left hand. When he didn't move she did it again.

Arthur could feel his hand breaking. Little breaking things moving in there as she hit him again. His mouth opened. His breathing sounded to him like an engine making noise. He watched her long Indian arm rise up into the air and bring down the beer glass on his other hand.

It's all right, Arthur thought. It's something that has to be done.

He felt good it was an Indian doing it. Somehow it made things better. It was as if he was a kid again and he was being tortured by the Apaches, by Geronimo or Cochise or someone. Their women were supposed to be even tougher than the men. For a moment Arthur could see himself lying on the desert with Apache women hurting him. They were very methodical.

These hands, these hands.

He hoped she'd pound them right off before the waiter saw what was happening.

"Don't worry," he said when the woman finally stopped. "I won't tell. You go away now. It's me they're going to want to talk to, not you. It's my hands they want."

"They sure ain't Indian hands," she said. "What is it they're supposed to have done?"

106

Whatever Was Going to Happen

Arthur didn't say anything. He was feeling his hands. It was as if he could feel them for the first time.

"You want to come with me?" she asked. "I got a little room around the corner in The Coldwater. Maybe I can help you fix up those hands?"

"No," Arthur said carefully. "I like them the way they are now."

"You come."

She took the beer from between his smashed hands and drank it. "You got any more money?" she asked as she picked up the change off the table. "You probably got lots of money, I'll bet."

I'll go with her, Arthur thought. I guess that's what I'm doing. That's what's supposed to happen next. I'll go with this Indian. At least she knows what to do. She's the first one who ever did.

Whatever was going to happen was going to happen next.

"Let's go," he said, "but I want you to know I'm bringing these hands."

"Sometimes I'm just a crazy Indian, I guess." Then she said, "Hey, I'm sorry I did what I did."

She had him by the arm, helping him to the door. His hands hung down off his arms like bags full of broken sticks. He could feel her pressing against him like the other ones.

"Don't be," Arthur said.

The Bear

Denny Secord sleeps on top of his trailer every night. He's got a little tent set up and a sleeping bag. The whole thing. Yeah, and a Winchester 30–30, loaded.

Denny's all ready for Dick Melstrom. As Denny says, "If that sonufabitch thinks he's going to sneak up on me, he's got another think coming."

Denny Secord is just a little bit crazy, I think.

On the other hand, Dick Melstrom isn't a guy to take chances with. When Dick says look out for the night, then you take it serious. He doesn't waste words. No sir, not Dick Melstrom.

The trouble is, if they've got a problem then so have I. Denny's trailer is just below mine. If it's going to come to shooting then I'm in what you might call a delicate position. I've got the last trailer on the hill.

Suzy says the trailer looks like something to be ashamed of the way it sticks out. She might have a point there. Personally, I think it looks okay. I know it's jacked ten feet off the ground, but that's the way I wanted it. I like standing in the front and looking out over the valley. We're the highest place in this jerkwater town.

I can see the North Thompson clear as a bell from here. Of course, the other thing I can see is Denny's trailer. If Melstrom decides to sneak up on Denny and they both start shooting, well, God knows where the

The Bear

bullets are going to go. Knowing Denny, half of them will go into my trailer. I'm glad we sleep at the back.

Denny thinks he's quite a shot. The guy used to be a mailman in Trail, for Christ's sake. What do mailmen know about shooting? So far the biggest thing Denny's killed is a crow and a few squirrels. What he dreams about killing besides Dick is a bear or a cougar. Denny's decided in that ex-mailman's brain of his he wants to be a taxidermist. You know, a guy that stuffs animals and birds.

That's why he moved to the north, to be closer to the real thing. Of course he wouldn't think about starting small and working up. Not Denny. He's got a crow without wings hanging by his window, and from there he wants to go direct to a bear. There's nothing half-way with Denny except his brain.

He got an address out of an old *Field and Stream* and sent away for a course. A hundred dollars! So far all he's taken is three lessons. As far as I can figure there's dozens more, but Denny's decided there's no point in paying for them. He thinks he can pick up taxidermy on his own. Practice makes perfect, he says.

I think perfect is something Denny wouldn't know if it bit him on the leg.

But to get back to the problem between Dick and Denny. Dick's the postmaster in Little River. He runs it out of his house. I don't know how he got the job. Nobody does. I figure it was the only way the government could get him off welfare.

Dick Melstrom's got a bent back and a withered arm. Deformities is what I say, though I'd never say it to his face. What else Dick's got is a tired wife and seven kids. They're a rangy bunch, the lot of them. There's only one exception and that's Sharlene.

Sharlene comes somewhere in the high middle of the family. She's about seventeen, though looking at her you'd take her for older. What Sharlene's got is looks. She stands out in that family like a tiger lily on a sandbar. It's like after the first two or three kids Dick and his wife prayed one night they'd end up with at least one that wasn't ordinary or worse, and something answered their prayers. Sharlene got it all.

She's blonde and blue-eyed and built like the brick wall of China. When she walks down the road to town there isn't a man who doesn't stop and just stare at her, she's that pretty.

The other thing Sharlene has is a bun in the oven and Dick thinks it's Denny Secord put it there.

I don't think Denny would know where to put it except maybe in his hand. "He's a type," Suzy says to me over coffee this morning. The

109

How Do You Spell Beautiful?

kids are fighting in the back while we're talking and both of us are doing our best to ignore them. We're sitting on the couch looking out the front window. Down below us Denny's sitting cross-legged on his roof cleaning his gun. He's jacking out shells and looking down the barrel as if he expected a spider to have holed up there while he was sleeping.

"What do you mean, a type?" I ask her.

"Just look at him," Suzy says. "The man's almost thirty and all the time we've known him have you ever seen him with a girl?"

"Well, no," I say. "But on the other hand, there aren't too many women here he could attach himself to even if he wanted. Most are either married or wall-eyed and crippled and permanently single."

"That's not the point," she says.

"Well, what is?"

"He's all talk and no action. Look at the way he behaves at a dance. Remember last Friday night?"

"I didn't see anything happen that says Denny's got a problem."

Suzy's got definite opinions on men, something that makes her admired by a few of the women in this town and generally disliked by the men.

"Don't get your tail in a knot," Suzy says. "You don't have to defend every man in the world."

"I'm not."

"I can tell from your voice," says Suzy.

There's no point arguing with Suzy. "Well," I say.

"Anyway," says Suzy, "Denny Secord spends his time drinking and talking, but you never see him walking anybody home but himself. He bumps into women when he can't avoid them altogether and he brags a lot, but I think he wouldn't know what to do if he got a girl alone. I don't think he could even get it up if he had the chance. Women know about men like that."

"It sounds like you've had a whole world of experience," I say.

"You weren't the first man I ever met," says Suzy, "and if you don't watch it you won't be the last."

"What's that supposed to mean?"

"Oh, for God's sake," Suzy says, "get your mind off yourself and think about the guy. He lives alone in a twelve-foot trailer. He sleeps on the roof and no wonder. The inside of that trailer is worse than a rat's nest in spring what with half-stuffed crows and squirrel skins all over the place. What woman would have him, especially somebody as pretty as Sharlene? She may be only seventeen but she's hardly a girl

110

The Bear

who'd spend her time getting pregnant with Denny Secord. It's somebody else give her that kid."

She says that and then she gives me a long hard look before heading down to the back to stop the kids from killing each other. You'd better believe they listen to her.

I wait until she's gone to Nancy Ditsky's house, the boys behind her like three savages looking for a meal. It's like she's saying it better not have been me. It wasn't, of course, though I wouldn't mind if it had of been, not that I'd want Dick Melstrom coming after me. Bedding a girl like Sharlene would be something else.

There's been a few times I've imagined it. Under a big cedar, say, or down by the river on a blanket. And I'm not the only one. There isn't a man in town who hasn't thought about it. But if it wasn't Denny, then who?

Before Suzy slammed the door she told me to talk to Denny. "I don't want him killing us all over this thing," she says. "You do something about it."

Exactly, I think. Why me?

After bit I get me a coffee and head down to Denny's. His trailer's only fifty feet away as a bird flies, but it's all straight down. When I get there Denny's climbing off the roof. He's built a ladder out of two-by-fours and nailed it to the wall. He hasn't had much sleep. His eyes are no bigger than two pee-holes in the snow.

"So," I say for starters. "How long do you figure this's going to go on?"

Denny leans his gun against the side of the trailer and rubs his face. He looks like he hasn't washed in a week. "What?" he asks.

"You up there with a loaded gun. Don't you know how dangerous that is?"

"The only guy it's dangerous for is Melstrom," Denny says.

"What about me and Suzy and the kids?" I ask. "You thought about that? Assuming Dick is stupid enough to come hunting you at night, and assuming he decides to hunt down on you so he can pick you off the trailer roof with one, maybe two shots, and assuming you're still alive and decide to shoot back at him, just where do you think that leaves us?"

"I'd get him with one clean shot," says Denny.

"At night?"

"Gun flash," he says.

"Oh great. And he's going to be sitting still all that time. I suppose he hasn't thought of that. And what if it's something else, like a bear or

How Do You Spell Beautiful?

something. What if you hear some thrashing in the bush? What then? You know there's a bear coming down to rummage in my burner. What if it's a bear? You going to shoot at it because you think it might be Dick?"

"I know the difference between a man and a bear," Denny says.

"Not at night you don't," I tell him. "You're as likely to go off half-cocked at an owl or a crow ruffling his feathers in a cedar. Look at you," I say. "You haven't been sleeping hardly at all. Your nerves are shot."

"My nerves are fine."

His face twitches when he says it.

"What I want to know is, are you the one knocked up Sharlene?"

"I'm not saying one way or the other. And don't talk about her that way. Sharlene's a fine girl."

"Shit, Denny," I say, "you know it wasn't you."

"So how do you know that?"

"Just look at you. Why the hell would Sharlene strip off her pants for you? Like or not it's the Swede down by the mill, or it's Bobby, or one of the other guys."

"I may have had her and I may not," says Denny. "And watch what you say about her," he adds.

"The hell you did," I say. "The closest you ever got to Sharlene was to smell her as she passed you by."

"Yeah, so what the hell do you know about it?"

"Jesus, Denny," I say.

"Dick thinks he can centre me out on this one he's got another think coming. I don't let no man tell me he's going to come hunting me down."

I look at him. Denny's about five feet four. A scrawny little guy, half bald with bow legs. Even his accent's weird, like he comes from way back East somewhere. The only thing that'd get into bed with Denny is a half-blind marmot with the mange.

"Denny," I say, "you've got to clear this up. If it was you knocked up Sharlene, then why don't you just out and say so. You could marry her, for God's sake. Think about it, Sharlene in your bed every night? Hell, there's not a man in town who wouldn't trade his wife in on Sharlene if there was a chance. All you got to say to Dick is that it was you. Sharlene'll do whatever her old man tells her now she's up the stump."

Denny picks up his Winchester and sights it on the top of a tree to the left of my trailer. "Nobody's threatening me," he says. "If it was me got Sharlene in the family way," and here he takes a look at me over

112

The Bear

the butt of his rifle, "and I'm not saying it was at all, then it's up to Sharlene and not her old man. The trouble with Melstrom, other than his gibbled arm and his bent back, is he's a pushy mean sonufabitch. Well, he's pushed the wrong guy."

"Denny," I say, "sometimes you're even dumber than you look."

"What's that supposed to mean?"

"Think about it," I say, and I head back up the hill.

What all this looks like is something out of a bad western. The only trouble is the movie's taking place on my front step and there's no sheriff in a white hat to clear out the bad guys. I'd shoot them both if I thought I could get away with it. The nearest RCMP is thirty miles away, but that doesn't mean they think killing people is all right. Some dumb corporal from God knows where would be in town and then I'd be cooling my ass in Oakalla.

What has to be done is to somehow get those two together so they can iron all this out. The question is, how? It better be soon, I think. Suzy'll only put up with this for a few more days and then she'll kill them and me to boot. Suzy's not a woman to be taken lightly, especially not over something like this.

Men with loaded guns on her front step is not something she'll put up with. What I have from her is what you call an ultimatum.

~

Two days later I come up with the solution. Suzy's stopped talking to me altogether and Denny's getting really strange. What with no sleep and Sharlene drifting through his brain like some wandering Rapunzel, Denny's a serious problem. Winning Chow's the answer. He's about a hundred years old but he's still the cook. You can't run a mill and a bunkhouse without one, and in a place like this cooks are hard to come by. Winning Chow's the best cook we've had in three years, and by best I mean he's the only one lasted more than a month. The ones before him were all drunks or crazy.

Winning drinks, there's no question about that, but he doesn't let it interfere with meals. Even if he was drunk you wouldn't be able to tell. He's definitely what you'd call your Chinaman. That's what Larue says about him. Larue's the manager and he says Winning is enigmatic. That means it's hard to read him.

It was Larue called me in this morning. He was sitting beside his desk in the office looking out over the yard. I'm a general handyman, millwright, carpenter, what-have-you, at the mill. I do a bit of this and a bit of that. Mostly I do what Larue tells me to do. It's not a bad living

113

How Do You Spell Beautiful?

and I don't have to keep regular hours. No shift work for me.

Larue's sitting there drumming his fat fingers on the desk blotter and staring past me out the window. Production's down since the mill started cutting cedar from the south slope, and Larue's getting antsy. His gold ring is blinking in what little light comes through the dust and cobwebs on the glass.

The mill's between shifts. One more and then it's down for the weekend. I stand against the wall and wait to see what he has to say. It doesn't do to interrupt Larue while he's thinking.

Finally he says something. He doesn't look at me at all when he says it. That's not Larue's way. "So what're you going to do about the bear?" he asks.

"Bear?"

I thought he was going to talk about the Denny problem.

He turns his head on his fat neck and looks at me with his black little eyes. "The bear at the cookhouse," he says. "Winning Chow is almost packed up to leave. If he goes then I know who I'll be asking to do the cooking."

"Who?"

"You," Larue says, "that's who."

"I didn't know there was a bear around there," I say. "I got one nosing around the back of my trailer, but I didn't know any was coming down here."

Larue looks at me as if I was a piece of snot on a sleeve and says, "I could fill an awful big hole with what you don't know. Of course there's a bear. Do you think I'm talking to cool my lips?"

"No sir," I say.

I can tell he's in a bad mood. The last time a cook left Larue lost half the crew. I was out with a couple of men four nights in a row running drunks and half-wits off the boxes and gondolas in order to fill a shift. Beating on steel cars with a ball-peen hammer will roust a drunk quicker than the promise of a drink. But trying to work a mill with a bunch of wet-brains is not a good idea.

"This morning Winning Chow gets up to start the stoves for breakfast. He always gets up at the same time. You know that, don't you?"

"Yes sir."

"Well, it's like this. Evidently he mixes up his pancake batter the night before so it's all ready to go. All he has to add is baking powder and it's instant cakes. Anyway, he climbs up out of the hole he calls a room under the cookhouse and walks into his kitchen. This's all an hour before the crew is coming to eat, right?"

114

The Bear

I nod. I don't know what's coming but I can imagine.

"He walks in and guess what's sitting in the middle of his kitchen eating raw pancake batter, with a side of bacon slung over its shoulder?"

"What?"

"A bear, that's what. I gawdam big black bear."

"Jesus," I say.

"No, not Jesus," says Larue, "a bear."

When I don't say anything, Larue continues. By this time he's got his feet up on the desk and his hands are clasped behind his head. His feet in his big steel-capped boots are tapping out some tune only he knows. "So what we have is a problem, right?" I nod again. "The men got breakfast all right but they had to fix it themselves. You ever see thirty men in a kitchen trying to fry eggs all at the same time?"

"No sir."

"Well, it's not a pretty sight," Larue says. "Anyway, I'm appointing you to get rid of the bear. If you don't then Chow is leaving on the first train through on Monday, and if he goes you'll either be going too or standing over a stove. Understand?"

"How do you want me to do it?" I ask.

Larue brings both his feet down on the oiled wood floor at the same time, making the desk jump and papers fall. "That gawdam bear's been at the cookhouse every night for a week. He's been rummaging in the garbage behind the kitchen, which has scared Chow silly, but now the bear's taken to coming right through the door. Now I can put on a better door but that's not about to mollify the cook. Winning Chow thinks the bear is magic. Do you understand? He thinks it's a ghost or something and it can walk right through doors.

"I don't know how you're supposed to kill it," says Larue. "I'd assume you'd do it with a rifle unless you're good at wrestling large carnivores. Whatever you do, I want it dead. Winning Chow's not going to believe it's gone until he sees it dead, fur, teeth, claws, and all. And you know what else?"

"What?" I say to him while he's glaring at me over the desk.

"He wants the paws and he wants the gall bladder. What for I have no idea. Maybe he wears them or maybe he eats them or maybe he does something obscene with them, I don't know. But he wants them so I expect you to give them to him. Is everything clear?"

"Yes sir," I say.

"And that's not my only problem. The edgerman didn't show up for work this morning. I've had to shuffle the crew."

"Where'd he go?"

How Do You Spell Beautiful?

"Who knows," says Larue. "And who gives a shit. It's what comes from hiring young men with nothing to hold them here. The next one I hire is going to be fifty with a woman and nineteen kids."

It's on the way up the road toward the trailer that I get the idea. It sounds amazingly simple.

All I have to do, I figure, is to get Dick and Denny to kill the bear. What I'll do is set it up so that they're in the kitchen at the cookhouse waiting on the bear. I'd put some pork chops or liver outside the cookhouse window, and when the bear comes the two of them can kill it. Before the bear comes they can talk out all their problems.

I think I'll try to explain this to Suzy when I get home, but when I climb into the trailer who do I find but Sharlene and Suzy sitting on the couch. Sharlene's crying and Suzy's sitting there with a cup of coffee in one hand and the other around Sharlene's shoulders, patting away.

In spite of myself and the fact Sharlene's crying her eyes out and Suzy's glaring at me, I can't take my eyes off Sharlene's legs. Her skirt's pulled up over her knees and her legs are splayed out in a kind of way that doesn't leave much to the imagination.

"You," Suzy says.

"What?"

"You, men, whatever," Suzy says. "Gawdam you all."

"What did I do?" I ask, trying not to look any harder than I have to at Sharlene's knees and whatever else is bare above them.

"You're all the same," says Suzy. "There aren't none of you worth nothing," she adds. "And put your eyes back in your head. What're you staring at?"

I back out of the trailer. Obviously there's not to be any talking about my plan with Suzy. Instead I go down to Denny's trailer.

It doesn't take much to talk him into it. Mind you, I don't mention Dick is going to be his hunting partner. Killing a bear is Denny's dream. I try to forget his other dream is killing Sharlene's father.

It'll work out, I say to myself as I drive down the road toward Dick Melstrom's. I've arranged with Denny to be in place at the cookhouse at nine o'clock with his rifle loaded for bear. I'll bring Dick along with me at nine-thirty. Once they're stuck in there together they'll work everything out. Either that or one'll kill the other or both of them will be dead.

Hopefully it's after the bear gets killed. I figure I'll bring along a bottle or two to keep things easy. They're more likely to talk drunk than sober. At least Dick is. Who can tell with Denny? Denny's got three

The Bear

things on his mind, which is two more than he can take. One is the bear, two is Dick, and three is Sharlene.

Melstrom's place is a quarter mile off the road. There's a tin sign at the turn-off saying Canada Post Office. Dick's got it nailed to a spruce.

If anyone was going to try and find the most inconvenient place for a post office, this'd be it. The trouble is, no one wants to complain. Dick Melstrom with a job is a lot better than Dick Melstrom without one. At least this way his wife and kids get enough to eat.

The house is tucked back into some cedars at the edge of a meadow. There are a few chickens around and a pig or two. The pigs are staked and chained by the ankle so they won't run off. A simple fence would've been easier but not for Dick. He preferred going out ten times a day and restaking them to forage.

The house is mostly junk. There's almost no paint left on it. What there is used to be a kind of yellow colour. You can see bits of paint up under the eaves.

When I pull into the yard there aren't any kids around. Who knew where Dick and Elsie kept them. Some are in school in town and the rest of them God knows where.

Dick's on the porch when I stop the truck. He's staring into an almost-empty Old Style bottle. From the way he's looking into it I can tell it's his last. I get out of the truck and walk over.

"Post office's closed," says Dick.

"What? At two-thirty in the afternoon."

"That's right," says Dick. "I'm the postmaster and it closes when I say so."

"Well, that's not why I'm here," I say.

Dick looks sharp at me. "What else brings you out?"

"We got a bear problem at the cookhouse."

"So, who hasn't," he says. "There's no berries this year. The bears are all down looking for something more than leaves and branches. I shot one last week." He stares down at the bottle in his hand for a moment. "Bear steak isn't half bad when you get used to it. Tastes a little like sugared pork."

"Is that right?"

"I just said so, didn't I?"

"Anyway," I say, and I go on to explain what it is I want. I also tell him there'll be a couple of bottles of rye to sip on till the bear comes. That's what gets him. Dick wouldn't shoot a bear unless he could do it off his porch. A bottle of rye is another thing altogether.

"You ain't seen Sharlene, have you?"

117

How Do You Spell Beautiful?

"Matter of fact I did. She was at our place talking to Suzy. Seems like she was crying a bit when I saw her. Don't know what about."

"The hell you don't," says Dick. He drinks the last bit of beer and throws the bottle into the weeds by the side of the porch. "She's up the stump and you and everyone else knows it. It was that gawdam Denny did it."

"How do you know that? It seems to me there's likelier candidates than him."

"Never you mind how," says Dick. "I know."

"Right," I say. "I suppose you know Denny's sleeping out on the roof of his trailer. Seems he thinks you're going to do something to him."

"He'd better not sleep at all," Dick says. "He better keep both of his little eyes wide open."

"There's no call for that," I say.

"Yeah, and what if it was your daughter he stuffed?"

"I don't have a girl," I say. "I got three boys."

"Then you got lucky," says Dick. "A daughter's more worry than a wife, especially when she's pretty like Sharlene. Men've been eyeing her since she was twelve."

He goes quiet on me for a minute and then he says, "What time do you want me down there tonight?"

"Come by and pick me up at nine-thirty," I say. "We'll have a few drinks before we go down. Light's about gone by ten. I'll set out some meat and stuff for the bear. When he comes to eat you can shoot him out the window."

As I drive out of the yard I start thinking maybe my plan might not be the best I've ever had. The alternative is to shoot the bear myself, but sitting in a cookhouse waiting for a hungry bear's not my idea of a good time. And there's no point telling the men at the bunkhouse. The last thing anyone wants is a bunch of young turks, half-drunk, running around town with rifles and shotguns.

More than just a bear'd get killed if that happened. I figure Dick's the more likely guy to actually kill the bear. Denny'd probably just shoot anywhere, hopefully not at Dick, though there was a distinct possibility he might.

When I get home Sharlene's gone. "Down at the cafe," is what Suzy says.

"So did you find out from her who did it?" I ask.

Suzy just looks at me.

"Was it Denny or wasn't it?"

"Of course it wasn't him," Suzy says. She gives me something I call

The Bear

her withering look. It's designed to kill anything within twenty feet. I get up and move toward the door.

"So, who was it?"

"It was Tommy Edel."

"He's the one left town according to Larue."

"You're all alike," says Suzy. "There's not a one of you a woman can count on."

I don't say to Suzy it takes two to tango, not when she's in this mood. Instead I say, "So what's she going to do?"

"Besides having a baby?"

"Well," I say, "yeah."

"She's going to have to get married, isn't she."

"To who?"

"To whoever will have her," Suzy says. "I told her she should just leave town and have the kid down in Kamloops, but Sharlene isn't old enough or smart enough to be able to do that. She wants the baby to have a father, why I don't know."

"How about Denny?"

"He's probably Sharlene's last choice in a man," says Suzy.

"So?"

"So you think about what it'd be like for Sharlene to be living with Denny."

"It wouldn't be so bad," I say. "Hell, she could adjust."

"And why the hell should she?" says Suzy. "Why the hell should any woman have to adjust? You think about trying to live in two rooms full of stiff squirrel skins and crow feathers."

"What about me?" I ask. "You live with me, don't you?"

Suzy gives me the look again.

"What's that supposed to mean?"

"I can't bear thinking about any of this," she says.

When she starts yelling at the boys to stop whatever it is they're doing I head down to the mill. There's Winning Chow to talk to and other arrangements that need to be made, like the meat I need for bait and the two bottles of rye I'm going to have to buy from the station agent. He's going to charge an arm and a leg for them. Larue's going to be mad about the cost.

~

"Spirit-bear," says Winning Chow, looking sadder than ever.

"It's only an old black bear."

"No," he says. "Spirit-bear. I see."

119

How Do You Spell Beautiful?

I pour myself another drink from his bottle of Scotch. It's not a drink I particularly like, but any port in a storm. Winning Chow has finished up the supper dishes and he's sitting on a stool, with two boxes at his feet tied up with binder twine. On the outside of the boxes is a lot of Chinese chicken scratches. Winning's holding a coffee mug of Scotch. His grey hair's hanging down around his face in long wisps. He looks like a little old tree you'd find in a swamp.

"Well," I say, "we're going to kill it."

"Can't kill spirit-bear," he says.

"Can kill," I say, starting to talk like him. It's one of the problems I get when I'm with him. First thing I know I'm leaving things out and talking like an immigrant just off the boat.

"I leave on train," says Winning. "If bear not kill."

"Bear no kill. Shit," I say. "I mean the damned thing is only a toothless bear who's come down in the world so far all he can do is rummage in garbage. I've got two good hunters coming in to kill him tonight. Your spirit-bear is definitely going to be dead."

"How you kill spirit-bear?"

"With bullets," I say.

He looks at me as if I'm some kind of fool. "Magic bullets," I say. "Spirit bullets."

He perks up at that.

"That's right," I say. "I've got special spirit bullets especially made for this kind of bear. They're the only thing that can do it."

"Maybe," he says, looking doubtful.

"Maybe, hell. These bullets are guaranteed."

"Hard kill spirit-bear."

"No hard," I say, trying to talk and not doing a very good job. I pour us both another drink of Scotch. Two more drinks and mumbling's going to seem natural. We sit there, me thinking my life's getting out of hand altogether and Winning thinking the spirit-bear will end his life in the night.

"Look," I say, "these bullets come from far away. I only have a few but they're enough to kill this bear."

"This special bear," says Winning. "Hard kill bear like that."

I explain what I can to him but he's sure he's going to die, or worse, be taken off to bear-spirit land. What happens there I don't know and I don't want to know. Whatever it is, Winning Chow's afraid of it.

Still, after he finishes his mug of Scotch he gets down off his perch and hauls out some liver he's had thawing since morning. "Won't eat,"

The Bear

he says when he gets back from throwing liver in ten directions. He's got a look that says everything's futile.

"Will," I say.

We have another drink.

I look around the kitchen. The door where the bear broke through last night is nailed shut with spikes. Beside it is the back wall, with a long low window looking out on an empty equipment lot.

There's garbage stacked up under the window in drums. On the dirt outside is the liver. If anything's going to draw that bear it'll be that.

I look at my watch. It's going on eight o'clock.

I tell Winning Denny'll be down soon and I'll be down a little later with Dick. I give him the two bottles of rye I bought for twice what they're worth and tell him to hold onto them.

"Give Denny a few drinks when he gets here," I say, and Winning nods. He's staring down into his fourth cup of Scotch.

"Spirit-bear," he says softly.

"No worry," I tell him, knowing it won't do any good.

~

After watching me eat a plate of cold weiners and beans Suzy heads out and leaves me with the dishes. Where she's going I don't know and I don't ask. I stack the dishes in the sink and sit down to a drink. Two sips and Dick arrives and I pour him one too.

We don't talk much. We have another and then I tell him it's time to go.

"I'll carry your rifle if you like," I say. He looks at me funny but he lets me pick it up and sling it under my arm. I figure he should be disarmed when he meets Denny. He's the more likely to shoot first. Denny'll just threaten him when he gets there. As long as I've got his gun it'll be all right.

We head out the door and duck back on the driveway to the road. The sun is long gone and the moon is showing light behind the mountains east of the river.

We pass by the swamp on the way to the cookhouse. The frogs are just starting to croak. It's late spring and our footsteps don't quiet them. They're lost in love is what they are. "Frogs," I say to Dick, but he doesn't answer. He's carrying the last glass of rye I gave him at the house.

"You sure there's a bottle waiting down there?" he asks.

"Yeah," I say. "Two bottles."

I let Dick go into the cookhouse first.

How Do You Spell Beautiful?

The lights are out in the kitchen and the moonlight isn't strong enough yet to lift the shadows. What I can see of Denny is him sitting on the floor under the window with his back against the wall. I can see his rifle leaning beside him.

Dick steps in and I follow close behind.

"That you?" asks Denny. His voice is already slurred. It's going on ten and it sounds like he's well into a bottle.

"Denny?" says Dick.

I close the door behind me and take three or four steps to where Denny's rifle is. I grab it and back up. "Dick," I say, "here's Denny. Denny, this here's Sharlene's dad. I think you already met."

"You sonufabitch," says Dick. "You been doing my girl Sharlene."

"The hell I have," says Denny as he puts down his glass on the floor beside him. He waves his hand to where his rifle was, and not finding it, flutters his fingers in the air.

"Gimme my gun," says Dick, and he makes a grab for it. I lever it up and back away from him.

"Take it easy, Dick. What say we all have a drink and talk about this." Before Dick can say anything more and Denny climb up off the floor I tell them both what Suzy told me.

"It wasn't Denny," I say. "It was that young edgerman Tommy Edel, who left town this morning on the early freight. That's who knocked up Sharlene. Not Denny."

Dick is standing in the middle of the room clenching and unclenching his one fist, while the other is still holding onto what's left of the rye in his glass. "Is that true?" asks Dick.

"I told you it wasn't me," says Denny.

"You never did."

"Did," says Denny.

"Didn't," says Dick.

"Look," I say, leaning the two rifles behind me. "What say we all have a drink and talk about this a bit more. I figure some kind of arrangement can be made. You'd marry Sharlene, wouldn't you Denny?"

"She's a helluva girl," says Denny. "A lot better than her old man here."

"Piss on you, you little runt."

"Have a drink," I say.

Dick still isn't sure whether he should outright kill Denny for just being there and Denny, who by this time is rocking on his heels prepared for the kind of attack he's read about in magazines, is staring

122

The Bear

at Dick. I gingerly pick up the bottle of rye from beside Denny and quickly pour all three of us a glassful. Winning's voice comes out of the corner by the stove. "Spirit-bear coming," he says.

"Fuck the bear," says Dick.

"I guess I'd marry her," says Denny.

"You think Sharlene'd want a peckerhead like you?" says Dick as he empties his glass and holds it out for more. I pour him another and splash a bit into Denny's.

"Seems like not a bad thought," I say to Dick.

"You're no catch as a father-in-law," says Denny.

"My daughter's elbow's got more brains than you," says Dick.

"Seems to me," I say, "Denny's making some kind of reasonable offer."

"Spirit-bear coming," says Winning Chow.

I turn and look but I can't see him. "Where the hell are you, Winning?" I ask.

"In here," he says.

"Where the hell is here?" I stare into the shadows and then I realize he's inside the bake-oven. The door is partly open and I can just see the top of his head.

"I'd be good to her," says Denny.

"The only thing you're good for is bear meat," says Dick, and just as he says that I look at Denny, who is by this time standing up in front of the window. He looks a lot bigger than I think he is and then I realize that it isn't just Denny I'm looking at.

Behind him on the other side of the glass is the bear.

I hear the door to the stove click shut behind me. Dick takes a step back and I yell at Denny to duck. He bends over just as the bear takes a swipe at the window and clears every bit of glass out of it with one stroke.

Spikes of glass spin across the room as both Denny and Dick head for the door where the guns are. Dick trips and Denny gets there first. The bear's still standing at the empty window as Denny shoots. He pops off three shots as Dick picks up his rifle, but by the time Dick gets a shell levered into the chamber the bear's dropped behind the wall.

"I got him," says Denny.

A muffled "spirit-bear" rises out of the stove behind me.

The room is still echoing with the sound of the shots and my ears are ringing. Denny's leaning out the window and I can see Dick lifting his rifle and aiming it at Denny's back. I reach out and push the barrel

How Do You Spell Beautiful?

down. "Not your future son-in-law," I say.

"Son-in-law, hell," says Dick.

I hold onto the barrel and we both look at Denny. He's half out the window by now. "The sonufabitch's gone," he yells.

"You dumb little shit," says Dick. "Three shots and you didn't kill him?"

"I couldn'ta missed," says Denny. "I saw him drop. We all did."

"Scared him more like," says Dick.

"Spirit-bear," says Winning Chow. The oven door is open and I can see him all scrunched up in the back of the oven. "No kill spirit-bear," he says.

"Shut the hell up," I tell him, and he pulls the door shut again.

Denny's outside by now and Dick is clambering out after him. "Look," says Denny, "blood. I winged him for sure."

Dick gives Denny a punch in the chest and knocks him over a drum of garbage. "Great," he says. "You've wounded a fucking bear. Now we're going to have to follow him to finish him off. What kind of gawdam son-in-law are you if you can't kill a bear five feet from you with three shots?"

"There's no call hitting me," says Denny as he tries to get up.

I'm still inside the cookhouse, where I intend to stay. Winning has climbed partly out of the stove. "No kill bear?"

"Bear almost dead," I say.

"Me leave on train," says Winning.

"No leave," I say. "Oh, shut the hell up."

Dick's down on one knee and he's looking at the dirt beside the window. "See there," says Denny. "I told you I got him."

"I see, all right," says Dick. He gets up and takes a few paces. "Damn thing's headed off into the swamp."

"Why don't we all have a drink and think about this," I say.

Nobody seems to think this is a bad idea, so the two of them climb back through the window and fill up their glasses. "Here's to getting that bear," I toast. Both of them look at me. Winning has crawled out of the stove and is on his knees at the window peering out.

"No kill," he says.

While we're standing there thinking about the various things we're going to have to do in order to find the bear and finish it off, I look out the window over Winning's grey head and see headlights coming down the road from town. One set and then two or three more behind it. It seems like half the town is coming.

The first truck wheels up with four of the boys from bunkhouse

The Bear

Number 1. As soon as they hear what's happened they wheel around and head back for their guns. The other vehicles follow them.

In ten minutes we've got twenty-five men standing around with rifles, some of them drunk and some of them with what they had on when they climbed out of bed—long johns, shorts, and not much more. All they did was pull on their boots when they heard the shots.

It takes only a minute or two to explain.

Dick is standing at the edge of the swamp with Denny beside him. The trucks and cars are all pulled around in a half-circle behind everyone, their headlights pointing into the mist. The frogs are quiet now except for the occasional peeper. "He's in there," says Dick. "Denny, you go first. It's you wounded the damn thing."

"That's right," says Denny. "It's my bear. I've a right to go first."

I'm thinking Denny is dumber than even I thought. The odds are if he ever gets to marry Sharlene he won't live long enough to be a bother to her. He'll probably see her naked, trip on his own shoelace, and brain himself half-way to the bed.

Denny takes a few steps into the swamp and then a few more. By the time he's lost in the mist the rest of the men follow, Dick with them. I watch them go and then head over to the cookhouse.

Winning Chow is still there peering over the windowsill. I figure Dick'll shoot Denny in the back and say he thought Denny was the bear. Either that or the bear will kill Denny. I hear two or three shots off in the mist and then I climb in beside Winning. I sit down against the wall, pour myself a drink of rye, and lean back.

"No kill spirit-bear," says Winning to nobody in particular.

"Have a drink," I say.

~

The next day I crawl out of bed late. The kids are off at the river throwing rocks at somebody's chickens and Suzy's in the living room. I sit up and peer down the long hall to the front.

"Suzy?" I ask.

"Get up," she says. "It's ten o'clock."

I pull on my pants and come out and pour myself a coffee from the pot on the back of the stove. "Well," I say, "we got everything worked out."

"What do you mean?"

"You know. The bear's dead, Denny and Dick have patched up their quarrel, Denny says he's willing to marry Sharlene, and Winning Chow is going to stay on and cook now he's got four bear paws and the gall

How Do You Spell Beautiful?

bladder. It took a bit of doing figuring what part of a bear is a gall bladder, but we did it."

"Is that right?" Suzy says.

"Of course that's right," I say.

"Not quite," she says. "Things have changed a bit since last night."

"How do you mean?"

"Sharlene's gone on the train to Kamloops to stay with my Aunt Isabel till she has the baby. The cook's gone too. He took his paws and whatever else there was and went out on the same train. Evidently he said you men only killed an ordinary bear. He said the spirit-bear's still out there."

All I can do is look at her.

"Oh yeah, and Dick Melstrom's still after Denny. Dick figures Sharlene left because Denny wouldn't do right by her. He says he's going to kill him."

She glances at me. Her look is worse than the ones Larue gives me. "Look out the window at Denny's place," she says.

I turn my head and look down the hill. Denny has got a huge frame built on top of his trailer and is busy stretching the bear hide on it. He hasn't bothered to scrape the fat off. In two days the whole thing will start to rot. It looks like a huge black sail on top of his trailer.

"Is that all?" I ask, burning my mouth on the coffee. I've got a terrible head from drinking most of a bottle of rye.

"Nope," says Suzy. "Larue dropped by this morning. He says you start cooking at noon today."

The Judge Sisters

I BOTH ADMIRED AND FEARED THE
Judge Sisters as only a small boy could who was lonely and half-blind
and whose favourite occupation, other than reading by candlelight
under his covers, was to wander the four blocks of back alley behind
Main Street to rummage in the huge green garbage bins in hopes of
finding some prize, some object a store had thrown away that I could
carry home and hide in my room.

Somehow, slipping silently down the street, some broken thing
hidden inside my shirt, I was met by the two women, who would look
at me askance, as if I were failing a more perfect world. It never
occurred to me such meetings were accidental. I was convinced the
Judge Sisters watched out for me. That they just happened to live
nearby and were often outside when I was heading home did not seem
to me to be a natural thing. Unlike my mother, who stayed home and
laboured from early morning until long after I was in bed, the Judge
Sisters worked in their garden or went out for walks that they called
strolls.

I asked them once where they were going and Emily Judge looked
at me strangely and said, "We are going out for a little air." She spoke
clearly and precisely, each word enunciated perfectly, as if to a boy
whose question had great meaning.

I was confused by this. Expressions like those that Emily used

How Do You Spell Beautiful?

bewildered me. I told my mother she should go out for air like the Judge Sisters did. She looked at me in much the same way Emily Judge had. She turned her head from her endless ironing, surprised I was there. "What's wrong with you?" she asked.

Prize stuffed inside my shirt, I did what I could to avoid the sisters' steady, quizzical gaze. Most times I managed to escape them, yet it seemed to me they saw me more often than not. "Well?" Emily Judge would say as I tried to slip away from them through a hedge. "Well?"

That *well* always unnerved me. It was not said in judgement, but was an all-inclusive word that encompassed what I took to be my failings. It was always spoken in the form of a question, Emily's high voice floating through the twisted branches of some scraggly caragana, her eyebrows raised and her head tilted slightly to the side.

Agnes, who was near-sighted and wore black-rimmed spectacles attached to her by a grey ribbon that went around her neck, would bend over and peer at me in the shadows. "Oh," she would say. "It's that boy."

"Are you being good today?" Emily sometimes asked. Her voice was not harsh. It was gentle, and yet that gentleness contained a distance, as if I were someone far away from their world.

Standing there, abashed, I would blurt out that I was.

"Very well," Emily would say, staring past me down the street. "The world has need of goodness." Then, having settled herself inside her severe black dress, she would take Agnes's arm in hers, and move past me down the wooden sidewalk in search of a little air.

I hadn't been good at all.

I may not have actually done anything bad that particular day, yet I believed I must have, else why would she ask?

Clutching whatever it was I had found in the garbage bin, a chipped vase or a few small bottles, I would scuttle into a hedge or behind a broken fence and move like a furtive shadow toward my home. I still had to escape the prying eyes of my brothers who would, if they could, stop and search me, taking whatever it was I had found for their own. As I ran I would curse my badness and promise to somehow be better, if not for myself, at least for the Judge Sisters.

Looking back now, I realize Emily and Agnes Judge's lives were governed by a firm gentility, yet they sustained that seeming vulnerability with a stern and powerful moral vision. They were *proper*. They were surrounded by a barbaric world and only a strict and uncompromising code of behaviour prevented barbarism from overpowering

The Judge Sisters

them and everyone else in that town on the southern rim of the high plateau of British Columbia.

The day I first trailed them through the park, I heard Agnes say: "Must that wild, ungovernable boy follow us?"

Perhaps I was wild, though I did not want them to think that. I believed that the goodness they wanted in me was an attainable thing, even though it had eluded me for all of my nine years. I thought that it might possibly be learned, but was more likely to be found, a prize hidden away in some obscure garbage bin on a street I didn't know. Perhaps someone had left goodness there, as hope had been left in Pandora's box, a story that had to be believed because it was written down. Hope and goodness, like bravery and honour, were virtues in a world I wanted to be part of. I thought someone may have misplaced goodness, putting it down somewhere and then not remembering exactly where they had left it. Goodness was somewhere, if only I could find it.

I was still young enough to believe that things were not discarded, but were only lost. My two greatest finds that summer were a leopard with ruby eyes whose foot was broken off to reveal the white plaster beneath the smooth black surface, which to me made it all the more mysterious and valuable, and a radio that did not work, though I listened to it for hours at night in my small room when my mother had taken out first the light-bulb and then, frustrated, her face in tears, my candle stub and matches. I believed the whole world entered me through that radio's silence. I would fall at last into sleep with that black box on the orange crate that served me as a bedside table, the dials turned as far as they could go, and my sleeping ears still hearing a music entirely my own.

But it was books that were my secret obsession, and in order to get books I had to confront Emily and Agnes. They ran the library in the basement of the fire hall.

They were always called the Judge Sisters, as if it were a title, and for the years I knew them they were never seen apart. It was as if they were bound together by something more than other people were. I know now they weren't sisters at all, but were companions and probably lovers. They were two old, grey ladies, who were neither old nor grey, but were simply women in their forties or early fifties. To a boy whose own mother at thirty was terribly old, they seemed ancient.

The two of them had emigrated from England to the desert country of the southern Interior after the First World War, a war that, according to my father, who had just come home from the second one,

How Do You Spell Beautiful?

had destroyed their generation of women. What my father meant by destruction I didn't know.

They lived in The Morocco House, a rambling structure with wide verandas encircling it that had once been the private home of Major Jonathon Ward Staples. He had built it before the First War for his tubercular wife. People in town said she died the day it was completed. My mother's friends said there had been talk back then that her death might not have been from tuberculosis as everyone had been told. Such dire comments were always made over coffee or tea at midmorning, the neighbour women with my mother shaking their heads while I hovered by the back door listening. Major Staples followed his wife two years later, a suicide.

Major Staples had named it The Morocco House because of the years he spent in North Africa in the service of the British Army. The common story among the old men who spent their days on the granite steps of the post office was that he had done something terrible somewhere in Palestine in 1905 and had been removed to Canada in disgrace.

He was said to have hanged himself in the basement of The Morocco House, and once I broke a window and climbed down into that basement with Willa. She was my only real friend, a year younger than I was, and because I always feared she would find out I was at heart a coward, I led her into the most terrible places I could find in order to frighten her.

In the basement of The Morocco House there was a thin bit of rope hanging from a rusted pipe in the ceiling. I told Willa it was the rope Major Staples had used to kill himself. That it was probably a piece of clothesline meant nothing. She believed me.

Willa's young life was full of darkness and doom. My mother said she had a gothic sensibility. I didn't know what that was, but I associated it with gargoyles and cathedrals, neither of which I had seen, but I had read about them in books. I made her climb to my shoulders, her body above me among the spider webs, her thin thighs tight around my throat. I know she thought the ghost of Major Jonathon Ward Staples watched us from the shadows, waiting for the slightest sign of fear before pouncing. I was her only protection.

Willa trembled as she reached up with her hands and worked upon the knot. She didn't manage to undo it and for months I tormented her, demanding she go back with me. I knew she wouldn't, which is why I asked her. When I knew I had pushed her too far, I would take her for a trip into the hills to find gold or rattlesnakes, or on a journey

130

The Judge Sisters

to Abercrombie's Coal Sheds by the railway tracks to catch black-widow spiders, which I told her we could sell to the circus when next it came to town. Her fear was important to me, her dread when I made her hold a jar of black-widow spiders.

Willa lived in a shack near Coldwater Creek at the edge of town, and she had no father. Her mother drank and was almost never home and Willa, an only child, wandered the streets of Mission Hill in cast-off clothing her mother picked up from the Salvation Army depot. She was a shy and quiet girl, and because I also wandered the town alone, she took to me, following me everywhere.

Emily and Agnes Judge lived on the top floor of The Morocco House, and every Saturday morning at precisely eight o'clock they appeared together on the veranda, Agnes's arm hooked through Emily's elbow, and Emily gripping a black purse that hung from her shoulder. They would stand in the shade of the Virginia creeper for a brief moment and then walk, arm in arm, down the wooden steps into the garden.

There they slowly strolled down the winding path that led to the gate, Agnes quietly exclaiming over the flowers that bloomed profusely in the beds she had planted in front of the lilac and caragana hedges.

Emily would nod as she spoke, stop for a moment to look down at some small cluster of violets or bleeding hearts, and then gently urge Agnes along to the gate before she could stop and worry herself about aphids or red-beetles or some other pernicious intruder.

At the gate they would stop again and peer out into the shade of the elms and chestnut trees of Schubert Street, as if they had to make sure the world had not changed somehow in the night. To them the wilderness, a scant ten blocks away, might have invaded the town while they slept. Southern England with its hedgerows and estates, its organized gardens and neat farms, was a dream they maintained in the face of the wild western hills with their cactus and pine trees, their coyotes, rattlesnakes, and spiders.

I watched them many times from my hiding place under Arthur East's front porch. I was obsessed by them, partly because they always seemed to know when I was hiding something, or lying, but mostly because of their power over books. It was also the way they spoke, the words they used, the way they carried themselves as they walked. They represented a world I knew nothing of, and they made me feel ashamed. I wanted to be a part of who they were, to escape from what I was.

How Do You Spell Beautiful?

I am sure now they knew I was there watching, but they never spoke of it to me, nor, when I was shadowing them, did they ever, after that first time, acknowledge my presence with so much as a word. I was the boy who followed them and they had become used to me.

I would wait under the porch across the street and watch for Emily to reach over the gate with her black gloved hand and unlatch it. Then they would step out, and with severe looks on their narrow faces, proceed down the wooden sidewalk to the fire hall. It was the same thing every Saturday and Sunday, the two days of the week the library was open.

Other women besides the Judge Sisters obsessed me. There was Mrs. Ogilvie, who had a goiter, a large red bag of flesh that hung below her chin, and the Countess Maletsky, who lived in a huge house on the hill surrounded by high fences, and who had never appeared in public since she arrived from Russia in 1918. The countess's daughter, who did appear occasionally, was the tallest person in town, taller even than Frenchie LeGrand, who worked with my father and who could pick up and carry a three-hundred-pound head from a TD-24 tractor, which he did whenever my father asked him to.

The skin of the countess's daughter was the purest white imaginable, whiter even than the albino boy who lived on the far side of town and had pink eyes and never went to school.

But the Judge Sisters were different. They were librarians. Somehow, the fact that they alone were in charge of knowledge gave them a presence, an authority, as if they not only dispensed books but had also written every word on those long shelves behind the counter.

The books had all been donated. The bulk of them had come from private libraries, the holdings of eccentric English and American expatriates who had died and willed their collected tomes to the town of Mission Hill for the furthering of enlightenment and education among the poor.

Most of the books were bound in faded stained leather. The leaves were touched with gold along their edges and bore the names of Longfellow and Hardy, Thackeray, Bronte, and Twain, and a thousand more. I believed the books were there for me and only for me. I thought if I could read them all I would attain the world the Judge Sisters lived in.

It was there I first read *Swiss Family Robinson, Coral Island, Beautiful Joe*, and *Tom Sawyer*. But I also read *The Mill on the Floss, Jude the Obscure*, and *She*, by H. Rider Haggard. Many of the books I read were far too old for me, but even when I didn't understand them I still read them,

The Judge Sisters

passing over the words I didn't know, following plots and characters that were mostly a mystery. Such a thing as a dictionary was unknown to me. I imagined meanings for the words I didn't understand.

Willa did not know how to read, though she often came with me to the library. Standing on the last step, she watched from the doorway as I received my book. Emily sometimes spoke to her, but Willa never came forward. Instead, at the sound of her name, she shrank back up the stairs to the street and waited there for me.

Each book was given to me by Emily Judge. She would take it from Agnes, who had found it on some high dark shelf in the far reaches of the stacks. The fact that they were guiding my reading had not occurred to me, just as it had never occurred to me that I was one of the poor children those expatriates had intended when they gave their libraries to be read. I didn't know I could have walked into the aisles and picked out my own books. Instead, I stood there expectant and dutiful as I waited for whatever book they might choose.

Emily took from me the book I was returning. Having lifted it carefully from my outstretched hands, she would turn the book to look at the spine to make sure it wasn't broken, and then reverse it to see if there was the hint of a page that had been turned down at the corner. Had there been, she would look across the book at me and I would say that it hadn't been me who had done it, but one of my brothers. I believed she could see into the farthest corner of my soul. She knew when I was lying, there was never any doubt of that. The fact that she accepted the lie made it all the more unbearable. I would swear to myself never to do it again. But far worse than a turned-down corner was one that had been torn off, and if she discovered one she would not allow me a book that Saturday at all, but, with a single gesture of her hand, would banish me from the library until the following day or week.

My greatest weakness was tearing off the corners of pages and chewing them. Why I did this, I don't know. It wasn't because I was hungry. Perhaps I was like some foundling who ate earth, or a child who needed to do more than simply read words, but must actually consume them.

I would stand there hiding my dirty hands, my bare feet itching in my torn running shoes, and wait while she sat and looked at me. I would smile at her in the hapless way boys do who wish to ingratiate themselves with a power greater than their own. I know now she thought me a boy who needed to be punished occasionally for reasons only she understood. Her refusal or her acquiescence made a great difference, yet she did not pity me.

How Do You Spell Beautiful?

I suppose she saw in me her own child, or perhaps, and I think this to be true, she saw the child of her imagination. Not some child she might have wished for in her womb, but a child she bore in her dream of a better world. I was the boy she had made out of the flesh of her own imagining. An *other* child, a small unusual animal she watched over, nurtured, cared for, and, ultimately in her odd wisdom, tried to guide. Her sternness was an act of subterfuge, a way of insinuating love into an alien flesh. Her wish was to give me grace.

Agnes was the dark one who searched out and found the titles that would form my thought. Unlike Emily, Agnes feared my maleness, though I was only nine years old. I thought then that Agnes Judge knew I spent my Sunday mornings at Gerald Gafferty's house staring down from his high bedroom window at Mrs. Cornwallis and her two teenaged daughters, who sunbathed naked in their yard behind the fence that Mr. Cornwallis had built to prevent eyes exactly like mine from watching. I was convinced Agnes knew I looked through the pages of *Sunbather's Magazine* in Kostopolis's Kandy Kitchen. I had two stolen issues in the strongbox under my bed, and many were the nights when I leafed through the sepia-toned pages, staring at the naked bodies of men and women who worshipped the sun in far-off places like Florida and Arizona.

Agnes Judge knew I did that. She could read it in my eyes no matter how I tried to hide it. She had a horror of me, though she rose above that fear. Agnes knew I could not be saved, I could only be prevented. Her guidance of my dreams was an attempt on her part to create a boy who would someday grow into a manhood that would sacrifice its base nature for king and country and not live long enough to wreak havoc upon women. What her dream of havoc was I did not know, but I believed in her mind there was a rich panoply of possible futures for me, and all of them ended with my death.

Yet she gave in to my desires, gave to me what I was right to want, and so made in me a conflict of centuries of English thought. There was no malice in her, just as there was none in Emily. There was only a long sorrowing, a faded gentility that feared my maleness and mistook it for a madness she herself had known. I wonder now if she had been a victim of some kind of violence, yet she rose above her memories and tried to make of me at least a sacrifice to virtue.

There were two things I always did on a Saturday. One was to go to the library, but first I went to the Courthouse, the largest building in Mission Hill. In the back of the huge granite building was a door that was always left unlocked. It led down a flight of stairs into a long dimly

The Judge Sisters

lighted hall with a number of rooms leading from it.

I had discovered it one day when I was trying to escape from Dirty-Neck Dronski, an older boy who lived nearby. Whenever he caught me, he hit me with his fist. He always hit me just once on the shoulder, but he did it with a knuckle extended and it hurt. His punching me was done with complete disinterest, as if I was not human, but was only some animal he was tormenting. "Do you want to die?" he would ask softly. "Is that what you want?"

Running from him one summer day, I had tried the door and, finding it unlocked, slipped inside. I stayed there and explored the long passageway. It was the section of the Courthouse where the provincial veterinarians and crop inspectors worked. I didn't know that then. I only knew it as a place full of forbidden things.

One Saturday I took Willa down the steps to the dim tunnel with its marble floors. I didn't tell her what was there. Holding her small hard hand in mine, I led her through the rooms. My favourite was an office with a single large desk in it and walls covered in deep high shelves. On one wall there were large jars full of animals and reptiles preserved in formaldehyde. Some of the jars held the foetuses of pigs. I took Willa into the room and told her they were babies that had been born to crazy mothers and had been killed.

They did look strangely human. Their grey bodies were crammed into the jars, their hairless skin pressed in folds against the discoloured glass, while around them in the oily liquid floated bits of pale tissue. While Willa stood there still and silent, I pointed to one large jar and told her it was the baby of Crazy Yvonne Gondor, who had killed her father with a hoe the year before. "And after she killed him, she gave birth to a baby," I said. Willa said nothing, only stared at the pink foetus, the tightly closed eyes, the red snout, and the tiny white teeth. "Look at it," I said.

As Willa stared at the jar, I knew I had found a great fear in her. The knowledge made me take the jar from the shelf and place it on the floor between us.

I unscrewed the lid and then, taking Willa's thin brown wrist, I drew her unresisting hand to the jar and lowered it slowly into the formaldehyde. Pushing on her wrist, I pressed her fingers and palm against the shrivelled head of the foetus. When I let her go she did not remove her hand. It was then I left.

I knew she would tell no one what had happened. And if she did, it didn't matter. If I was ever asked about it, I would simply lie. I also knew Willa would never talk to me again and I didn't care. As I walked away

How Do You Spell Beautiful?

from her, I felt triumphant, vindicated by something I didn't understand. I was also angry, though I didn't know what I was angry about. I did not know why I had terrorized Willa. Yet I had enjoyed doing it, the meanness, the cruelty of it. I had felt a power in that hidden place.

I went from there to the library. I stood in front of the counter and Emily looked down at me and asked where Willa was. Her question was a casual one, yet at that moment I thought she knew what I had done.

I blurted out that it had been Willa who had taken me to the Courthouse and showed me the things in the rooms. I told them it had been Willa who said the jars were full of dead babies and that Willa had made me touch one of them.

Emily simply stared at me. She knew I was lying. So did Agnes, who stood beside her companion with a look that I thought then was hate and know now was merely distaste.

Emily picked up the book she had waiting for me and handed it to Agnes. Neither of them spoke a word. Empty-handed, I raced up the stairs of the library and past the scarred green doors that led into the public lavatories.

I ran down the alley past the huge garbage bins toward home. When I got there I opened the screen door and walked into the kitchen where my mother stood over her wringer-washer in front of the woodstove that, even in summer, was burning. I said nothing to her as she stood with her arms up to the elbows in soapy water. She did not notice me as I went past her and up the stairs to my room. I stayed there for hours and then returned to the library.

Hidden behind the cenotaph in the park across the street, I waited for Emily and Agnes to close the library. At five o'clock they came out the high oak doors and I shadowed them up the street.

As they passed through their gate and walked up the path to the veranda, I picked up a stone from the gutter and threw it at them. The stone hit the sloping roof of the veranda and rattled down the grey shingles to the path at the foot of the steps. Neither of them turned around. They walked to the door, opened it, and went inside.

I stood on the wooden sidewalk and gazed at The Morocco House. I had never been in their apartment. To my knowledge, no one but them ever entered that separate world. What they did there, how they lived, had always been a mystery to me, yet at that moment, as I stood in the shade of the hedges, I wanted to know. I wanted them to come back outside and ask me to come into their sanctuary.

In the weeks that followed I went to The Morocco House in the

136

The Judge Sisters

evening to look up at their windows. The summer was advancing inexorably toward another year of school. But in the early evening, with the darkness gathering in the elms and chestnuts, I would glance upward and look at the high soft glow of their lives.

I imagine them now on one of those summer mornings before Willa and the Courthouse and my lies. I can see them hesitating at their gate before stepping out of the garden at The Morocco House, and I imagine Agnes saying to Emily, That boy is there, isn't he? And Emily says Yes, and that *yes* is one of only a very few I have counted on all my life, just as I have counted on the tentative flinching steps of the countess's daughter, who walked like a narrow wolfhound into the town, afraid and very lonely, to shop for the goods her mother needed behind her walls.

I have counted too upon Mrs. Ogilvie, who suffered me as I followed her home, her goiter, which she never hid but wore as something more than an affliction, that swollen flesh hanging like some strange beautiful thing grown out of her. And Mrs. Cornwallis, who sometimes walked alone into her yard and stood there with her body facing the bright desert sun, her full breasts and belly pulling the light into them, knowing a boy watched her from afar. She did not flaunt her body at me, but neither did she prevent my seeing her.

I count on Willa as well, the shy, slim girl who rode on my shoulders, afraid and struggling with a knot in a rope that had hanged a man in her imagination. I count on the girl who reached into the jar to hold in her small hand the aborted child of the mad Yvonne Gondor.

I know that when Willa held that face, there was not a thought in me that was not fear. I know I gave her dreams and they were the ghosts of dead mad babies who floated in formaldehyde in the room below the Courthouse, ghosts she must have carried with her for many years, just as I carried ghosts each night into my sleeping, though they were not the same as hers.

Willa had trusted me and I betrayed her. I would have to live with that. I would have to think of it when, book in hand from the new library at school, I would course down the dusty streets home to my mother, who, if I could convince her I was sick, would leave her work and lay me down on my bed under a bright red Indian blanket, and with the light spilling from the autumn sun, read to me of boys hunting gorillas in darkest Africa, and of a perfect family building a home on a lost island somewhere in a tropical sea.

The Morocco House, with its obscure saga of death and suicide, would rest in the evening of the desert autumn, the lights in the high

137

How Do You Spell Beautiful?

windows floating far above me in the darkness. Standing inside a maze of lilacs, the deep shade of chestnut trees upon me, I would watch those lights, thinking of Emily and Agnes Judge reading to each other from books they would never share with me.

What did I want under those windows with those two women not knowing I was there? I thought then, standing in the shadows, it was love I wanted, but know now what I meant was not love but, strangely, something to do with forgiveness, though who was to be forgiven and how, I did not know.

Marylou Had Her Teeth Out

MARYLOU HAD HER TEETH OUT. No one ever seemed to notice Marylou. She wasn't exactly ugly or anything. It wasn't that. If she'd been real ugly then I guess people would've noticed her. People notice ugly people just like they notice beautiful people. They stand out. Marylou didn't stand out. She was just there. You know, ordinary.

No. More than that. Sort of like a post in a fence. Once the wire is hung the post is just there. That's what she was like ever since she'd been born. Of course, it was a big family. I'd say there must have been at least fourteen or fifteen of them. I never counted. No one did. I wonder now if even her folks counted them. When you get past six or seven they kind of all blend together I think.

Marylou's teeth had always been a problem. When they grew in, they grew in wrong, all pointing every which way. Some kids are like that. People say it's what they eat, but I don't know. Some kids have just got bad teeth I think. She never complained at all. None of the kids in that family complained. What was the good of that? And who'd you complain to if you wanted?

That family never had much money to speak of. Marylou's old man was born to be poor. It was like he'd aimed his whole life at having

139

How Do You Spell Beautiful?

nothing and it'd worked. He had nothing. They had a house, if you could call it that, and a few other things, but not much. How Jack Trackle even got a house I'll never know. They'd been living there for years. I think that old farm had just been deserted and Trackle moved his whole brood onto it. There's still lots of old places around here from before the war.

Jack Trackle had a clubfoot and he was a little guy. Always complained about that foot. Said there was no way he could work it hurt so bad, though you'd see him at a dance on Saturday night at the Odd Fellows Hall and he'd be kicking that foot six feet up a wall. That never seemed to bother him.

Dancing was one thing Trackle could do. Saturday night he'd lock that house of his so the kids would stay put, and he'd bring his wife to the hall. Just her, not Marylou or anyone else. The wife would hang like a fly by the sandwich table and never move while Jack would dance with anyone he'd a mind to. Most would. You didn't say no to Jack.

Anyway, Marylou had them out. The whole mouthful. Had them pulled out down in Kamloops one day when she and her mother went out. I think that's all they went out for, Marylou's teeth. They were welfare people. Jack Trackle didn't work, like I said, and I guess she had her hands full looking after all those kids and Jack. There was no way she could work. Trackle wouldn't have let her anyway. He was way too proud for that. I don't even know her name come to think of it. No one talked to Jack Trackle's wife. Anyway, out they went on the CN Mainliner and Marylou came back with all her teeth out. Came back the same day. Down in the morning and back by six o'clock. That's when the east-bound comes back through.

I still think it had a lot to do with that young first-aid man they had down at the mill. Not that he interfered with people all that much. People sort of interfered with him. The mill reopening after all those years really changed things in Little River. There were a lot more people in town, that's for sure. The bunkhouses were filled. They'd been empty for years.

The first-aid man was one of the biggest things to happen to Little River besides the mill starting up. We all knew he couldn't do things like a real doctor, but it was a lot better than the health nurse who used to come up twice a year. Now she used to interfere a lot, I'll tell you. But it was him, I think, who arranged the teeth thing for Marylou. So out she went and came back with no teeth.

I guess I should say something more about Marylou, seeing as how what happened. She was about fifteen or so. Around there. I said she

Marylou Had Her Teeth Out

was ordinary. They were all ordinary. She had long black hair and a kind of straightforward face. You couldn't say she was good-looking at all. Oh, she had a body on her in a way. I never paid attention. That kind of thing was never too important to me at all. It might've been once a long time ago, but not really. I guess I just missed out on all that. I'm glad now I did.

So that was her. There's not a lot more you could say. Fifteen about. Black hair. Ordinary. What else can you say? The whole family was that.

I talked to her a few times. She used to come in to get things once in a while. Her teeth were terrible. I only saw them the once. She was scared this one day by the Dutchman's dog, and she opened her mouth real wide. I was standing right there and you couldn't miss them. That was the only time. The rest of the time she talked, when she talked at all I mean, she kept her mouth kind of closed so the words came out muffled. Or she'd say something to you and keep her hand in front of her mouth so you had to figure out what she said by what was happening. If she was coming it was hello. If she was going it was goodbye. That's almost all I ever heard her say.

I guess those teeth really embarrassed her, I don't know. When they're young like that things like teeth can seem real important. Kind of a lonely girl now that I think of it. But there was a big family. How can you be lonely when you've got that many brothers and sisters?

So it was that young first-aid man who started it all. At least that's what I figure. Anyway, there she was, back. I saw her come in on the train with her mother. I meet the train regular. I don't nose into other people's business. Don't get me wrong. I like to see who's coming and going, that's all. I saw her that day. Her cheeks were all sunken in like one of those old people with only gums. Jack Trackle was there to meet them and he was mad.

I don't know what it is with little guys. They're always trying too hard. I hardly ever saw a fight yet that wasn't started by a little guy. Seems like they're always looking for trouble. He was there, Jack Trackle, waiting. When they got off he grabbed his wife. He twisted her arm so hard I thought he was trying to take it right off. She didn't yell or anything, just stood there and let him do it. Marylou just stood there too with her hand covering her mouth. It looked sore. Jack Trackle was yelling at his wife real bad and just twisting that arm. I felt like maybe going over and stopping him, but what good would that've been? He'd a real reputation for that stuff and if you got in the way it just made things worse.

141

How Do You Spell Beautiful?

The first-aid man was there too. He'd been picking up some stuff off the express car when Trackle started yelling. He was saying things like, "Don't you never go nowhere unless I say so!" Things like that. He was swearing at her too. I thought for sure he was going to kick her with that heavy boot he had on that clubfoot. I saw him once kick a guy right in the head at a dance after the guy had danced, or maybe just tried to dance, with his wife. Kicked him with that boot. That guy never came back to Little River. They shipped him out on a fast freight to Kamloops and the hospital there. He was a bad one was Jack Trackle. Nobody had anything to do with him or his family for that matter. They just left them alone. It wasn't worth it, him being the kind of man he was.

I'd have told the first-aid man if he'd asked me. I'd have told him to let her alone and to stay out of Jack Trackle's way. It was asking for trouble. But he didn't. I'm not saying he was the interfering kind, but in this case he troubled himself a little too much. I guess he heard Trackle yelling and he ran down the cinders by the track there and grabbed him and pulled him off the wife. I could've sworn I heard her arm pop when Trackle let go. That young guy was mad as hell. He wasn't from Little River that's for sure. Somewhere back east I think.

Well, I don't think anyone had ever right out and grabbed that man in his whole life. Nobody in Little River. Jack Trackle just stood there and looked at the first-aid man. He was totally surprised. That's when the wife ran over and put her arms around Trackle. Real thin arms she had. Pipe stems with a bit of gristle attached. She yelled at the first-aid man and told him to leave them alone.

Marylou didn't say anything. She was still standing there with her hand over her mouth, watching it all. I could tell by her look she was seeing it all in slow motion. People when they're doing that have a certain kind of stunned look about them. The same as a steer does when it's hit between the eyes with a ball-peen hammer. Still-like, as if the whole world just slowed right down.

That first-aid man backed off then but he didn't go. No way. He went over to Marylou and said something to her. She gave him a piece of paper and then Trackle grabbed his wife and her. Not with his hand or anything. Just with a look. It was like they were attached to him by his eyes.

They headed up the road from the station there, Trackle's boot kicking up the dust with every step, and his wife behind him walking with her head down, and Marylou behind her with her hand still over her mouth. I watched them go. I wouldn't have wanted to be those two

Marylou Had Her Teeth Out

when he got them home. You'd think they'd have known better, knowing what he was like and all.

The first-aid man stood there watching them and then he read the piece of paper. After he finished he threw it away. He took off then. Grabbed a box from the cinders by the express car, walked down to the head of the train, and went around the engine to the mill on the river side. There were people on the train looking out watching, but when I looked back at them they all turned away. It was the dining car. You'd think they were watching some kind of movie. Those eastern people, all dressed up and going to wherever it is they go, Montreal or Toronto. Places like that.

The first-aid man was just a young guy. He was walking real stiff-like in jerks, like he was mad, and I guess he was. His hard hat was pulled right down to his eyes. That's when I picked up the paper and read it. I know it wasn't any of my business. It didn't say much. It had a printed name at the top. The dentist who'd pulled all of Marylou's teeth I guess. I don't remember it now, some kind of foreign name like the Pakis up on the hill. Underneath it said: Stitches to be removed in three weeks. That was all. I guess when you've had all your teeth pulled they stitch up the gums. That's what Karl Arnverg's wife says. She says they pack the gums full of cotton stuff and stitch them over so they won't bleed. Helps them to heal, she says, and it keeps them right for when you get your false ones. What you do, Arnverg's wife said, after the gums are healed, is to cut the stitches and pull them real gentle through the gums so they don't tear or anything. Sounds simple enough to me.

It made sense. The paper I mean. What you had to do was take those stitches out. I figured Marylou and her mother would be heading back down to Kamloops in three weeks for that. Well, that's not what happened. Talking like this, I remember it all.

I was pretty busy around then. Oh, I still found time to sit down at the Dutchman's store and meet the trains, but I was pretty busy all the same. I'd shot a moose up on Mad River and I'd had to cut that all up and freeze it. Then I had to bring in the cordwood I'd stacked up above town. Good wood. Nice seasoned fir. I'd knocked a tree down that spring and let her dry real well all summer. Full of sap. Still, it was a lot to do.

Thinking back on it now I never saw Marylou or her mother in Little River during those weeks. I saw Trackle once but I didn't say anything to him. He looked the way he usually did. He'd walked into Little River from that house of his six miles up the road, picked up a box or two of stuff, and walked right back out. Never said anything to anyone as far as I could tell.

How Do You Spell Beautiful?

No, that's not right. I almost forgot. He didn't come in alone. He had one of his kids with him pulling that wagon he'd made. It's true. I wonder why I forgot that? Strange how things get to be so ordinary you get used to them. That kid, one of the boys it was, about thirteen or so, was hitched up to the wagon just like he was a horse or something. I mean, he didn't have a bridle on or reins, but he did have on a leather belt with loops attached to it. The loops were there to hold the two-by-fours sticking out from the wagon box. Two bicycle wheels. That's all. Just like a damned horse. Can you beat that?

Well, Trackle filled the wagon with the stuff from the Dutchman's and that kid of his hauled it back. Trackle never paid for any of that stuff. It was all welfare food. The Dutchman made good money from welfare, I'll tell you. Down the road they went, Trackle walking on ahead, and coming along behind was the boy leaning into it and pulling the wagon. I never laughed when I saw that. It looked funny in a way, but he wasn't one to take too kindly to people laughing at anything he did. Or his family did either.

I minded my own business, especially when it came to him. I think if I took pictures, though, I'd have taken a picture of that. Can you imagine hitching one of your kids to a cart, just like a horse? I'm glad I never had kids. Glad all that sort of thing passed me by. It's enough looking after yourself. You look after yourself and let others do the same. That's what I say.

Anyway, things went on for a while. It was a few weeks later and I was sitting on the steps of the store when I saw Jack Trackle coming into Little River. He had Marylou this time pulling the wagon and his wife was with him too. There she was, Marylou I mean. Same clothes, same black hair, bare feet, same look about her. In they came. They stopped in the dirt outside the Dutchman's and he left them both there and went in to do whatever business it was he had.

I never said a thing, just minded my own business. You live a long time if you do that. There they stood, right in the hot sun. Marylou's feet in the dust like brown frogs run over by a truck, the wagon hanging from her belt, and looking straight down at the dirt between her feet as if she could see something there so important she couldn't take her eyes off it. She had her hand as usual over her mouth, but I could tell just by looking at her there was something wrong. Her face was all swollen. Even from where I was sitting I could smell her. There was something terrible wrong in her mouth, that was for sure.

Trackle's wife stood in front of her and just stared straight ahead, right through the wall of the store and past it to the poplars down by

Marylou Had Her Teeth Out

the river, and over the river and right into the side of Green Mountain. That kind of look. Not stunned. Not like Marylou's look down at the station that time when they first came back from Kamloops. It was different. She was looking right through everything. It was like her eyes would've burned you if she'd looked right at you.

I just sat there.

That was when the first-aid man drove up in the company truck. He always came right at that time to pick up the mail. Everybody knew that. As soon as he saw Marylou and Trackle's wife he started walking fast. He went right over and stood in front of the wife. She was standing in front of Marylou. There wasn't much room to get around. I remember the conversation real well. It's not like there was a lot said.

"Move away," he said to her. "I'm supposed to take those stitches out." Trackle's wife didn't say a word. She just looked right through that young guy like he wasn't even there. If he doesn't have two holes burned right through his chest to this day I don't know. He asked her again and she didn't move.

It was Marylou who spoke. She said, "I'm okay, mister. You leave us alone." She didn't say it scared-like at all, and she didn't look up either, and for sure she didn't take her hand away from her mouth. Just said it muffled and flat. You'd think a rock had talked to you to hear her. That's it exactly. Just like a rock talked to you.

The first-aid man stepped back like someone had hit him. That's when Trackle came out of the store. There was Marylou looking straight down at the dirt, and the wife burning holes through the first-aid man's body, and him standing there looking at what he could see of Marylou.

Trackle came down those steps solid. That clubfoot of his banged every second step like a hammer hitting iron, and the iron wasn't winning I can tell you. I never moved an inch, just felt the whole porch trembling. He walked down with a step-bang-step-bang-step-bang-step-thump into the dirt and threw a big box of groceries into the wagon. The two-by-fours jumped and lifted Marylou six inches in the air he threw that box in so hard. I thought, well, this's it now.

The first-aid man stood there stiff, those two eyes of the wife burning him, and Trackle about one foot away from both of them. "What d'you want?" Trackle asked. I never heard anyone say anything like that in just that way. I saw a snake once strike at a stick in a circus when I was a boy. A rattler it was. The man who ran the snake pit used to make them strike so the people who were watching would get their money's worth. If he didn't, they'd get mad. I mean, a snake will just

How Do You Spell Beautiful?

lie there still as a stone forever unless you make him mad deliberately. That's what the man would do. I went there every day for the three days the circus was in town, just to see him make that snake strike at a stick. That's what Trackle sounded like. A snake someone's poked a stick at. "What d'you want?" Just like that. A snake jumping so fast and so cold you could damn near die hearing it.

The young guy just looked at him. I give him credit. He didn't back away or anything. He stood his ground, what there was of it. "If it's Marylou you want then you can just forget it."

That's when the first-aid man spoke. "I'm supposed to take those stitches out," he said. He was trembling from holding himself so stiff, and Trackle standing there a good head and a half shorter.

"That's looked after."

I swear everything stood still for a while. Everything just got still. Trackle on that clubfoot, the first-aid man, the wife staring right through everything and everyone at God knows what, and Marylou looking down with her hand over her mouth. I could smell her right inside my own mouth it was that bad.

The first-aid man said it again, but this time it wasn't quite the same. It was like he didn't understand something suddenly. He was young and he wasn't from around here. Like I said, from back east probably. "But I have to take them out," he said again.

Trackle moved then. He held out his hand in a tight little fist and opened it right under the first-aid man's nose. "Here," he said. "You want them stitches so bad you can have them."

The first-aid man didn't move.

Trackle reached out with his other hand and took the young guy's hand and emptied into it what he had. "Here," he said. Then he kind of cut his hand at Marylou and the wife and said, "These here ones are mine." That's all. He turned then and walked up the road, him in the lead just like always, the wife right behind him, still staring, and then Marylou pulling the wagon. I can see it now like a picture inside my eye. Their backs all in single file and the wagon with the bicycle wheels behind. The wheels didn't have tires on them. You could hear them grind every time they hit a bit of gravel. We watched until they rounded the turn by the poplars up at the corner above the store.

I went over to him then. I felt kind of sorry for him. He was an important man in Little River, even if he was so young. He was looking down at those stitches in his hand. There were about thirty of them like little black spiders on his fingers. "Jesus," he said. "They aren't even cut."

Marylou Had Her Teeth Out

I brushed them out of his open hand so they fell on the ground. I didn't say anything. What was there to say? He looked at them lying there in the dust between his boots. "He didn't even cut them," he said. He wasn't talking to me, just talking to himself.

I left him there. It was almost five o'clock. The CN Mainliner was due in an hour and there were still a few things I had to do. I just left him standing there looking down into the dust.

Burning Wings

The DUTCHMAN WAS WIPING DOWN the counter and when he got to where I was sitting I told him the girl he'd brought up from Kamloops was grief in a box. "What you got there is trouble, pure and simple."

He lifted my cup like it was something dead, wiped underneath it, and then set it back down on a counter that was no cleaner than when he started. "You want more coffee?" he asked.

"No, I'm just nursing what I got."

Willem looked at me like what I was saying wasn't worth the dime I was paying. "It ain't your business," he said.

"No. It ain't anybody's right now, but it soon will be."

"What's that supposed to mean?" He was holding a sugar jar and looking at it in a way that begrudged anyone who liked his coffee sweet. The Dutchman was someone who put more rice than salt in a shaker.

"If you don't know, then you're the one that's got to live with it."

That's when Wally down at the last booth hollered for another cup of coffee. "Hey," he yelled, making sure everyone in the place could hear him, "How about some more coffee here."

He wasn't yelling at the Dutchman, that's for sure. What he wanted serving him wasn't wearing pants.

We watched the new girl come out from behind the counter with a pot of coffee. She wasn't more than fourteen. She walked over with

Burning Wings

everyone's eyes on her and reached out with the pot to pour.

Wally moved his cup.

She reached out a little further and Wally moved his cup again.

The two guys with Wally sat there as he moved his cup. They grinned, glancing back and forth from the girl to Wally. "C'mon," Wally said, "gimme some coffee."

She leaned a little further. By this time she was way out over the table, trying to reach and not touch anyone at the same time. Wally moved his cup an inch or two more and then he took a long look down her blouse. "Would you look at them," he said. She jerked back and some of the coffee spilled.

Wally started laughing, and when he did, the others started. The girl stood there with the pot in her hand. She looked scared and turned her head, trying to find the Dutchman.

Wally stopped laughing suddenly and moved the cup back. "Coffee," he said. "What's the matter, don't you know how to serve a customer?" That's when she poured it, but her hand was shaking so bad she slopped the coffee into his saucer. The others pushed their cups toward her and she filled them up the same way, coffee sloshing everywhere.

Billy Ackerman, who'd been sitting down the counter from me, got up then and headed out the door. He was looking agitated but I didn't think about that too long. Billy'd always been strange. A kind of lost kid who did odd jobs down at the mill.

He was sixteen or so and didn't belong to anybody but himself. One day he just got off a freight and stayed. I think Simard, the boss down at the mill, kind of took pity on him and gave him casual work to keep him alive. He was just a kid from nowhere in particular. You'd get that kind around milltowns, kids who're runaways or just drifting from families who didn't know or care their kid was gone.

"You know it," I said.

Willem just looked at the girl one more time and then started wiping the last of the counter, as if that's all there was in the cafe to concern him. The Dutchman's wife came out of the kitchen at the back looking mad, as she always did, and said something and the girl turned around and carried the pot back to the burner.

She followed the Dutchman's wife into the back.

"Hey now," Wally yelled after her, "don't you go away mad."

The Dutchman left me with my half cup of cold coffee and headed down to where Wally and the rest of them were. I couldn't hear what he was saying, but I could hear Wally and the others laughing. The

How Do You Spell Beautiful?

Dutchman's wife pushed the door at the kitchen and told Willem to come and he did. The girl was standing by the steam table crying. I caught a glimpse of her before the door swung shut.

Whatever was between Wally and the Dutchman I didn't know, but the Dutchman owed Wally from somewhere, sometime. There was no other reason for him to put up with what Wally did.

I left then, but I knew what I was talking about. The girl had been there only two days and already things were tense.

There weren't more than twenty women in Mad River and all of them were married, locked up tight as sheep in a short pen. The problem was there were more than a hundred men.

You figure it out. It didn't take much to see that a fourteen-year-old who looked a whole lot older was going to be the cause of nothing but trouble.

It's not like it was her fault. It was the Dutchman who'd done it. This one was different from the last one who worked there. That girl was only here for three weeks before she ran off to Jasper with an edgerman. And she was twenty or so, someone Willem hired off the train.

It's how he got the new girl made it different.

From what I could figure, he made some kind of deal with people down in Kamloops. It was that government place, you know, the one that kept girls who've got into trouble with the law or with their families or whatever. The Dutchman set up a deal with them and arranged for this girl to work in exchange for room and board.

He got her till she was sixteen.

After that, of course, she was on her own, but while she was there she belonged lock, stock, and barrel to him. He owned her for two years is how the deal worked.

There was Indian in her from what I could see. She had that colour and that straight black hair no white woman ever had. She acted different too. There never seemed to be anything you could read. Her face was bare, flat-like, with no expression.

Indians've got a certain way like they're not there half the time. In her case it was just as well.

But seeing her working at the cafe got me thinking about Wally. He was the kind of man who talked a lot about women, but I never noticed him with one. You'd see him at the hall and he'd be talking it up on the front steps with the other men, drinking beer and bragging about how he'd had this one or that one in town. Somebody's wife or daughter.

Everybody'd laugh with him about it but I don't think anyone

Burning Wings

believed him. Things like that went on in town but it wasn't Wally doing it. He was nothing but talk.

I think he was afraid of women. There are men like that and what they're more afraid of than women is another man maybe finding out.

I had me a woman once but she's long gone, and wherever she is I hoped then and hope now she stays there. The years I spent with her were hell from the day I said I do to the day she said I don't. I got me a few books and that's better than any real woman. I figure the woman you got in your head is easier to live with than the woman in your bed. The one in your head only talks back when you want her to.

Wally had problems, there's no doubt about that. Bullshit baffles brains, somebody told me once. There's nothing truer. If you believed everything Wally had to say about life then you'd believe anything. One half of him was bullshit and the other half was the bucket that held it.

The guys that followed Wally around were just bigger losers. What they saw in him is what a loser sees, someone they think can make things happen.

The trouble was the grief Wally made. Grief for me and grief for you and grief for anyone else who got in his way. Wally was afraid, you see, and he had to show everyone he wasn't.

Anyway, I was heading up the road toward my cabin when I saw Billy cutting across the field behind The Sacred Heart Church. Well, you could call it a church if that's what you wanted. A log hut with a tin roof, a cross mended with shingle nails, and a priest who came through once a month, dragging his beads out to hear the confessions of any fool who'd go to him.

Billy went to him every time. Seems like wherever Billy came from was Catholic. He probably needed something when he was growing up. He wasn't too swift was our Billy.

So I saw him angling over at me and I slowed a bit. He wasn't nothing more than a big kid really. Lonely as a skint tree in Saskatchewan. He caught up right where the fence meets the corner.

"Mr. Zadic," he says to me.

"Hey, Billy. How're you?"

"I'm fine, I guess."

"Saw you at the cafe," I said. "How come you left like that?"

"That Wally. He oughtn't to treat her like that."

"Who?" I asked.

I knew who he meant but I said it anyway.

"The girl at the cafe. Myrtle."

"That her name?"

151

How Do You Spell Beautiful?

"Yessir," Billy said.

"Well, you're right there, but that's the Dutchman's job to be looking after that."

"She's an awfully nice girl," he says to me. "Nobody should be doing things like that to her."

He said that and then he looked down at his boots and started kicking at a clump of dried clay, just like a little kid who's got worries too big for him. I could tell the way he was talking he had a thing for the girl, but how that made him different I didn't know.

"Listen," I said, "I'm not much for giving advice but if I was, I'd tell you to steer clear of the Dutchman and that girl he's brought up here. And keep clear of Wally. He's trouble, and a kid like you's got no business getting in the way of it. Wally's less than warm piss in a short bottle, but that doesn't mean he's not grief for someone like you. And that girl down there's a fire waiting to get started."

"Well, Mr. Zadic . . . " he said.

"For Christ's sake, just call me Charlie like everybody else."

"Yessir," he says. "It's just I don't want them bothering her like they're doing. You know what I mean?"

"Listen, Billy, you stay away from all that. You're just a kid still, and Wally's grown. He's got ten years on you. You get in his way and he'll walk across you like you were a thin board over a deep hole. You hear?"

"Well, I've talked to her and she says she's afraid of him."

"She's right to be," I told him, "but it's the Dutchman who's in charge, not you. He's the one bought her in Kamloops for the price of beans and bread. You got no say in it one way or the other."

I said that, thinking I couldn't get any clearer, and Billy just looked at me from under his yellow hair. Nobody'd cut it for a long time. It hung over his face like a crow's nest bleached by the sun. What I was saying was going right by him.

"Look," I said, "if you're lucky you'll live long enough to know what I'm telling you. The world's made up of all kinds of men and some are like Wally. You got to learn to step sideways from people like that. You do and you'll live a good life. You don't and a man like Wally'll catch you on a dark road and leave you blind or worse."

"Well, he still shouldn't."

"Shouldn't?" I said.

I couldn't believe what I was hearing. "Wally'll do what he wants when he wants to. There'll be a day someone's going to do something about him, but that day isn't now and you're not the man, not by a long shot."

"Well, I don't know," Billy said. "It's just . . . "

152

Burning Wings

"Billy," I said, slow and clear. "You think on what I just told you. Meanwhile, I'm heading to my cabin to do whatever's there for me to do. I advise you to do the same. Stay the hell away from the girl and stay off Wally's track."

Billy nodded at me with a troubled look in his eyes. I could tell he was all caught up. There's a first time for everyone. When it happens it's like your blood hurts. I left him holding up the fence with his elbows.

Sure, I thought, as I was stepping off the road onto the path to my cabin, that girl was going to think Billy was just right for her. He was young and dumb and she knew that.

She knew there was no finding a man who'd look after her without her having to pay some kind of price for it. But not a kid like Billy. All she had to do was smile at Billy and he would've jumped in front of a train to show her how thankful he was. She may have been only fourteen, but I'd seen into her eyes and they were scared enough to grab hold of a dumb kid who wouldn't ask more than a look at her ankles.

Her problem was she was young and pretty and the Dutchman owned her and could do whatever he wanted with her.

God knows he was probably doing her whenever he could already. And he wouldn't have been the first. She'd been owned before, by her daddy or an uncle and then whoever else in that government place. To the Dutchman she was less than nothing, and to the Dutchman's wife she was just cheap labour.

Hell, I thought, finally sitting in my chair and putting up my feet on the stove. Pure grief. Plain and simple as that.

The Dutchman was making money off her by not having to pay wages, and he'd make anything else he could off her if he got half a chance. A hundred men with nothing to do but whistle on a Friday or Saturday night?

I'd been there and back, but a kid like Billy? He hadn't even arrived yet.

I knew if he kept thinking he'd arrive a whole lot quicker than he wanted to.

~

The mill had finished with the peckerpole pine they'd been cutting for a month. It'd gone over to fir from the slope above Catlin Lake. Everyone was working like there was no tomorrow. It was bonus wood, even with the peelers being pulled aside. Men were counting their side money and dreaming about breakup and a few wild weeks in Vancouver or Calgary.

How Do You Spell Beautiful?

Every morning I was down at the cafe having my cup of thin coffee and listening to whoever wanted to talk. Billy was there too whenever he could get away from the mill. He'd found the last stool at the end of the counter down by the kitchen. It's where the girl stood when she wasn't serving coffee or whatever.

I watched them looking at each other, Billy with sad eyes and her looking like she hadn't got a friend in the world but guess who.

Billy figured they'd found each other.

I'd seen them one day when I was down by the river. The mill had started the river run and I was watching to see if any of the logs made it through Little Hell's Gate. Simard thought they would or he'd never have started running them. I knew they'd jam in that narrow canyon.

That's when I saw Billy and her.

If you could believe it they were sitting on a rock holding hands. Neither of them was talking at all, just holding hands and gazing at the drift going by, snags and broken logs and the occasional spruce that finally leaned too far and fell in. There's a sound to that falling, a kind of a sigh, the needles whispering all the way into the river.

Kids, that's all they were, except she'd gone through a lot more by the time she was five than Billy ever dreamed of in all his sixteen years. I knew he didn't have a clue. He was in love, that's what he thought.

What she thought was anybody's guess.

Wally was in and out the cafe with whoever else would follow him around. There was a whole group of them. Wally'd taken over Number 7 down at the crook in the road by the swamp. It was just a shack and Simard never bothered getting it fixed. Wally didn't live there himself, of course. He had his own little cabin up in the townsite. He just wanted a place for poker games or whatever.

No one complained. People stayed out of Wally's way.

Simard didn't say anything to any of it. All Simard wanted was things to run smooth and simple. Men timed in and they timed out, and in between they waited until they could time in again. What they did while they waited wasn't Simard's concern. So long as that was how it was, then Simard was happy. A hundred thousand feet of lumber a shift, that's what he wanted. If he was getting that and no breakdowns and nobody disappearing on a slow freight south to the Coast, then Simard wasn't about to complain if Wally wanted an empty bunkhouse. Wally did his job and his buddies did theirs.

Bosses and men and sawmills. Straight and simple, like a piece of clear coming down off the rig.

Burning Wings

So it was Friday, the middle of the month, and everyone at the mill had got their pay. The train was coming through from Kamloops on its way to Jasper and points east, and in it were the groceries and things for the men with wives and families, and booze for those without.

It was the payday shipment and everyone who was staying in had his order, rye whisky, and beer.

I headed down to get my own at five to six. One case of Seagram's 83 every week, no more no less. Two bottles for me and the rest to sell when everyone else ran out. Eight dollars a bottle on the platform and twelve on a Sunday morning after the night before. Twelve bottles to the case, which meant ten to sell at four bucks clear profit.

Some weeks it all went and some it didn't, but one way or another it all went eventually. People could get awful thirsty on a Sunday when they were staring at what crapped on them the night before.

"She on time today?" I asked Fred Melrose.

Fred ran the station. For some strange reason he was a happy man. He liked the north and living where he was. He spent most of his time trying to get baseball games on the radio. At least he said he could, but all I ever heard when I was down at the station was static. You couldn't get anything between those mountains on the North Thompson, but Fred didn't seem to mind.

Fred had risen to about where he was going to be the rest of his life, station agent in a milltown where he was chief cook and whistle-blower. A wife and five miserable little pale kids with bleached hair, sunburns, and blackfly bites. Fred's wife never seemed to notice. To her, sharing Fred's bed was about as good as it could get for a woman. You could tell by looking at her she was straight happy.

I could never figure what made a woman like her attach herself to a man like him. Maybe it was growing up in Nowhere, Saskatchewan, in a town she wanted to forget, and Fred was the first chance she had to leave.

Some women get trapped by their bellies, but for Fred's wife it was all heaven, babies, and baseball games. It seemed to me she was always either pregnant or trying to get that way. There're women like that.

Fred took out his railroad watch and looked at it like it was the final word on time. It was as big as an apple. "Six o'clock," he said.

I heard the whistle blow at Stearman's Crossing, long and low and sad like train whistles always are.

Everyone was down to meet the liquor train, even Martin Graff, the Jehovah's Witness. He was walking through the crowd passing out leaflets to the men, who dropped them where they stood. "Liquor's the

How Do You Spell Beautiful?

devil's drink," Martin kept saying in his hopeful wheedling way, but no one was listening.

The Dutchman was there with the girl.

"Look at that," Fred said, shaking his head.

"What?" I asked, knowing who he meant.

The girl was all dolled up in a pink dress two sizes too small, and her hair was combed long and shining down her back. She even had what looked like new shoes on. Little black ones, the patent leather kind with straps and hooker heels. She was looking like she wasn't there.

There was nothing behind those eyes but a hole you couldn't fill.

"That's one sad girl," said Fred.

"Ain't that the truth."

"She wouldn't be here at the station if the Dutchman's wife was in Little River."

"Where's she?" I asked.

"Gone out Thursday to Edmonton. Something family, Willem said. A sister dead or something."

"Huh."

"Lookit the way she's looking."

I did and it seemed to me she was purely not there at all, just a brown body stuffed inside a pretty dress with half of it trying to get out. There wasn't a man there, even the married ones, who wasn't staring at her like Saturday night steak.

That's when the train pulled in. Fred started acting important and telling everyone to get back so they could unload the express car. While everybody was milling around I saw Billy sidle up to the girl. She was standing in her shiny shoes looking at nothing and no one.

You could see she was scared of what he was saying. And anyone could see Billy was getting mad.

He said something to her again and then Wally pushed through the men around her. Wally was all dressed up in his Friday night outfit, a rhinestone shirt and cowboy boots with plates on the toes. I'd moved a little closer over the ties. Nobody was paying any attention. The men were either helping unload the crates and cases or lining up for their orders.

"Why don't you just fuck off and leave her alone," Wally said to Billy. "She don't want any part of you."

"What?" Billy said. He was stepping up and down on the same small spot, crushing cinders with his oversize boots. "What?"

"You heard me," said Wally. "Go ahead and ask her. See if she wants you bothering her."

"Go away," the girl said to Billy in a voice as quiet as dust.

Burning Wings

"She's scared of you," Billy says to Wally. "That's why she's saying that."

"Hey, Willem," Wally called to the Dutchman, and the Dutchman came over.

"What?"

"Am I right or am I wrong about this here girl not wanting this kid bothering her."

Willem looked hard at Billy. "I told you," he said.

"Well," said Billy. "Well."

It was like he had to repeat himself in order to make sense of what was happening.

Wally put his arm around the girl's shoulders and I could see her kind of get small under the weight of him.

"You heard Willem," said Wally. He looked down at the girl. She was half his size and only came up to his chest. "Tell him again," he said to her. He took his thumb and pushed his hat back on his head. He said it like he couldn't believe this kid was still there.

"Go away," she said again.

Billy turned around then in a complete circle, as if he had already gone somewhere and was coming back to see where he'd been. As he came around to face where he was, Wally's fist was waiting and caught him on the shoulder, hitting him hard enough so Billy almost stumbled and fell down. Wally did it fast, and the girl jerked forward at the force of it.

Billy staggered and the Dutchman took the girl by the wrist and pulled her away from Wally. "Not here," he said.

Wally watched her go from under his arm and then he turned to Billy. "What's the matter with you?" he asked. "Don't you understand nothing, or are you as dumb as you pretend to be?"

He stepped toward Billy and gave him another shove, this time with a straight arm so Billy went backward, tripping over a tie and falling into the cinders by the track.

Wally made as if to kick him and Billy moved away on his heels and hands like an upside-down spider making dust. The girl just stared at him. The Dutchman still had her by the wrist while he was making sure the right number of boxes were being stacked in his pickup truck. Her hand was hanging like a brown leaf from the Dutchman's fist.

The look on her face told it all.

I turned away then and carried my case of Seagram's to the truck.

There was nothing could be done about that, I thought.

I was lifting the case into the box when I saw Billy out of the corner

How Do You Spell Beautiful?

of my eye getting up and brushing himself off. His hands were flailing away as if there was more than dust and cinders he was trying to get shook of. The girl had turned away from him by then, and Wally was standing by the Dutchman laughing about something Willem said. The girl's hand was still hanging like an empty glove from the Dutchman's.

"Hey, Billy," I said. "You want a ride up?"

I didn't really want to ask him, but he looked so useless standing there beating on himself.

"C'mon," I said, hating myself already and going round to the door. "Get in. There's nothing here to do but get mad at what you can't do nothing about."

I should've left it alone. I knew that even as I said it.

Billy looked at me and then at the girl with her back to him. He spun then and came over to the truck, almost tearing the door off as he got in. He slammed it just as hard.

"Take it easy," I said.

He sat there staring out the windshield, his hands balled up in his crotch. "Well," he said, "go if you're damn well going."

So I did.

~

The first bottle was empty and the other was standing beside it waiting. I'd had maybe five drinks and Billy'd drunk the rest. He was sitting there with his one hand wrapped around a jam jar and the other holding on to the table. His fingers were stiff from gripping it. He was all slack-jawed and white across his cheekbones. His hair was gone wild from pushing his hand through it a hundred times or more.

I'd figured I might as well get him drunk as see him sober and a danger to himself. It was a lost bottle as far as I was concerned.

There was no point in feeding a kid as young as Billy. Most of what he'd got in himself was going to end up in a ditch. But what else was there to do with him?

I'd been young once too, but I don't think I was ever as young as Billy. It's like he'd grown all the way to where he was without learning a thing from the world he'd been travelling through.

I took another long look at the second bottle and said the hell with it as I screwed off the cap. To me it was good whisky wasted, but the kid had got to learn. When he was puking out his guts somewhere he'd roll over and look up at the clouds and he'd know something he didn't know before.

158

Burning Wings

I poured him another and he stared into the glass. "What do you say, Billy? Had enough?"

"I loved her," said Billy. "I really loved her."

"Well, yes," I said. "There's no denying that."

What could you say?

"She said so. She said she loved me too."

"I guess she would."

"We was going to run off together when I got a little money." He lifted his jar in his skinny hand and took a long look at it, as if he had to fix it exact in his eyes. He finally did, and the whole of it was gone down a throat that was starting to learn what whisky was.

"It's too late for running off. She's with Wally now."

"But why?"

Damn, I said to myself. Why was it the questions he asked had answers a half-dead horse would've understood? "You know why," I said.

"No, dammit."

He was talking slow and heavy, like it was taking him an hour inside his head to make the words come out.

"I don't. I really don't."

"Look at it this way," I said, pouring myself another and him a bit more. "You ain't near a man yet, Billy, and that's the plain truth of it. Even a girl like her knows that, young as she is. And she is young. Too damned young for what's happening, but what's there to say to that? It's nothing new under the sun, I can tell you. Man or boy, woman or girl, it's all the same. If you were all of a man she'd have gone with you, but you're not. For whatever reason, the Dutchman's given her to Wally. I wouldn't give him a dog because he'd kill it out of meanness, and I don't know why the Dutchman's doing what he's doing, but there it is."

Billy locked his hands around his jar, trembling a little.

I went on.

The only shape he was in was to listen.

"She's a girl who's got herself all tied up in the middle of grief and there's nobody can get her out. She's owned, and if Willem wants to give her to Wally or whoever, then that's up to him."

"She's trash," Billy says. "She's nothing but trash."

"Well, you could say that if you want. In most everyone's eyes she's trash, sure enough. She's trash to the married women in town, that's for sure. They hate her 'cause she's young and pretty and all the men in town would like a piece of her, including their husbands, especially their husbands. They haven't had something as good as that in bed for

159

How Do You Spell Beautiful?

years. And the single guys want her because she's got tits and legs and can walk. Your problem's Wally."

I thought he'd react to that, but it seemed like he was tied up inside himself, or maybe he was untying himself from some knot he'd made there. I couldn't tell.

"Wally doesn't want her, don't you see? What he wants is other men not to know he doesn't. Wally hates women."

Billy said nothing to what I was saying. He just stared at me through most of a bottle of whisky and nodded his head.

"But the big question is, why do you want her? We got the answers for everyone else's need, but how about yours? You say you love her, but what does that mean?"

"I'd marry her," Billy said. "I told her I would."

"What's that got to do with it? You'd marry her so what would happen? So she'd climb into bed with you and wrap her legs around you and say 'I love you, Billy, I love you' while you're doing what every other man in town wants to do too? Is that it? You want to own her just like the Dutchman does."

"Fuck you," said Billy. "Just fuck you. You're bad as the rest of them. I loved her and she just looked at me like I was nothing."

"Where were you when she looked at you like that? On your back in the dirt scrambling like a bug away from Wally's boot, that's where you were. Love, shit. You were just a big scared kid at that point and you still are. She had keeping alive to do when she looked at you, and she knew you weren't ever going to be any part of her future. You think holding her hand down by the river's going to save her? What do you think is going on down at Number 7?"

"What was I supposed to do?" said Billy. "What? Punch Wally? He'd of tore my head off if I did."

"That's right," I told him. "That's purely right."

"Just trash and shit is all she is. It's what they all are," he said, his chest moving heavy with the air he was pulling in. "I should've known."

"No," I said, knowing there was no explaining to him what he couldn't and maybe never would know. "No, they're not."

Billy got up then. As I watched him I expected him to fall right over, but he didn't. He gripped the table hard and pulled himself up so he was standing skinny as a stick on a pair of boots a size too big for him. I waited a minute but he didn't fall.

"Sit down," I said. "There's nowhere to go tonight. You can flop here if you like. There's a couch by the stove."

"Nope," said Billy. "I got to go."

160

Burning Wings

And as I sat there, he did.

He turned very slowly like drunks do and took a half-step, like he was walking over wet rocks, and then another, and finally, moving almost steady, he made it to the door and pushed it open. The door slammed behind him without as much as a thank you for a bottle of good whisky.

I heard his feet stumble down the steps and then he was gone into the night, home or wherever, but probably a ditch fifty feet down the road.

I took another drink and watched the moths burn themselves out on the coal-oil lamp. They'd been battering it all night but there were still a few left. You'd have thought they'd see all the dead bodies of the other moths, but they didn't, or if they did, they didn't care. What they wanted was the light and they'd die to get it, burning off their wings to try and climb inside anything that beautiful.

I thought I knew one clear thing. He wasn't going to Wally's bunkhouse.

He'd think he was going to go, but he wouldn't. If he could stay walking without falling, he'd start that way for what only he thought he knew, but he wouldn't go in. Not in there.

No, I figured he'd start that way but he wouldn't make it. He'd circle around and make a dozen false starts, but every time he'd find himself on the wrong path or the wrong piece of road. He'd keep doing that until he either fell into a ditch or into his own bed, where I figured he'd lie until he'd slept off whatever else besides the whisky he needed to sleep off.

When he was done that he'd be finished with it.

That's what it was to be someone like Billy or Wally or the sad girl who'd found herself with nowhere to go.

They were who they were. There was no changing any of it. The Dutchman had given the girl to Wally for whatever he owed him. She was a debt paid off. No different than a truck or a chainsaw to them.

Billy'd wake up in the bright morning and feel himself thick in the mouth and one day older, and he'd stare up at the ceiling or at the sun from a puddle of water and he'd say, "I loved her," and then, knowing what I knew of him, he'd cry for a while, and then he'd roll over and go back to sleep and that'd be it.

That's what I figured, sitting there looking into a jam jar with two fingers of whisky in it.

What else was I supposed to think? I'd got him dead drunk and sent him on his way. That was it, right?

161

How Do You Spell Beautiful?

~

Four in the morning with what's left of a bottle of rye's a place I'd been a lot of times in my life, but it wasn't somewhere I ever planned on being.

Drunk or sober, what I got is me and that's how I like it. You could say it gets lonely sometimes, and maybe it does, but lonely's just two hours from the sun rising. The worst is when you're with someone, and that's a lonely I can live without.

It seems to me you spend the first fifty years of your life chasing what a woman's got between her legs, and the next fifty running away from it.

I look back on the woman I had and I'm amazed at how I thought she was different. She wasn't. She was the same square inch of flesh. A man spends most of his life trying to own that flesh, and why?

What is it drives a man to near killing not just any other man who might want what he thinks he owns, but the woman whose flesh it is?

I know there's no answer to that but I wish there was. I'm damn sure women would like to know. Or maybe they're doing the same thing in reverse, trying to own what a man has hanging between his legs? They say they're not, but they keep climbing into bed with men they wouldn't spit on if they thought about it.

But climbing into bed with a man like Wally was something else. Anyone who'd lived as long as me knew what was wrong with him. It takes one time for any man and then he knows.

And Wally?

Wally was quiet crazy, the kind that's buried deep.

It was about four in the morning, or maybe closer to five, because I remember the false dawn and the first crows stirring in the spruce outside the door. I was sitting there at the table and I'd drunk the better part of the second bottle. A few trucks had wandered by in the night, their tires skittering across the gravel, with whoever driving them three sides to the wind.

It wasn't up to me to save the girl. Save her from what? From Wally?

There'd just be another after him, and maybe worse. And I'd tried with Billy. I tried to tell him what was what.

You've no idea how quiet it can be when a mill's shut down. You listen and there's something makes you uneasy. Then you know. It's quiet, that's what's bothering you.

When a mill's running three shifts, six days a week, all you hear is the sound of chains on chains, that clank, clank, clank, and the screech and whine of metal scraping metal in the belts. The saws are eating their way through timber and you get used to it until finally you think

162

Burning Wings

that's all there is, the scream of saws and chains banging.

I got up then and stepped outside and looked down at the mill. The burner was still hot. The cleanup crew had poured chips and bark and dust till midnight. Sparks were twisting out of the high cone of the burner, rising into the night like a snake in the clouds.

There's nothing more crazy beautiful than that.

Staring down at it I thought of Billy.

I was drunk you understand, drunk and tired, and I should've been long gone to bed, but I thought of the kid and his maybe blundering into the swamp down by the mill.

I'd interfered with him, you see. I'd got him drunk and I'd yapped at him like some fool who thought he knew every answer there was.

I'd stepped in the way of his life is what I'd done, and I knew, standing there drunk looking at that burner pour its fire into the night, that I'd tried to turn him from where he was going, and if I had, then I was part of it now.

It's the sort of thing you think when it's almost day and you've spent the night staring at yourself through a bottle.

I knew where I thought he wasn't, and I hoped I was right.

I did up my shirt, pulled on my boots, and started down the hill to where Wally's bunkhouse was. Number 7, just at the crook of the road where it bends toward the tracks and the mill beyond it. It sits off by itself with its back end on pilings at the edge of the swamp. Dead trees and still water.

I could see a light or two in a cabin or a shack, and knew whoever was sitting by those lights was trying to stop the night from eating him. Guys who couldn't find their lives.

The bunkhouses were mostly dark as I went by. Wally's truck was in the ditch by Number 3. There was no one in it. The door was hanging open and a shirt was thrown like a rag across the seat.

It was Wally's.

I took a look at it, half expecting blood, but it was clean. I kept on going. I knew there'd be light in Number 7 and there was.

The door was closed. Wally'd hung blankets over most of the windows, but one or two had torn off their nails and light was glimmering out from lamps he'd lighted. Greasy light is what I thought, from lamps whose chimneys weren't too clean.

I stood in the road for a few minutes. I knew what he had in there and I wanted no part of it.

I listened for a while. The light was coming on over the eastern range. I couldn't hear a thing. You'd of thought the place was deserted

How Do You Spell Beautiful?

except for the thin light coming through those windows. A crow rose up from a dry snag in the swamp and made a cry. A yearling's what I thought. The older ones stay buried in their sleep. They know enough to wait for day.

But there was no stopping on the road. I couldn't just turn round and head back up to where my bed was. It was Billy who'd drawn me down and the least I could do was see if he was there. What I thought I'd do if I found him in that place I didn't know.

You see what happens to you?

The only thing there was Wally.

The room was empty except for a bunk at the back end and some tables and chairs for playing cards. There were bottles all around. The blanket Wally'd hung for what privacy the men had needed was lying on the floor. I went down to the bunk and looked at it. It smelled of men, the sheet all wet with what they'd left.

Her shoes were sitting underneath the bed, still shining. Her dress was folded on a chair by the far wall. I remember thinking Billy wouldn't have wanted her in those.

I covered Wally with a blanket and went to wake up Simard.

As I walked into the night I knew there'd be two fresh Regina corporals up from Clearwater on the morning train. They'd take Wally out. Simard would have him in the cooler at the mill. Number 7 would be all cleaned up by then.

I didn't know what Simard would say when the police arrived.

One thing for sure, he wouldn't mention Billy and the girl.

And there wasn't anyone who cared for Wally anyway. The Dutchman would keep his mouth shut.

Willem.

There were other girls where she came from. Kamloops was only a hard ride away. The corporals would be around for the day and then they'd leave, just like they always did when there was trouble. A question or two, a shrug, and then they'd go. No one troubled much about things in the north.

There'd be people wondering what exactly happened, but I knew. Those kids would catch a ride on a long freight passing through. There were two every night, and the engines had to crawl to hold the grade at the crossing.

It'd be easy enough.

They'd leave that way. Billy'd be smart enough not to steal a pickup. They'd track him down for that. Billy'd come on a freight two years before from Edmonton. He knew how to do it. Once down in

Burning Wings

Kamloops there were twenty ways to go to disappear.

Who knew how long they'd last? They were both of them kids and running too, afraid the law would follow them. The Kootenays maybe, or out on the prairie, Alberta or Saskatchewan.

Yes, that's where they'd go. A kid like Billy'd find some harvest job and she could always work in some cafe.

What I think of is their going. I can see them riding south into the wind, the girl wearing whatever Billy'd stolen for her, and Billy in those boots one size too big. I can see the two of them flying in the night like they'd put wings on grief, their backs against the steel.

Burning wings.

They'd be holding each other and staring at whatever life they thought they had, the morning coming on, high clouds and crows and the first light burning cold on the eastern range.

Sing Low

It's past midnight, the last light of the moon sliding off the foothills. This day of sleep is long over and now it's dark, the thin road winding as we ride the shadows. I'm with him, going into night.

I look at those tight hands gripping the wheel, his face above them a kind of mask hanging off the skull, with eyes inside made of the palest blue. Above is his red hair combed back slick, and his white white skin that burns in any kind of sun.

He's like he was from the beginning, still trying to find a way out of whatever he believes he's in, convinced in the same way animals are, that if they walk around the edge of a field enough times they'll find the fence has fallen down somewhere.

It's been years now and he still keeps doing it, his mouth making that same noise, a kind of melting cry, as if out there somewhere was a place different from where he is.

His pale skin's right for this, I think. It's best only at night, for that's when it shines. In the day the sun eats it, pulls the thin blue veins out of him like threads with blood in them. Pulls them out and drains them onto the hard ground.

Behind us in the back seat are the women he stopped the car for. It was outside Crow's Nest Pass, just before the highway tilted and everything became one long run to the prairie, down through the

Sing Low

foothill country where our father came from long before the war, and into the plains, the true prairie where nothing grows but sky. I know why he stopped for them, know he thinks the one with the yellow boots is the one he dreamed.

"She will be beautiful," is what he said down by the creek when I found him wandering alone. "I dreamed her when I was walking out the night. She filled the whole world. The leaves and branches, even the water was full of her."

He said.

"It'll be like the last time," is what I said, feeling the hour hold me like a fist around a beak.

"No, it won't."

"Goddam you, Tom."

He laughed then, a kind of snicker, his mouth only opening at the corner, as if he was afraid of what might come out. His narrow laugh, a noise that gathered me into him just as it always did and does. He knew I'd go even as I said I wouldn't. Looking at him I knew nothing was changed, nothing at all.

"There's a woman out there," he told me. "I dreamed her. I saw her dancing in my mind. There's something about her shines."

The car rolls and I keep hoping it isn't either of these that shines, even as I know if it isn't them, all this will still end with him gone wrong, and me having to help.

They're not who I'd have stopped for.

Had it been me there would've been no stopping. Had it been me there wouldn't have been a going at all. I'd have stayed by that creek. I'd have held him if I could.

"It's her yellow boots," he said, when I asked him why. "I like the way they shine. It's like I saw them long before I was here. She's the one. I know it. You do too."

They're all that shine on her, is what I think.

She's back there holding onto the other woman, who's staring out the window. This other one's barely a woman. Yellow Boots is what I'm calling the shining one and she's no longer young. Her name, as she's told us, is Alibet.

The young one who's being held is Matilda, though Matilda hasn't told us that. She's said nothing since she was helped into the car by Alibet with the yellow boots. Matilda, the young one, is wrapped in the blankets I was smart enough to bring, two red Bay blankets from the back cupboard a night and a half away from where we are.

The first of winter is all around us with that same hard small snow

How Do You Spell Beautiful?

that's more sand than snow. It cuts the windshield before all our eyes. Yes, it's her rubber boots made him stop and now we have them in here with us. Now there are four of us going to wherever it is my brother thinks we're going. If he'd looked above those yellow boots he'd have seen enough to keep us going without them, but he's always been like this since I have known him in this lifetime.

Yellow Boots.

She's holding more than a woman in her arms. She's holding woe. It's Matilda, the young one who's said nothing, who's been lying back there with her eyes wide open. Her face tells what she won't say.

Someone, somewhere, has worked it over good with at least a pair of fists, if not boots, cut as it is, although a fist can cut if there are rings on the fingers. So maybe not boots then, maybe only with fists and rings.

She's in bad shape is Matilda.

Yellow Boots holds her, crooning a song I can't make out the words for. I've decided now the song is not made out of words but is only sound made just to soothe her. It's like she's a child who's imagined something terrible in the night, something not there, come out of a closet or the bush. My brother hums with her. He learns the song as it goes, making it up along with her. The one I call Yellow Boots hears him, thinks she knows he's doing what he can.

I only listen. I don't know what it's about, don't know the words, the sounds.

What I've done is gone along with him. I swear to myself as I stare out the cracked windshield of his red Dodge Dart, this time's the last. After this there'll be no more. I know my brother believes otherwise. He believes we're here because of what he dreamed. That's why he pushes harder at it, almost as if he can keep ahead of time by moving fast.

He's convinced.

The way he understands it has to do with what he calls relativity. He thinks he can go and return younger than he is. He says it's like being in a spaceship. I've heard him talk about this and I've always listened, but I don't argue about it any more. There's nothing left to fight about. It's what he means when he says, "It's in the going, the way she shines."

I don't know what he means.

It just happens.

Whatever's going on in the back seat I don't want to know. I turn to my brother and I ask him what he thinks we should do. He slides at me that fish-like sideways look he makes and drops his eyelids, that slow grin with the snicker behind it almost coming out, as if to say: You see, you see? I told you we would find her.

Sing Low

And what he doesn't say, but what I know, is he thinks he's found one for me. Mine will be Matilda, the young one. But she isn't shining, not like Yellow Boots.

I feel only the old rage at who he is and has always been. His idea that he can maintain anything as impossible as what is going on. He's always been like this, allowing things to happen to him as a stick does in a river, and how people trust him for that, believing he's the river when he's not and is only the stick.

I've watched the river. I know.

What I don't know is what is happening behind me, and it's because I'm afraid to know, and my brother doesn't need to know what is happening behind him because he thinks he already knows.

And this is what I get when I do this, what I've always got each time I've gone with him, chance getting us deep into it as if we were at the cross of two lines drawn on a page and instead of leaving that point, taking it with us, pulling the moment forward or backward, without wanting, space and time travelling with us, as these hills are now, or the moon is as it's seen when you're a child, travelling along with you so no matter when you look it's always there, that ghost-light in tall trees, face-white, the hard flat moon like a round knife cutting there.

And behind me is the moaning of Matilda, her sound having built slowly and steadily, ringed by Yellow Boots and my brother's song, their murmuring together circling her moans and holding them in the air as if with hands, that soft steady song going low, their voices without words just singing low. And I don't want to know, but ask them anyway, sending my question out at both of them, sending it out.

"She's got a child in her, hasn't she?" I say. "Is that what it is? Is that why she's moaning?"

"Yes," my brother says.

"Jesus, Tom," I say.

"It's ones like you have done it," the one called Yellow Boots says from behind me. "Men like you."

"Oh no," my brother says and then he laughs.

"Look at her cut up," she says.

"Not men like us," Tom says. "It's not us who've done this. We're the ones found you."

And then, "It's your yellow boots. They make you shine."

"What?" she says to that.

There's a silence then except for Matilda's moan, smooth and hollow rising from her belly to her cut lips.

"I'll find a place," my brother says.

How Do You Spell Beautiful?

He reaches out with his right hand and lays it on my shoulder. I shake it off. He puts it back on. He's jumpy, I can tell. This is not like the other times, not with two of them, and one of them having a child.

"You'll have to do it," he says. "You're the one who can."

Why not you, I say to myself, knowing he can't but wanting to know why.

"She can't and I can't. It's you," he says. "It's always been you. You know that."

~

It's right in the centre of night he stops, the car suddenly quiet on the side of the highway. We've talked and talked. Yellow Boots has agreed with him.

I stare into the car. My brother is sitting behind the wheel, still holding onto it with his thin hands and staring out straight ahead as if we were still going, still moving forward even as we're not. The road is riding him. The one called Yellow Boots is in the back seat. I can't see Matilda but she's there, resting her head on Yellow Boots's chest.

I open the back door on the side away from the highway, the snow draining down out of the dark sky framing the opening so before me is pale light and behind me is the cold and dark, the road-hard ice below.

Yellow Boots is holding Matilda's hands above her body. They're grey moths fluttering in the air. Matilda has one leg over the front seat and she starts to kick with it. My brother grabs her ankle and holds it, bending her at the knee. The other leg's braced hard against the frame. Her belly's barely swollen.

The car door's open to the night. Yellow Boots is holding her wrists and Matilda's making her sounds, and I am kneeling on the hard shoulder of the highway, not knowing what it is I will precisely do, but ready to do it when it's time.

Why not him or her, I think, but already know there's no answer to that, just as there's no answer for why it's me.

Except it is. It's me to do it.

Behind me, down the falling hills of withered cactus and wild rose bushes and bunch grass cut by snow is the Old Man River. It's a cold mountain river, glacial, a hard blue come down from the high Rockies. My brother sits behind the wheel, his teeth slowly eating a stick he's pushed into his mouth, a thin white spear of wood he is chewing into nothing, swallowing the bits of pulp and dust. His foot is tapping on the gas pedal as he hums, the motor rising and falling. He holds Matilda's ankle. He's crooning to her leg and I am waiting.

Sing Low

This is what is happening, is what must always happen when my brother goes and I go with him, a something he can no more avoid than he could avoid himself in a room made entirely out of mirrors.

I've given up trying to let whoever else is here do something with it, this moment I know as chance and he knows and accepts as given, this moment when we've floated into the centre of something out of our control.

That stick, that river.

And it's of course me who must do the doing, and what I'm thinking on my knees with the snow cutting my back is why he knows it will be me and not him, how sure in the world he is that he knows it will be me.

This now, I think, and what later?

This is the question I want answered on the cold highway beside my brother's slant-six red Dodge Dart with the one broken headlight. This is what I want to know above the valley of the Old Man River as I help the young one called Matilda push her half-made child into my hands as she cries out.

I wait and watch the mouth between her legs open and throw out what it has held for months inside her. It comes out slow and wet. And now I hold it. This small, this half-jelled thing I hold in my cupped hands, this thing even as I look at it still alive, if only for a moment, made out of cartilage and blood that is not yet fully human, a thing that cannot breathe or see or do anything.

I hold it and I watch it die.

I do not look at my brother. I know he's chewing his stick and it's almost gone. And I don't look at Yellow Boots. She hasn't moved from where she sits, holding Matilda's head on her chest. She's lowered Matilda's hands down out of the air and crossed them on Matilda's breasts. Yellow Boots's hands are holding that cut face, cupping it with her palms, the fingers stroking the broken skin where whoever it was hours before beat her and caused what I have lifted from between Matilda's throttled legs.

I have taken off my shirt and placed this thing in it, there being nothing else to hold it. I wait for the blood to stop, which takes what seems a long time, thin clots and mucous, and then I clean her with the cuffs of my shirt and the snow from the side of the road. I see her closing around herself, the opening becoming smaller, the vent closing up as a door does when it closes, leaving only an entrance where there was an exit before.

"The hell with you," I say out of the cold night.

He says nothing, only chews.

How Do You Spell Beautiful?

I say, "It's dead."

I take the corners of my shirt and I pull them together and knot them down hard, until all I have is a small round sack with a half-child in it with its blood and membranes around it. The rest of the shirt makes what is a long tail. I say nothing more. I hear my brother's slow chewing and Yellow Boots singing, and then I get up and go down the hills to the river, silver far away.

I can think of nothing else to do with what dangles from my hand. To leave it on the side of the road for the magpies and crows is not what I can do. This is not an animal who's stumbled into the travelling light only to find a hard death under the wheels. It's a human thing I carry through the hills, down through the dust and snow and cactus to the bank of the Old Man River where I stand, the snow cutting skin on my bare chest.

I hold it here, her blood and her child's blood all over my hands. I hold it here and say nothing, not having anything to say, only swing it around and around my head in great wide flying arcs until I suddenly let go, watching it lift into the night and then descend out of it, the distant splash of it in the hard smooth running water, my shirt and its frail cargo being borne away east into the plains. And I imagine as it goes a great strong rainbow trout rising out of the deep pools and currents below, lifting its silver body with its flecks of blue and red upon it, up out of the heaving water and taking in its great jaws that bound sack and swallowing it whole, the child sliding down the warm red gullet past the gills and back into life, becoming even as it slides, the muscle and blood and bone of the fish, that long sweet whisper of colour carrying it back to where it came from in the deep.

I kneel among stones and mud and clean my hands in the glacial cold. The blood circles my fingers and drifts away on top of the water, drifts away like oil. In the moon there are cold rainbows.

It's not my blood. It's hers.

I look up the long rise of prairie to those lights blinkering in snow where he waits, hard-hunched and tapping high above. Wolf willow and stunted saskatoons bend under snow, their thin stick limbs like bones. There's where I'll be climbing, holding nothing in my hands but her lost blood.

～

I shiver as my brother turns the car around in a hard sharp spurring of frozen gravel and heads it back toward the mountains out of which we came. Behind us the sun will be rising soon, and Matilda

Sing Low

is wrapped in the one clean blanket on the back seat, awake and smoking the cigarette I've lighted for her. I'm sitting where Yellow Boots sat, and Matilda's head is in my lap.

We are two here and my brother in front with the one he dreamed, his one white hand on the wheel moving us back. There is the smell of woman and woman's blood all around me. Matilda is smoking, staring straight up into the roof, where the felt is ripped. Her eyes are held there as if they were two small animals trying to find a place they can live in far from the world. She has only looked at me once since she threw out her dead child, and she said to me when her pale eyes caught me looking back, "You saw me," and I said nothing, only nodded yes.

I have one arm on my leg and the other rests across Matilda's high breasts. Her head presses into me. She's staring up. In front of me Yellow Boots is sitting next to my brother, his arm around her shoulders, the hand hanging down in front where I can't see it but know it is upon her breast, his fingers inside her shirt holding onto her, stroking her nipple. I don't know where her hands are. Her head is tilted against him, at rest in the corner of his long neck, listening to him tell her of the house he's taking her to and what it will be like there, him and her together as he dreamed it. They are drinking from his bottle of whisky.

"It's in a valley," I hear him saying. "It's like a garden it's so beautiful. There's fruit trees, apple and peach and cherry, and a huge garden where anything you throw into it grows. Close your eyes," he says, "and you can dream it like I say. A green, green place with sprinklers going and swallows in the evening and a chicken house with Barred Rocks sleeping. Can you see it?"

"Yes," says Yellow Boots.

I don't want to think about it. How does he know anything? What garden? Where?

I have that trout in my mind. He's settled in the current, his gills moving in and out like curved silver saucers, his belly resting heavy on the gravel. Matilda's child is there.

I look away from his words. I don't listen any more. I look down instead, all the time thinking this will be all, this will be all there is.

I have cleaned up Matilda, even her face, so what at first looked like deep cuts are now only shallow ones, the blue markings rising in her skin, swelling her eyes and her jaw. She is still looking up at that hole in the roof. I take the cigarette from her and smoke it for a moment before returning it to her mouth, where it sits burning slowly in her lips. She drags on it, exhales, the smoke rising around us. I look down

How Do You Spell Beautiful?

at her eyes that aren't looking at me, and she says to me quietly, "Is that true?" she says. "Will we be there too in that beautiful place?"

I only look at her.

"Yes," my brother says from the front seat, above the murmured sounds of Yellow Boots's song.

That's when Matilda looks at me the second time. "You won't hurt me, will you?"

"No," I say.

"Was I your dream, like Alibet was your brother's?"

Before I can answer, my brother rolls his head around his shoulders as if he's pulling snakes from his muscles, his hair brushing Yellow Boots's brown cheek, and says, "I dreamed you all. I dreamed you and Alibet here, and I dreamed my brother too. I dreamed us all together."

～

"This's perfect," Tom says.

When none of us says anything, he says, "We'll stay here for the day and sleep. Tonight we'll drive to the valley."

He has brought his bag from the trunk of the car, the one I put there, and he's laid it on the floor beside his chair. He and Yellow Boots are sitting at the table in front of the window that looks out on the thick trees at the end of the parking lot of The Foothills Motel. It's the end cabin, detached from the others.

We're the only car here. The two of them are sitting across from each other, the bag beside him.

"It's nice," Matilda says in her small voice. "It's a nice room."

She's sitting on the couch leaning into me. I have my arm around her. On the coffee table is what remains of the bread and cheese and sausage I brought from home. The TV is on. The Saturday morning cartoons. It's a roadrunner cartoon and Wile E. Coyote is busy falling off cliffs like he always does. "I love cartoons," Matilda says. "I just love them."

We will return with these, I say to myself. We've left the child behind us in the river. We've gone through the night and now it's day and we'll rest here and then we'll go on. Matilda is here beside me, the one I have delivered, though I didn't know I would until I did, and Yellow Boots is with him. She will be okay with him. He's taken me down this road and found what he said would be here, and now we are returning. I've done what I was supposed to do in this, just as I've always done with him. He is there and I am here. Matilda is watching the cartoon and I'm watching him.

174

Sing Low

Next we'll have a drink. That's how it begins.

As I think this, Tom opens his bag and takes out three bottles of whisky and then he reaches back down into it and takes out his hunting knife.

Yes.

I take my shirt with the child wrapped in it and I put it in my mind. I stand again by the river and I see the rainbow hanging in the current, his tail a great high wedge moving back and forth as he holds himself in the driving water. He's waiting for me to place my cargo in the river.

Then the rainbow goes and I am back, the cold moon and the cactus left somewhere.

My brother lays the knife beside the bottles on the table between him and Yellow Boots.

"So," my brother says, "you and Matilda take the bedroom and we'll make do in here. Okay?" As he says this he gets up and brings a bottle over to me. I take it out of his hand and he grins his narrow grin at me. His face is a shadow in wolf willow.

He goes back to the table, unscrews a bottle, and takes a long drink from it, his head tilted back so I can see his thin neck and his throat moving up and down as he swallows. He takes the bottle away from his mouth and holds it out to Yellow Boots. She takes it and has a long drink too.

"Have some more," he says, so she does.

It's all unwinding, is what it is.

Yellow Boots looks straight at him as she drinks. I wonder what she's seeing as she looks at him, but I don't ask.

I know what I would see.

There's something moving now. He's drumming his fingers and looking right back at her. His fingers are hammering away on the table and he looks at her and says, "Is that okay with you?"

"What?"

"Them in there and us out here?"

"I guess," she says. Her voice is slurred now. Whisky-wrecked, all throat and whispers. She throws her head back and wipes at her hair with her hands. I've seen that shaking, that wild throwing of the hair and hands.

I hold onto Matilda and I'm thinking maybe it will be all right this time. Maybe Alibet with the yellow boots is the right one after all these years.

It's like everything in this room is a kind of movie. Me, Matilda, him, and Yellow Boots. We're all in a picture and the picture is unwinding, sometimes fast and sometimes slow.

175

How Do You Spell Beautiful?

"Well," says Yellow Boots, "if you think that's the way it should be, then I guess that's the way it should be." She laughs. "This is your dream, so I guess you can arrange it how you want."

Oh yes, her voice is going gone.

"Right," he says, half snicker like a scissor in spare cloth. "Oh, you're the shining one. I knew that when I saw you on the highway there. I knew it sure as I've known anything all my life. Isn't she the shining one?" he says to me.

Yellow Boots just laughs. Her hair is all over her face and she tries to wipe it away again, her hand mostly missing, so the hair hangs smeared on her cheek. She takes another long drink, her throat pumping.

"Did you really dream us all?" Matilda asks. She looks slow into my eyes. "Did he?"

"You guys go on," my brother says.

"I want to watch the end of this," says Matilda. "Maybe Wile E. Coyote will beat the roadrunner this time."

"He never does," I say.

"But maybe he will," she says. "You never know. Maybe this is the last roadrunner cartoon. Maybe this is the one where they let Wile E. Coyote catch him forever."

"It's only a cartoon," I say. "It's not like it's real."

"You watch this one," Yellow Boots says, "and then you go with him to the other room." She says this to her, but she never takes her eyes off my brother's face. She never lets go and neither does he.

What does she see there? What is it in that pale skin with the red hair that she sees?

Maybe she's as crazy as him.

Maybe.

Matilda squeezes my leg and goes on watching the cartoon. I watch it with her. Wile E. Coyote is on the top of a mountain and he has a huge rock he's pushed there, with dynamite underneath it. When roadrunner goes by I know he'll set off the dynamite, and instead of blowing up the rock and dropping it on the roadrunner, it'll drop on him. It always does. That's the story. It's the same one every time.

I watch the cartoon and wait for it to end, but I'm also watching my brother and Yellow Boots. My brother has picked up his knife. He's asking Yellow Boots if she wants to see something he can do with it.

"Tom," I say.

But he doesn't answer. I watch him lay his hand out on the table and spread his fingers in front of Yellow Boots. Then he takes the knife in

Sing Low

his other hand and starts raising it and lowering it. Each time it comes down, it comes down in the space between his fingers, as if the blade was afraid to touch his skin, one space at a time, and each time he gets to the end where the little finger is, he starts again, each time a little faster, so soon he's going fast, the blade of the knife a silver thread ticking on the table top. All the time he's doing it he doesn't move his eyes from Yellow Boots's face.

"See that," he says. "I bet you can't do that."

"What's he doing?" asks Matilda. The sound of the knife tickety-ticking on the table has drawn her away from the cartoon. It's like a clock in the night, counting hard the time.

"Why don't you two go into the other room?" my brother says. He says that and he never misses a beat of the knife. Yellow Boots is watching the knife go. It's like she can't take her eyes off it. They flick a little each time the point of the knife touches between his fingers. "Isn't that something," he says, and starts his laugh. "I bet you can't do that."

"I don't know," says Yellow Boots. She says it slowly so I barely hear the words. "I never tried anything like that."

"Go to the other room," he says, flat and hard and quick. "You and Matilda. Leave us here in this one."

"Is it going to be okay?" Matilda asks.

"You go," Yellow Boots says. She's looking at the knife my brother's holding. "It's okay, for Christ's sake. We're just fooling around."

But her head doesn't move.

"C'mon," Matilda whispers to me.

I get up off the couch and then I help Matilda up and we go together toward the other room. As we go Matilda says, "I've got to go to the bathroom first."

"Are you going to be okay?"

"Yes," she says.

I go into the bedroom and sit on the edge of the bed with my face looking out through the door at my brother and Yellow Boots sitting at the table by the window. He has started humming some song only he knows, singing low.

He has taken her one hand and laid it flat and he's moving the knife slowly between her fingers, tick, tick, tick. As he does this I feel my own hand moving on the bedspread. I look down at it and watch it move as it traces out the shapes of the flowers in the cloth. My fingers go around the blossoms. They are like yellow clouds floating there.

"Like that," I hear my brother say. Yellow Boots doesn't say anything. I see her take the knife from my brother and hold it in her

How Do You Spell Beautiful?

free hand. Her other hand is still splayed out on the table. My brother has that hand by the wrist and he's pressing it down. His blue eyes are flickering. I know they are even if I can't see them.

I feel like this is all I can take. "This is it," I say out loud.

Matilda comes in then and closes the door behind her. "I don't feel so good," she says.

I get up and help her onto the bed. I lay her down.

"You won't hurt me, will you?"

"No," I say.

She smiles then and I help her get her clothes off, everything except her underwear, which looks padded with a towel. I look at her breasts. "It's okay," she says. "You've seen me anyway." Then she says, "Do you like them?" I pull the yellow-flowered bedspread back and then the sheets, and I help her under the covers. She looks up at me. "You too," she says.

"In a second," I say. I go back into the other room and pick up the bottle by the couch. I look at my brother and Yellow Boots. They are both drunk, but she is drunker than him. She doesn't think she is, but she is. One bottle is beside them, empty, and he is opening another. She is on the couch now with her dress up around her. Her head is lying back. She is wearing nothing underneath her dress. Her panties are on the coffee table. He looks at me then, his face like a ferret. It's a weasel-look, there and gone.

He laughs. He knows I won't do anything.

I turn and head back into the bedroom with the bottle. I close the door behind me. There's nothing I can do with him. There never was, there isn't now.

"You want some?" I ask Matilda. I don't know what else to do, what else to say. "This, I mean."

"Maybe just a little one," she says.

I open the bottle, take a drink and then give it to her.

She drinks a little and then takes it away from her mouth. "You too," she says. "Take off your clothes too. But first give me a cigarette."

So I do. I light her one and put the package and the matches on the table by the bed.

"Your body's nice," she says.

I look down at myself. It's like I'm seeing myself for the first time. My whole body just kind of drops away below me down to my feet, which are far away.

Matilda smiles, shy now.

I don't say anything. When I'm in bed beside her she gives me back

Sing Low

the bottle. We lie there on our backs not touching each other as I take another drink. She hands me the cigarette.

"Your brother's strange," she says. "Did he really dream Alibet and me?"

"I don't know," I say. "He says he did. It's what he always says."

"I like you better," she says.

She puts her hand on my arm then and she says, "You saw me, didn't you?"

"Yes," I say.

"I saw you too now." When I don't say anything, she says, "I never had a baby before."

"It wasn't a real baby," I say. "It was only partly."

"I know," she says, and we're both quiet for a while.

"What did you do with it?" she asks.

"I put it in the river that was there. The Old Man River. I put it back into the waters. It came out of you and I put it back into the same kind of place. A rainbow has it now."

"That's beautiful," she says.

I say nothing.

"What was it?"

"You couldn't tell."

I look at her then. She's got the spread pulled up under her breasts so they're there outside the covers and she's above them staring at the ceiling. When I look, she looks at me. "Is it really beautiful where we're going?" she asks. "Is it like your brother says?"

"Yes," I say. "It's like that if you want it to be."

"With apple trees and peach trees and everything?"

"It's winter now, but yes," I say. "You sleep. You've had a night of it. Sleep and then when you wake it'll be tonight and we'll be going again." I take her hand.

"I don't know if Alibet will like a place like that," she says. "But I will. It's like a place I've always dreamed."

"She might not be here anyway," I say. "She might leave."

"Today?"

"Maybe," I say. "It's what they do when they're with him. They go."

"I should say goodbye," she says.

"No," I say. "Not now."

We're quiet for a while. I take another drink and so does Matilda, and then I put the cigarette out in the ashtray by the bed.

"I can't do anything," Matilda says. "I still hurt. But we could do something if you want."

How Do You Spell Beautiful?

She puts her hand on me.

I say, "Later. Maybe later."

"Is Alibet okay, do you think?"

"Don't worry about her," I say.

"Your brother's different than you, isn't he?"

"Forget that now."

"Okay," Matilda says, and she closes her eyes. "Will you be here when I wake up?"

"Go to sleep," I say.

She curls toward me then and I put my hand on her hip. She still has her hand on me, but it's like there's nothing there.

"It's gone to sleep," she says.

"You too. You sleep too."

It'll be okay, I think to myself. I take a drink and look down at Matilda as she starts to sleep. Her hand is still on me. It is soft and still.

They're just fooling around out there is what they're doing, I think. That's all he ever does is fool around. What he's always done. Him and that knife. But maybe not this time. Maybe it's different this time. There was the baby. Surely that's enough.

I lie there in the bed with Matilda sleeping and I think that over and over. It'll be okay, that's what it'll be. Okay, I say to myself. I have done this much but there's no more. I'm here with him and this's as far as it goes.

There's Matilda now. Matilda is going to be with me.

Yellow Boots will be gone.

When we get back and Matilda's better, she and I will leave and go somewhere far away. Australia maybe, or North Dakota.

She is beautiful, I think.

I feel her hand on me and I look at the door. I try to see through it but I can't. I stay in bed, watching and listening. Matilda is beside me.

Yellow Boots is his shining one, I think.

You stay in there, he says. That's what he says to me. But he'll not have this one. Not Matilda. Not after the rainbow. Not after the rising. There was the river and the child. That has made this different. It's what I know.

I'll lie here and I will not sleep. I'll stay awake and keep on watching and listening. Yellow Boots is gone even if she knows it or not. He is doing it to her is what he is. Behind the door with his red hair hanging down upon his face and his laugh.

180

Ned Coker's Dream

He chose to bury what dreams he had, Ned Coker, and I for one would not take that away from him, would not dig them up myself nor ask him to do it, for what is buried is buried and that is an end to it. I know, for I have buried some dreams of my own, put them down under in the place where certain dreams must go, as each of us has in our time. It is only here in the hills I remember, these things that rise into the mind, watching as I am the whiplash that is my daughter weave thin through the brush on the path ahead of me, her dark hair flowing to her shoulders, thick in the sun.

It is not that Ned Coker had all that many dreams in the first place. There are those who start out in this world with only a few to their name, just as there are those who have many. Ned Coker was not one of those with many. It was as it was with all his family. They were, as my mother said, small potatoes and few to the hill, and that meant in my mother's terms not the number of them in the family, for they were as many and varied as Eveline Jean Coker could make, but rather they were in her eyes a stunted runted clan whose future was only as good as their past, and that to my mother was a worthless one.

The Cokers come from poor seed she would say, though I felt it was Eveline Jean Coker's eggs that were as much at fault as the seed that

How Do You Spell Beautiful?

was poured into her. You could say they were a dreamless people and that was true of most of them, but not all. Not Ned anyway, who was made as they all were, small and quick as if they'd been half-starved, though I knew they weren't. Ned was as the rest though he was different. At least to me.

Where are we in the middle of things? That's what I ask myself, my daughter ahead of me knowing somehow where we are going, that nowhere clear to her in this the last year of her childhood. Where is there ever a place where things can be explained? I knew Ned Coker when he was only a boy not more than five feet high, though he was already fourteen years old. I knew because I was twelve years old myself, just a slip of a girl, and when you are that age you know the ages of everyone who is also a child.

It was to the Coker's place I'd go whenever I had the chance. To play or just to be, and if the truth be known it was mostly the being I wanted. The Cokers were different from everyone else I knew, not that I knew all that many people. What child does? A child's world is bound by a few square yards of earth, a street, a hill, a corner in a town, a place that is within a place, though the child does not know that when she is a child. She does not know she pushes at the margins of that small place each hour and day and year as she grows, making it larger as her own need demands, another yard, a bit of earth, a stone.

When I discovered the Cokers my life changed. Perhaps it would have anyway. A child's life changes no matter what or who she knows. It was just that they all of them held a clarity for me, from Eveline Jean Coker with her dark black hair and her silver earrings that made a small impossible music whenever she turned her head, right through to Ned, who was not the youngest of them at all but was the special one. Ned was, as Eveline Jean Coker said I don't know how many times, the best of the last. I'm near to being done, she'd say to whoever happened to be there when she said it. This one here, and she'd point at Ned or rumple his thin golden hair, which touch Ned loved more than even the wind's touch, is the best child I ever brought into this world. And then she'd laugh out loud and give Ned a push if he was close enough and say, Isn't that right, Ned Coker? And Ned would grin, the best of the last.

So that is where I should start because that is where I first knew him, in the Coker yard, which was full of broken machines, cars and bits and pieces of trucks and washing machines, huge wooden crates and cardboard boxes with their tops torn off, piles of lumber and tires and cans full of rusted nails and bolts, and everything else a child could love

Ned Coker's Dream

in a world that was more ordered than not, or at least was in my case, where home was a yard covered in grass and where there were flower beds with flowers arranged according to their colours, types, and sizes. A place where my mother had constructed a certain world that obeyed her in everything. I thought as a child even the trees leafed out when she ordered them to.

But at the Coker's everything found its place as best it could. I have always thought of it as a place that was somehow akin to what the real world is and was and will be, a kind of glorious chaos with everything in it being born and dying, growing and shrinking all at the same time. Things came and went at the Coker place. Things accumulated of their own wild will and just as easily disappeared into oblivion never to be seen again. One day there would be an old woodstove leaning precariously against the front steps of their house, and the next day it would be gone, only to be replaced with three forty-five gallon drums with bullet holes in them. A tree would grow inside the body of a car, sending its crazed branches out through the broken windows to the sun, or cucumbers and melons would appear from between the porch planks, with leaves bigger than my head and fruit even bigger than that. And no one seemed to notice that they did, just as no one of the nine Cokers who were still at home noticed the many men who came and went over the months and years. They were the uncles, according to Eveline Jean Coker, and were accepted as such. Each one brought with him when he came a desolate vehicle piled high or low with more of the same things that were already there in plenitude, and as they left they left behind some of it and took other away.

And sometimes they left their seed for Eveline Jean Coker to mix with her eggs and grow into another child. Each time she began a child it was with a strong and powerful will, throwing it out in its time into what could only be called a tribe. Their house and yard was I believe a kind of cornucopia of a child's dreams. All was ranged around them, the flotsam and jetsam of a world that didn't know what it had and didn't care where it ended up.

I would go up to the Coker's whenever I had the chance to slip away from the narrow eye of my mother, who watched over me as only her kind of mother could. I was her only daughter, her youngest, and she feared me in a way she never did my brothers. What that fear was I never knew until I was much older, but I knew it was there. My father would tell her to let me go when I'd ask. Nan, he would say, let the child go. She's only a few more years of being a child. Let her have that. God knows it'll end soon enough. And he'd smile at me and put his arm

How Do You Spell Beautiful?

around my mother and give her a kind of hug that meant all is well.

My mother would shake him off and say, That's exactly what I think too, and it's exactly that which makes me want her not to go traipsing off up to that place where anything can happen and usually does.

Now Nan, he would say, and while he was saying it he'd give me a look that said, Get going while I've got her occupied, as if she was an alien force he had to surround and hold. And I would. I would slide out of the kitchen or off the back porch and slip through the caragana hedge and be gone as fast as I could go down the alley to where it ended and the trail up the side of the hill began. I never took the road.

Somehow it didn't seem right to go that way. It was always better through the brush on the hard-packed trail that the Coker children had worn smooth over the years as they came and went to town. No Coker child ever thought of travelling in a straight line when there was a shortcut to be taken. Or even a longer way if it somehow seemed more interesting, a pond or a marsh where a muskrat could be seen, or a high dead poplar on a hill with a single hawk or owl in it. Those were the things that took them off the beaten road and those were the things I loved as well.

Whenever I went up there I would meet Ned. He'd be waiting for me where the trail slipped over the edge of the hill and down to where their house was in the crook of a small coulee. He'd be sitting on the third bare limb of a cottonwood tree, or on a huge rusted boulder that grew out of the hill like a rounded tooth that had scratched and worried itself up out of the deepest earth to find the sun.

I'd reach the crest and there he'd be, small and hard and quick as if anything might set him off to running in any one of a thousand directions, his thin blonde hair sliding in the wind as he disappeared forever for the day. He never did, but I believed it of him just as I believed he knew exactly when I would appear, for why else would he be there when I came? I know now he waited for me in that spot each day of the summer in hope that I would come.

How'd you know I was coming? I would ask, and he would say back, I don't know, I just knew. Hey, he would say then, look at what I've got here, and I would look at whatever it was he had and it was always something so beautiful, so completely strange that it seemed to change me forever. Once he had a baby crow with a red ribbon tied around its neck that he kept for months, feeding it bits of meat until he let it go with that ribbon around its neck so that we saw it for more than a year in the woods and fields until the ribbon fell off, and Ned said he could still tell which crow it was by the way it cried to him. And once he had

Ned Coker's Dream

an eight-ball from a pool game, a shiny black orb with its number on its sides, which he said weren't eights at all but the signs for infinity, and they were. He said he could tell the future and the past in it and I believed that as well, just as I believed he knew the secrets of frogs and pheasants, motors and magic. He even had a pet gopher that lived in the pocket of his jacket. It would crawl up inside him until its small bright head appeared out the hole of his sleeve to eat the sunflower seeds he had there waiting for it.

And that was Ned Coker, a quiet shy boy I know now, but then thought only that his silences were of a deeper stranger kind, and perhaps still do believe that, for who knows what is pooled beneath the surface of such quiet? Shy, yes, I know that now. Shy and strange because his whole family was looked on as being so different from everyone else that they were made to feel it. Or Ned felt it. Some of them didn't. Some of them found their way out of that web of strangeness. Some left and some stayed, some married and got jobs in town, and some went bad and went to prison, from where they returned only to go to prison again for some hopeless crime as theft or drunkenness. Mrs. Coker rode through all such times as she always had. She was there in that place living as she could, doing as was done, being as she willed herself to be. She was the maker of all that was around her and though she couldn't reach beyond her life to them, she was there when they returned. And Ned was her own, her special one, her best of the last, the one who stayed with her and by her through all his young years. And more.

It was that summer I learned Ned's dream, his dream of what he willed to be his life. In the labyrinth of cars and trucks and broken things that was his backyard he told me of himself as only a boy could who was as he was. It was in the deepest dark where he had made a place for himself and me, a hollow between and beneath two old truck beds that was a hiding place for him against the world, and where we first explored each other, taking off our thin summer clothes to touch and smell and see the differences we were. It was hot in that place, though not the heat of the hard summer sun, but rather a kind of soft full heat that surrounded you as water does in a shallow pond. It was there we lay naked together and did what all children do when they first discover themselves as other. It was there I saw him throw his pale seed into the slow air and it was there he touched me, there, so that I knew what I hadn't known before. And it was there he told me he would marry me and we would live forever in our love.

There was such a rage in him when he told me that. Such an anger.

185

How Do You Spell Beautiful?

I didn't understand it then, didn't know what he already knew, though he fought against it, willing to take on a whole world in order to find another. I said we would. We will, we will, he said, his quick body all bones and thin hard muscle standing in that secret place before me, his eyes as blue and cold as early winter rain, his small fists shaking. Yes, I said, and held him as I could, though I was but twelve years old and still a child. I held him as a woman does who must hold a man when he is ranged against a world that doesn't want him. I know it now as the thing that comes in a man before he has fully learned sorrow and pain and loss. It is the knowing those things will come that makes him so. The thing that is a man's rage and which precedes his first crying, as over a child's small death, or for a moon that rises into him, which is the first of all his moons and which he has never known before though he be twenty or fifty or a hundred. Or fourteen.

His mother knew. Her touching him when we appeared from the wreckage and walked up on her porch to drink the cold clean water she had waiting there. Her look at me, which held no judgement I could see, but was only a long far understanding of what was. Her touch of him, her long hands in his hair. My best of the last.

That was Ned Coker's dream. The dream he buried that was of all his dreams the first and last he told to only me. He stood in the secrecy of that wild wreckage and told it to me. No, perhaps that isn't fully true. I was there, yes, and it was me he meant, but he spoke over and beyond me to something or someone else, someone not there who could, if she wanted, somehow stop the dream being made true, but who it was I didn't know then and don't know now. He knew. It was what he looked at standing there above me, and it was that looking made me rise to him, a girl only, a slim thing half made of water, to rise to him and take him in my girl's small arms and hold him there, hard and quick and shaking. We will, I said, we will. And even as I said it I knew it wasn't true, knew it for the dream it was, a thing to be imagined, nothing more.

For my breasts were to grow that were only then small buds as soft as flowers, grow into the things that are a woman's to give to a man or a child, to suckle or to praise, for what is a man's mouth at a woman's breast but a child, though he thinks he's more, believes he is a sullen secret thing, a trickster whose caress is only need gone begging for desire. Oh, I have known that trick, have given my breast to be succoured by a man's warm mouth, the trick of teeth, the whimper of desire, as I have known a child's wild suck, that terrible demand, that thing that makes a woman into only animal. Oh, animal I was. And am.

Ned Coker's Dream

So I had small Ned Coker at my breasts. As I had small Ned Coker in my mouth, that small hard rigid thing that was still a boy's that I suckled on. Is there a man who knows a woman's dream? For we also sucked on stones, the streaked rare things we'd found in ponds and brooks, the chipped bits of blue and yellow flint we turned with our tongues into shining, only to let them lie on our palms in the sun, where we watched them turn from jewels back to stone. The moments when we simply slept.

Yes that. I remember that. That sleeping far from the garden where every flower was known, my mother's garden, ordered and arranged. I remember. I remember. I remember holding Ned Coker in my mouth, the all of him, the whole of what he was. I remember looking at my father and thinking my mother holding him like that. There were the stones.

So I am here in the middle of things, my daughter not looking back, her hard bare heels on the trail leaving their mark in the dust. Of course I knew, I knew it all the time. For me there was always an away. It was in that I fooled him, for my dream was other than his own, though then I couldn't name it. That was the trick. I could give him everything because there was nothing given. What? My body?

Oh, Ned Coker, you small miserable boy.

But what of that dream? There is this. Let me tell you this. Today I am out walking as I have always walked, going nowhere, drifting through the lighted afternoon far from the man I live with and the house I live in with the garden that is as my mother's was, arranged and ordered, every flower placed, each bush, each blade of grass. I walk where I am wont to walk. God, there's a word. Wont! But I did and do. And my own daughter is with me, though I hardly noticed her at first and, yes, I know the fear my mother knew, and I walked into the brush land with this fierce young girl of mine following along who is now ahead of me, tough and kind and fierce and mellow, like a turtle that has come at last from her sharp shell to smell the sound of summer. Proud and lost within herself as all of us are lost. No, she's not lost.

And far from home in the bright hills I saw her stop and bend above a stone. It was only a few feet back on the trail. It was only a small and nothing stone, a little blue and nothing thing, but she picked it up and held it to herself. I saw her there in the bend of a hill's shadow hold that stone to the light of her own wild eye before she slipped it in her mouth. A little thing she is, not more than I was at her age. Hold your blue stone, my daughter, in the wreckage of things.

How Do You Spell Beautiful?

Ah, Ned Coker, your sweet dream. For one of us was a fool as only a fool can be. But I held you that day as only a woman could, fierce and small in my arms, and didn't understand. Oh yes, your rage I knew, it was the other I didn't know. God, I could wish to know it, here where I am in a hill's shadow far from my negligence.

Patrick Lane has worked as a common labourer, truck driver, salesman, and first-aid man in sawmills. He is intimately familiar with the territory he writes about in these stories. He is best known, however, as a poet. He has published thirteen volumes of poetry over the past thirty years and has received numerous awards, including the Governor-General's Award for his *Poems: New and Selected* and the Canadian Authors Association Award for his *Selected Poems*. He was nominated in both 1990 and 1991 for the Governor-General's Award for Poetry, most recently for his collection entitled *Mortal Remains*. He received a National Magazine award in 1987 for his short story "Rabbits," which appeared in *The Canadian Forum*, and in 1991 his story "Marylou Had Her Teeth Out" was selected for the anthology *Best American Short Stories*. Patrick lives with poet Lorna Crozier in Victoria, BC.